Cathy's Christmas Kitchen

BOOKS BY TILLY TENNANT

The Waffle House on the Pier
The Break Up
The Garden on Sparrow Street
Hattie's Home for Broken Hearts
The Mill on Magnolia Lane
The Christmas Wish
The Summer Getaway
The Summer of Secrets

AN UNFORGETTABLE CHRISTMAS SERIES
A Very Vintage Christmas
A Cosy Candlelit Christmas

FROM ITALY WITH LOVE SERIES
Rome is Where the Heart is
A Wedding in Italy

HONEYBOURNE SERIES
The Little Village Bakery
Christmas at the Little Village Bakery

HOPELESSLY DEVOTED TO HOLDEN FINN
The Man Who Can't Be Moved
Mishaps and Mistletoe

MISHAPS IN MILLRISE SERIES
Little Acts of Love
Just Like Rebecca
The Parent Trap
And Baby Makes Four

ONCE UPON A WINTER SERIES
The Accidental Guest
I'm Not in Love
Ways to Say Goodbye
One Starry Night

TILLY TENNANT

Cathy's Christmas Kitchen

Bookouture

Published by Bookouture in 2020

An imprint of Storyfire Ltd.
Carmelite House
50 Victoria Embankment
London EC4Y 0DZ

www.bookouture.com

ISBN: 978-1-83888-963-0
eBook ISBN: 978-1-83888-962-3

To the people who cared for us when we needed it most.

Chapter One

Not for the first time Cathy wished her mum had written this stuff down. Her gaze swept the worktop as she tied a band into her honey-blonde hair to get it out of the way. Whenever she did this there always seemed to be one stubborn, greying lock that wanted to escape, and it did so now, falling into her eyeline. She blew it out of the way, not bothering to try to tether it back with the rest of her waves – it would only come loose again anyway.

Flour, eggs, butter, baking powder… all the usual ingredients, but Cathy knew there was a secret ingredient – if she could just remember what it was. But the days of her mother writing it down were long gone, along with the days when Cathy could have watched more carefully and made notes. There were other recipes, of course – there were books and books, recipes all over the internet – but they wouldn't be the same. They wouldn't be her mother's recipe.

With a heavy sigh she went over to the kitchen table and sat down. Her eyes were drawn to the window, where the November sun streamed in and lit the room with the sort of clean, fresh daylight that came only with the brightest and coldest of winter days. The tiny kitchen of her even tinier cottage was a little dated and in need of redecorating, but it was as welcoming as any, and right now it was warm and cosy, while outside a hard frost glinted on the ground.

The cottage stood on the outskirts of the northern town of Linnet-ford, a small path through a rose garden leading to its wisteria-garlanded front door, and had once been the dwelling of the tollkeeper in the days when travellers had to pay to use that stretch of road. The road that ran alongside was now covered in tarmac rather than cobbles, and it was far quieter these days as most people travelled through Linnetford and the surrounding Staffordshire countryside on the motorway or ring roads. In fact, it wasn't often the road outside Tollkeep Cottage was troubled by much traffic at all, and it was certainly never troubled by the tailbacks that plagued the nearby A road.

Cathy had been for a brisk walk early that morning, soaking up the views, marvelling at how much prettier their grimy old canal path looked with an azure sky above it. And every so often she'd almost make some comment along those lines to her mum, but then she'd remember that her mum wasn't there and the loneliness would threaten to overwhelm her again. But of course it was silly anyway because her mum's wheelchair wouldn't have made it along the towpath – they hadn't been walking that way for years, not since her mum had been confined to that chair. Still, she would have liked it.

She turned back to the ingredients lined up on the worktop.

'Nutmeg!' she said with a sudden smile. 'See, Mum, I worked it out after all.'

But then her smile turned into a vague frown. She was talking to her mum as if she was here again and that really had to stop. Spending her days talking to an empty house wasn't good for her. She needed to get out, make new friends, find new things to do with her time now that her duties as a carer were over – but what? She'd spent so long caring for her mum she hardly remembered what sort of things she'd liked doing before.

There was cooking, of course. They'd both liked cooking. They especially liked baking and had often baked together, right from when Cathy had been a little girl barely old enough to reach the tabletop. She'd stood on a chair, tongue poking from the corner of her mouth as she mixed the batter, her mum hovering close, soft brown eyes the exact same shade as Cathy's own watching every tiny wobble, ready to catch her if she fell. Cathy's arms would ache and the batter would be lumpy but her mum would put it into the oven for her anyway and they'd eat the cake together and Cathy's mum would pretend it was delicious. And then, one day, Cathy's practice paid off and what she made started to become delicious for real.

She pushed herself up off the chair and returned to the worktop, reaching into a high cupboard to look for the nutmeg. 'Come on, Cathy – snap out of this!' she admonished herself. She knew her mum wouldn't want her moping around forever.

And the truth was, Cathy was sick of moping, even though she didn't know how to stop. It had been three months since her mother's death but it had been no shock, and she'd had plenty of time to prepare herself. Even so, it had still caught her off-guard, still left her with a hole that she didn't know how to fill. She'd got herself a little job now on the flower stall of a local market, but it was only for a few hours a week and it still left her alone a lot.

Relatives and acquaintances had all offered advice on how she could fill her time, ranging from joining a gym to putting herself on Tinder, but none of it had particularly appealed, and some of it had sounded downright horrifying. As for friends, she didn't have many of those – tending to her mum's every need hadn't left a lot of time for socialising over the last few years. At thirty-eight she was almost beginning to feel too old to be starting again like this, rebuilding a social life and forging new friendships at a time when most women her age would have had all that firmly established. And as for hobbies, she wasn't much good at anything really.

She weighed out the flour and tipped it into the same stoneware mixing bowl her mother had used for all the years Cathy had lived in that house with her. That mixing bowl was older than Cathy herself and she certainly had no idea where it had come from. Her mother had always said it made the best cakes and Cathy was inclined to agree. Then she measured out the baking powder and the butter and counted out the eggs before putting the oven on to heat.

That was when she heard the letterbox clatter the arrival of the post and went to look. She was still getting letters to do with her mother's estate, not to mention various other official documents that she had to deal with, so she'd found it was better to go through the post as soon as it arrived in case she needed to make any lengthy phone calls before office hours were over for the day. She'd had to do all that alone too, and at times the sheer volume of official things she'd needed to sort had felt utterly overwhelming. She'd found she could cope slightly more easily if she didn't let it build up.

Picking up the little bundle, she took it back to the kitchen and sat at the table for a moment while she opened everything. It was all fairly routine and boring – nothing to worry about today. But right at the bottom of the pile was a leaflet from a cancer charity advertising a coffee morning at St Cuthbert's – the local church – and asking for attendees, as well as donations of cake and hot drinks.

St Cuthbert's… it was funny. Cathy had fond, if rather vague, memories of that old church. She hadn't been there for years, but before his death, her dad had been a regular. He'd even persuaded Cathy's mum to go to the odd service too, which had been some feat because, as she'd got older, Cathy had come to realise that religion was one thing her mum was no great fan of. After the death of her father, neither Cathy nor her mum had ever set foot in there again, but Cathy still had those flashes of memory – of holding her dad's hand as they filed in, the tuneless singing of hymns, the feeling of the smooth cold wood of the pews as they took their seats, and the smiles of old ladies after the service as they patted her on the head and told her dad what a pretty little thing she was.

Those memories gave her a melancholy smile now, as they always did, though she thought less and less of them the older she got. Nowadays, she wondered whether half of what she remembered was even true at all. She'd been five years old when he'd died and so five years old the last time she'd been to that church service, and memories that old couldn't always be reliable.

Cathy read the leaflet carefully, glanced back at her mixing bowl and then put it down again. She wouldn't know anyone and it would be terribly awkward. What if everyone there already knew each other? What if nobody talked to her? What if she spent the whole time sitting alone and watching everyone else chat? It would be horrible and certainly wouldn't do much to make her feel better.

But then, what if the people there were lovely? What if, by going, she helped someone, even if it was only in a small way? Wasn't helping the one thing she did really well? She'd cared for her mum for all those years, after all, and if she didn't know how to do anything else, she at least knew how to do that. Wouldn't that give her the sense of worth she was so sorely missing now that her mum – her reason to get up in the morning – was gone? Wasn't it worth the risk? Surely the people who went to the coffee morning couldn't be that dismissive and uncaring that they'd sit by and see her there alone without coming to talk to her? They must be nice people if they were there for charity, surely?

She glanced at her mixing bowl once again and smiled slowly. She'd cared for her mum and she'd done a decent-enough job, but maybe that wasn't the only thing she was good at. She didn't have fancy qualifications, but everyone had always said she sure could bake.

Chapter Two

'Not that I'd ever want you to leave me, of course…' Fleur dumped a large vase of carnations onto the display stand currently positioned at the entrance of her market stall, French for Flowers. She'd called it French for Flowers because her name was Fleur, and someone had once pointed out the irony that she ran a florist. Before that it had been called Moody Blooms but then someone in the next town had decided to call their florist Moody Blooms and, on a whim, Fleur had decided to change hers. That was a long time before Cathy had started working for her. 'But you could do a lot worse than set up your own stall in here,' she continued. 'There'll be one coming up when Ernest retires and closes his key-cutting business.'

Wiping her hands on her apron, she turned to face Cathy.

'I couldn't do that.' Cathy glanced around with more than a touch of anxiety in her expression – even though it was unlikely anyone would be listening in on their conversation. The other stallholders were busy setting up for the day themselves or chatting to staff and early customers; they certainly didn't have time to stop and strain to hear what Fleur and Cathy were talking about. She lowered her voice anyway. 'I'd be in competition with the cake stall that's already here.'

Fleur hauled another vase filled with pink roses to the display. 'So?'

'They'd hate me.'

'I reckon there'd be room for the two of you. Anyway, if their cakes are as good as yours then they'd have no reason to hate you. Half the time they sell out before the end of the day so I think there's trade enough to go round.'

Fleur sniffed hard. It was always cold in Linnetford's old stone market building, even during the summer, and Fleur's nose was always running. There had been a brief but doomed campaign by a few stallholders to move the market into a newer and more comfortable location, but most of the townsfolk were so fond of the old place – which had been a commerce centre during the Industrial Revolution, where goods were bought and sold by the gentlemen of 'new money' and the town made its wealth – that the bid was quickly snuffed out. And so Linnetford kept its draughty old market building, complete with vast glass roof panels, scrolled iron joists where pigeons nested and constantly plagued the caretaker, and wheat-coloured stone walls. The few who had complained were invited to leave and find themselves shop premises if they didn't like it.

'Last thing they've usually only got the factory-made ones they buy in left over; nobody wants them like they want the fresh ones.'

'I couldn't bake enough in my little kitchen to last all day on a stall either.'

'Maybe you could if you got help. Or even hire a kitchen space… I mean, I don't know how you'd do that but you could look into it.'

Cathy shook her head. 'Even if I wanted to, I don't know the first thing about running a market stall. And I like working with you anyway.' She paused, a worried expression casting a sudden shadow over her face. 'Unless you don't want me to work here anymore?'

Fleur started to laugh. 'Of course I do, you daft lump! I was just saying people would queue round the block to buy your cakes!'

'I don't know about that…'

'Trust me – they would.'

Cathy shrugged, though she was blushing from the compliment. 'I like baking for friends, when there's no pressure. If I baked to make a living I'd get so stressed about it, I'd end up cocking every recipe up and making everything taste horrible.'

Fleur poked a finger between her dark braids and gave her head a lazy scratch as she studied Cathy for a moment. And then she seemed to shake herself and shrugged. 'You'd know that better than anyone else.'

Cathy wasn't sure how to respond to this, so she didn't. She guessed that Fleur was touching on a lack of confidence in her abilities that even Cathy knew everyone could see plainly. She wasn't offended by the comment; if she was totally honest with herself, she felt it was probably a fair appraisal.

'Do you want the gerberas out front too?' she asked instead. 'It won't be too draughty for them?'

'Oh yes, they're hard as nails are gerberas. Stick 'em out – they won't mind a bit of cold.'

'It's funny,' Cathy said as she cut open a parcel of vivid orange flowers and dropped them into a large vase, 'they look so tropical you wouldn't imagine they'd survive a British winter.'

'A bit like me then,' Fleur said with a raspy laugh. 'Looks can be deceiving. Although…' she continued, 'sometimes I dream of a nice mild Barbadian winter. I've got my dad to thank for that, moving us to England without even asking me.'

'I thought they'd come to England when you were very little?'

'Exactly!' Fleur tipped a bag of coins into the till for the day's float.

'But you wouldn't go back, would you?'

'I don't miss the hurricanes – that's for sure,' she said with a wry grin, 'and I'm more British than anything else. No, cold or not, I'm happy enough in England. I've been here since I was five, after all, and I hardly know anything else.'

'It must be lovely having such a gorgeous place to visit when you go to see family.'

'I wouldn't know; it takes me so long to get round to all the family, I hardly see any of the islands! I suppose it is though.' She nodded at the vase Cathy was carrying. 'Be a darling and straighten those out a bit, would you? They look like they're having a fight in there.'

Cathy nodded and then set it down. 'Talking of baking, I'm going to bake some cakes for the coffee morning at St Cuthbert's next week.'

'Oh yes, I had a leaflet through about that. It's for cancer research, right?'
'Yes.'

Fleur nodded. 'You should make those gorgeous red velvet cupcakes you brought in last week – they'd go down well.'

'I thought about those too. I'll probably make a few different things – what do you reckon?'

'Everything you bake would get a thumbs up I would imagine.'

'I hope so…' Cathy paused. 'I wondered if you might come with me.'

Fleur reached for a pair of scissors with a frown. 'To the coffee morning?'

Cathy nodded.

'What for?'

'I don't know… I thought it might be fun.'

'I'm sure it would but I'll be here, won't I?'

'But couldn't the Saturday girl… Jade, is it? Couldn't she cover for an hour? Didn't you say earlier she'd be off college that day?'

'I also said she'd be off college all that week; she'll be in Corfu – remember?' Fleur said with a half laugh. 'I think someone needs to go back to bed and start again this morning.'

'Oh.' Cathy smiled and twisted a gerbera so that its head faced the same way as all the others. The vase looked like a sunny little choir in the middle of the drab wintry building, and Cathy thought vaguely that Fleur was right – they would bring customers over to have a closer look because their little orange faces couldn't fail to cheer. 'I think I do – I clean forgot about that bit. Must have gone in one ear and out the other.'

'Don't worry about it, love. But I'm sorry I won't be able to come.'

'That's OK. Ignore me; I was being silly.'

'It won't stop you from going, will it?'

'No… of course not.'

Cathy forced a smile. It wasn't that she was particularly shy, but sometimes social situations could overwhelm her, particularly when she was faced with lots of new people at once, and for some strange reason she had become particularly sensitive to this since her mum died. She could only imagine that it was perhaps because her world had changed so drastically now that she was on her own and it had made her so much less certain of herself than she used to be. Or perhaps it was because she had nobody to fall back on in the same way she did when her mum was around; even though her mum was physically disabled she'd always been able to offer moral support, encouragement and love whenever Cathy had needed it.

'It'll do you good,' Fleur said with a shrewd look.

'I'm alright, you know.'

'I know,' Fleur replied with very deliberate carelessness. 'But even so. And they'll love your baking.'

'You think so?'

Fleur laughed. 'You've tasted your cakes, right?'

Cathy's smile was genuine now. 'I know, but I don't think… I mean, they're quite nice, I suppose, but I don't think they're all that special, and if they are then it's down to what Mum taught me, not any talent I have.'

'Honestly, accept a bit of praise from time to time,' Fleur said with the barest edge of impatience in her tone. 'Take it where it's due – it wouldn't kill you to feel good about yourself for once.'

Before Cathy had the chance to think of the right reply Fleur was across the stall greeting a customer she'd just spotted approaching. 'Alright, love, come to pick up that birthday arrangement?'

Cathy left them to it. Her gaze caught that of the woman on the cake stall across the aisle and she gave her a guilty smile. Cathy would never admit it but her own cakes *were* pretty good, and perhaps they were even better than theirs, as Fleur kept saying. Hopefully the people at the coffee morning would think so too.

Chapter Three

Though Cathy had some recollections of attending church services at St Cuthbert's with her dad, she couldn't recall ever being inside the adjoining church hall. Those dim memories (along with the desire to do some good and share her baking) were part of the reason she'd been drawn to come today, because she recalled feeling happy and content during those visits. Even if they were false memories, she'd take happy and content right now over feeling lost and lonely.

It was funny, though, because her mother had forsaken religion completely soon after Cathy's father had died and so Cathy shouldn't have felt any kind of pull to this place at all, but strangely, today, she did, and it was strong. If there was a God, her mum had said, then why would he make people suffer like she was forced to? Why would he or she (probably he, she said) take husbands so suddenly and before their time and curse the grieving widow with a horrible illness?

Cathy had taken a more philosophical view of things – some people were just unlucky, God or no God – but she could understand why her mum would think that way. And even though she now found herself alone with no parents and no siblings and precious little other family, she still didn't feel like she could blame anyone, least of all someone she couldn't see or hear or prove the existence of in any way.

The church itself was fairly standard – a dark old building of grey stone and tall, heavily leaded windows in need of some repair, just like many churches in many towns across Britain. So Cathy had walked into the more modern church hall tagged onto the back in a separate building, expecting some draughty old space with peeling window frames and paint that had been on the walls since Margaret Thatcher had been in power. But the room she was sitting in now had a pink carpet with pretty handmade rugs strewn across it, lots of squashy armchairs and a pair of huge beige sofas. All the furniture was clearly old, but it would have been expensive when new and was still quite serviceable and very comfortable.

She was fairly certain that all church halls weren't like this, but then, she hadn't set foot in one for a very long time, perhaps twenty years or more. Perhaps churches had cottoned on at some point in those twenty years that people didn't want to sit in freezing old rooms being stared down on by a tatty Jesus on a dusty crucifix; no, they wanted to be in a homely room where they felt welcomed and comfortable. Or maybe it was just this one.

On her way through she'd seen another, bigger room with a wooden floor and high ceilings. The lady who'd shown her and her groaning basket of cakes in had informed her that that was where the Brownies and Scouts met weekly. Cathy had been to Brownies once. She couldn't remember where the meeting had been held and how old she'd been when she'd tried it out, but she'd never really settled and had spent the evening longing for her mum to come and pick her up. The other girls had all known each other and seemed so much more confident and clever than her, with badges for this and that achievement crammed onto every spare inch of tunic space. They'd played some elaborate game with beanbags and a whistle and Cathy had been awful at it, and then they'd discussed at length a camping trip that Cathy wasn't altogether sure she wanted to go on. When her mother had finally come to reclaim her, Cathy had announced that she didn't want to go back the following week.

Balancing a chintzy cup and saucer on her lap and longing for a good solid bucket of a mug, Cathy gave a polite smile to the woman who had just spoken to her, dredging her recent memory for the woman's name. So many had been fired at her as she'd sat down and everyone had introduced themselves that she could hardly recall which one belonged to who – apart from Colin, who was the only man present, possibly in his seventies, with a thick head of white hair and the only person she'd ever seen in real life wearing a cravat. This was… she wanted to say Iris, but she couldn't be certain.

'We haven't seen you at church before,' the woman – possibly Iris – said. 'We haven't seen you at all. Don't you go to church?'

'I haven't been for a long time,' Cathy replied, dimly recalling that the last time she'd been to a church service (at a different church outside Linnetford) was probably for a family wedding when she'd have been about twelve. Her mum hadn't wanted any religion at her funeral at all, so the service had been conducted in a forest clearing, her ashes scattered in that same forest. Some of their relatives had been horrified at the lack of tradition, which had annoyed Cathy a little because if any of them had bothered to pay the slightest bit of attention to her mum they'd have known that she was never going to take the traditional route to her final resting place. And why would she have embraced religion in death when she'd never done so in life? It would have felt like slapping her in the face, a smug dismissal of all she'd believed in, as if her daughter knew better. Cathy would never have insulted her in that way.

'Perhaps you'd like to come now you know where we are?' Iris said cheerfully, seemingly working on the twin assumptions that anyone who lived in these parts could somehow have missed the huge spire that rocketed into the sky, and that everyone of sound mind would want to give up all their other Sunday activities to sit inside it and hear someone drone on about kingdoms of heaven and how blessed meek people were. Cathy considered herself meek, but she hardly felt she was blessed. She didn't feel cursed either, just somewhere in the middle – pretty much like everyone else was.

Still, Iris seemed friendly enough and that was one thing Cathy could appreciate – almost all the regular churchgoers she'd ever met had been very friendly. She certainly didn't want to offend her, having just arrived and not even got started on the cake yet.

'If I'm not too busy I might do,' she said, hoping that would be enough.

Iris looked faintly stunned at the notion that anyone might be too busy to attend, but she nodded uneasily and turned to Colin.

'You'll be able to play organ for us this week, won't you?' she asked. 'Only Mr Pettigrew still isn't right since his bypass. Between you and me, I don't know if he'll ever be right again, and all that flailing around at the organ won't do his recovery much good.'

'I didn't think you'd want me again after last time,' Colin said sombrely.

'I don't think anyone's going to worry about the odd wrong note,' Iris replied.

'It was more than the odd wrong note, Iris,' another lady chipped in. Newly arrived, she settled into a nearby chair. 'It was like that time Morecambe and Wise had André Previn on their show.'

'Dora!' Iris scolded. 'Why would you say that?'

'Because it's true.'

Colin gave a wry smile. 'Don't worry, Iris,' he said. 'I know I'm terrible, but I also know you don't have anyone else and I won't let

Dora's frightening honesty put me off. I'll play for you on Sunday if you need me to.'

'You just might have to hand out ear defenders as the congregation files in,' Dora said as she helped herself to the teapot.

'I'd better go and buy about four pairs then,' Iris said wearily. 'It's hardly a congregation these days, is it?'

'You want to get *Songs of Praise* in,' Dora said. 'You'd have a full house then, let me tell you.'

'Yes, but you'd also have me playing the organ,' Colin said. '*Songs of Praise* certainly wouldn't come back after that and neither would all the new parishioners.'

Dora let out a laugh while Iris gave a haughty sniff.

This was all very well, and Cathy was quite enjoying listening to this conversation, but she couldn't help wondering if everyone who was going to be coming to this coffee morning was a member of the church community. Obviously, the venue was the church hall, but she'd been expecting some people a bit more like her to come – in fact, she'd been banking on it. She'd feel very out of place if it turned out she was the only person who didn't already know everyone else.

Quite a few had arrived already, and they all seemed to know each other and were engaged in their own little conversations. Most of the people she'd seen arrive were retirement age too – or at least close – and she was starting to wonder whether she didn't feel a little incongruous for being so young in comparison. But if anyone there thought it was odd that someone of her age had turned up, they certainly didn't show it; in fact, quite the opposite – they seemed pleased to see her there. Cathy, on the other hand, was starting to wonder if she ought to make her excuses and leave. Perhaps this wasn't the place for her to be today after all.

But then she looked up to see the door open and another lady arriving with carrier bags. Cathy would have put her at perhaps her late thirties, early forties. Her mid-brown hair was cut into a neat bob, with a clean grey streak framing one side of her face, and she was dressed in a fitted grey sweater, bootcut jeans and black-heeled boots that flattered what was a neat figure.

'Hello!' she said, giving a warm but slightly apprehensive smile to everyone in the room. It looked as if she was in the same situation as Cathy – not knowing anyone – and Cathy relaxed a little. At least she wasn't the only person starting from scratch – or the only person under the age of sixty.

'Welcome!' Iris got up, apparently deciding to be the spokesperson for the whole room. 'I see you have goodies there.'

'Oh, just shop-bought, I'm afraid,' the woman said. 'I'm hopeless at baking but I know a good brand of Jaffa cake when I see one.'

'Anything is welcome,' Iris said. 'We were just about to start actually.' She placed a hand on her breastbone. 'I'm Iris; I'm the church secretary, and treasurer and keyholder and… well, just about everything really.' Then she proceeded to point out others. 'This is Dora, Colin, Myrtle, Julia, Janet, Karen, Lulu and… I'm sorry, dear.' She stopped at Cathy. 'I've quite forgotten already. How rude of me.'

'That's OK,' Cathy said. 'You can't be expected to remember everything.'

'That's the problem,' Dora said. 'She remembers nothing.'

A low snigger rolled around the room. Iris didn't seem to notice the comment or, if she did, she didn't seem too offended by it.

'I'm Cathy,' Cathy said.

The newcomer smiled. 'I'm Erica.' She gave the room an approving once-over. 'I've never been in here before – it's nice, isn't it? Much cosier than I imagined.'

'We do our best to make it welcoming,' Iris said with obvious pride. 'Shall I take those bags from you?'

'Oh, lovely,' Erica said, handing them over. 'I hope it's OK that I only got shop-bought cakes. I can't bake to save my life!'

'Anything is gratefully received,' Iris said. 'Whether they're home-baked or not, we're still doing our bit for charity, after all.'

'Well,' Colin said, 'I make it eleven o'clock and I vote we get things started. If we get any latecomers, they'll just have to take what's left over.'

'There's plenty to go round,' Dora said.

Cathy got up from her seat and went to the table where her own creations were currently stashed inside large Tupperware containers. 'Shall I uncover everything then?' she asked.

'Might as well,' Dora said.

As Erica unwrapped her offerings, she glanced across to see Cathy prise the lids from her tubs and gave a little gasp of approval.

'Oh, I feel so ashamed now,' she said, laughing. 'Look at those! Mary Berry couldn't do better.'

'You haven't tasted them yet,' Cathy said, blushing. 'Looks could be deceiving.'

'I doubt it,' she replied. 'No cake could look that good without tasting good too. And you've made so many!'

'Well, I didn't think it would be enough to be honest,' Cathy said.

'Did you think we were feeding the multitudes?' Colin asked with a smile.

'Sort of,' Cathy replied.

She sat down without taking a cake and waited. It felt polite, somehow, to make sure everyone else took what they wanted first. Though she'd feel it improper and a bit arrogant to think that everyone would want to eat hers, secretly she couldn't help feeling that they did

look better than all the shop-bought ones and certainly better than the
sorry, sunken little fairy cakes that one of the other ladies had brought
in. And she didn't think this because she believed for a minute she
was better or more talented than anyone else, but because her mum's
recipes were so good that it was more or less impossible that anything
baked to one of them could turn out wrong. That was all Cathy had
done – followed the recipes to the virtual letter, her mum having never
written anything down and Cathy having memorised them over the
years. It was her mum who had been the real talent.

'Aren't you having anything?' Dora asked her.

'I just thought… Well, I was waiting for everyone else.'

'You've baked them – you get first choice; to hell with this lot of
scroungers.'

'Dora!' Iris cried, but Colin simply threw back his head and laughed.

'Say it like it is, Dora!'

'Nobody is scrounging!' Iris said testily. 'Everyone has donated and
deserves their fair share.'

'Oh, don't be so sensitive.' Dora waved an airy hand to dismiss Iris's
possibly misplaced outrage.

'I'll have a cake after all,' Cathy said and shoved a coconut madeleine
into her mouth with some haste, just so she wouldn't have to offer an
opinion on scrounging either way.

'Oooh, I'm having one of those,' Erica said, leaning over to help herself
to one of the cakes she'd just seen Cathy eat. 'Did you bake these too?'

Cathy nodded.

'Oooh!' Erica exclaimed again warmly. 'That's fantastic!'

Then Colin made a beeline for the banana loaf, while Dora took a
Black Forest muffin and Iris popped a square of millionaire's shortbread
into her mouth with a satisfied sigh.

While Cathy's sense of pride grew with every expression of absolute cake-induced rapture, so did her embarrassment. Accepting compliments wasn't something that came easily to her, regardless of how well-intentioned they were. She was beginning to wish she'd dumped her cakes and left before anyone could eat them.

'How do you get this so light?' one woman asked as she marvelled at a cherry scone.

'Oh, I can always taste baking powder in mine no matter what I do,' another said. 'Nothing worse... You must give me the recipe for yours, Cathy.'

'Oh, me too!' the first woman said.

'No point in giving me the recipe for anything,' Erica said with a laugh as she took her second coconut madeleine from the tub. 'But any time you feel like baking some for me, I'd be glad to take them off your hands!'

To be polite, and because she felt sorry for the sunken fairy cakes, Cathy took one and bit into it.

'Oh, I don't suppose that's a patch on yours,' the lady who'd brought them in said. Cathy thought she might be Myrtle but she couldn't be sure.

'No, no, it's lovely,' Cathy said, forcing a smile. There was nothing wrong with it – a perfectly adequate little cake – but it wasn't very thrilling. Cathy swallowed it down anyway.

'Would you like another?' the lady asked.

'Ooh, yes please. Makes a change from eating my own, doesn't it?' Cathy said, taking one but wishing she *was* eating her own.

'More tea?' Iris asked, coming round with the pot. There was a chorus of 'Please' and 'Thank you' and a forest of hands holding up cups to be filled, Cathy's included. It was almost like being at primary school again when the table server asked if anyone wanted the leftover jam roly-poly before it went back to the kitchen and there'd be a veritable scrum to get it before someone else did.

'That's a good cup of tea,' Erica said as she slurped from her cup.

'Special teabags,' Iris replied, tapping the side of her nose, and Cathy couldn't imagine what kind of teabags required being kept secret, though she did agree it was pretty good tea.

The door opened, a faint draught coming from the larger space beyond it, and another man walked in. Cathy noted straight away the black shirt and jacket and starched white dog collar. He was far younger than she'd have expected a vicar to be and actually quite good-looking, in a gentle sort of way, with an abundance of mousey hair stylishly dishevelled, a button nose and deep blue eyes. A sort of vicarish version of a young Michael J Fox.

'Oh, hello, Vicar,' Iris said, looking up and suddenly sounding rather breathless. 'I didn't think you were going to be coming over this morning – we haven't had time to tot up all the donations yet.'

'Oh, don't worry about that,' the vicar said, shrugging off his coat. 'I had a meeting cancelled and thought I'd come and join in the fun. If you don't mind me staying, of course. I haven't brought any cake obviously, but, to be honest, you probably wouldn't want my cake if you tasted it.'

'As long as you make a donation like everyone else, we'll let it slide,' Iris said with a warm smile.

'That sounds like a fair-enough deal to me.' He took his coat over to a stand in the corner of the room and hung it there with everyone else's. 'It's a good spread today,' he added, casting an approving glance over the tubs and packs of cakes and biscuits.

'Oh, most of that's down to this new lady, Cathy,' Iris said, and when she looked at Cathy, Cathy wanted the ground to swallow her up. She didn't want to be singled out when everyone had contributed. Admittedly, she had brought more along than anyone else but that was only because she'd got carried away planning what she was going to bake and made far more than she'd really needed to.

The vicar dug his hands in his pockets and stood at the table, examining the goodies on offer.

'I think I'll take a scone if that's OK,' he said. 'I'm quite partial to a nice scone.'

'There's cream to go with it in the jug,' Cathy said. 'And a little pot of jam too.'

He picked up the jam. 'Home-made as well?' he asked.

'Yes.'

'Wow! Must have taken you days to make all this?'

'Oh, no,' Cathy said, that funny mixed-up feeling of pride and embarrassment at the compliments rearing up in her again. 'Besides, I really like doing it, so I enjoyed myself. If anything, it was like my version of a day out.'

'Funny day out if you ask me,' Dora said, crumbs spraying from her mouth.

'Tea, Vicar?' Iris asked.

The vicar had found a vacant seat and settled there with his scone. 'That would be lovely, Iris. Your special teabags?'

'Of course,' Iris said.

What was in these teabags? Crack? They were good but they were getting people way more excited than teabags ought to. Perhaps Cathy would ask Iris for the name of the brand later on.

'Is everyone having a good morning?' he asked the room at large.

'Oh yes!' Iris said, before anyone else could draw breath. 'I'm sure we'll have raised lots of money today.'

'The charity organisers at Cancer Care for Britain will be pleased to hear that,' he said.

He turned to Cathy and Erica. 'It's good to see new faces too. Welcome to St Cuthbert's.' He shook both their hands. 'If you don't mind my asking,' he continued, 'did you have a particular motivation to join us today?'

'I lost my dad to cancer,' Erica said. 'So anything I can do for cancer charities I'm happy to.'

The vicar pulled a sympathetic face. 'I'm very sorry to hear that.'

'It's not much just turning up at things,' Erica continued. 'I know people run marathons and all sorts, but I'd like to do something good to redress the balance a bit, even if it's only small.'

'Nothing is ever too small or insignificant,' the vicar said.

He looked at Cathy and waited. She wasn't sure whether she liked his expectation, but then she thought if she was here and people were sharing, maybe it wouldn't be a bad thing for her to share too. It might even help her.

'I lost my mum,' she said. 'I'm sort of the same – I wanted to turn my loss into something that can do some good.'

'You lost your mum to cancer?'

'Not to cancer – lung disease. A couple of months ago now.'

'Then I expect it's all still very new and hard, isn't it? I am sorry to hear that,' he said, and when people said that usually there wasn't an ounce of sincerity in their voice. But with this man, Cathy could see he meant every word. 'You've got a good network around you? Friends? Other family members?'

'Oh yes,' Cathy said, although she wasn't sure why she was lying about it. She had some family – mostly disinterested, though she saw them from time to time – and her friends had gradually drifted away over the years because she'd never been able to find the time to see them. There had been a boyfriend too, once; a fiancé in fact – Jonas. Cathy had loved him and he'd loved her, but that had ended as well, unable to take the pressure that caring for her mum had put on their relationship. The last Cathy heard, he'd married a veterinary nurse and was living in Scotland with her. She wasn't mad about it and she wished him well, but sometimes she felt sad for what could have been.

'More tea for you, Cathy?'

Cathy looked up to see Iris hovering with the teapot.

'I've still got this cup – maybe in a little while?'

'Well,' Iris said as she moved to the next chair, 'just whistle when you're ready and I'll be right over.'

Cathy could have got her own tea easily enough, but she realised that Iris wanted to do it and it probably made her feel useful. Cathy got that, and gave Iris a tight smile and thanked her, suddenly feeling very useless indeed.

Chapter Four

Cathy had enjoyed the coffee morning more than she'd ever thought she would. Of course, she'd been hoping it would be a good distraction from the hours spent alone at home, but when she finally made it back to her own little bubble, she was content and happy, her head full of the conversations that had taken place. Almost instantly, she seemed to have gained a whole new social circle. Iris and Dora, she soon discovered, were not only lovely old ladies but also a hilarious double act (whether intentional or not). They were cousins and seemed to simultaneously hate each other and yet love each other to pieces. They bickered and threw out sarcastic comments constantly but their affection was always on show, no matter what they were saying. Dora would rush to make sure Iris was OK if she stumbled, and Iris would rub Dora's arm affectionately as she handed her a plate of cakes.

Cathy had got on well with Erica and had even arranged to meet her outside of the coffee morning sometime. Colin had regaled her with thrilling tales of his time in the navy as a young man, while Myrtle had told Cathy she had eight children and thirty-two grandchildren (number thirty-three was on the way). She insisted that there was nothing special about her until Cathy pointed out that anyone who had raised eight children and regularly babysat another thirty-two was pretty special.

Janet and Karen seemed to be a couple (although nobody said it explicitly, it was fairly obvious) and ran a centre for underprivileged children to participate in various sports, and Lulu – just like her more famous namesake – had a very successful (albeit very local) career belting out sixties classics in pubs and clubs. Cathy had asked if she'd called herself Lulu for the sake of her job and was more than a little surprised to discover that she'd actually being christened Lulu by her parents. Julia was a bit mysterious and volunteered very little information about herself; in fact, she'd barely spoken, even when prompted.

By the time the coffee morning was over they'd raised almost one hundred pounds for charity and Cathy had finally learned which face went with which name. In the heady spontaneity of the moment she might well have agreed to attend a service that Sunday too. She'd have to deal with that at some point because she had no intention of going, but she felt that her new friends might like her enough to forgive her if she reneged on that small promise. She hoped so; as much as she didn't want to offend anyone, church just wasn't her thing.

As if all this wasn't enough, Cathy's cakes had been an unqualified success and so many people had asked her for recipes that she announced it would take her until the next coffee morning to write them all down. So Iris had said that if she wanted to jot them down, she'd do photocopies for whoever wanted one. It seemed like a good plan and Cathy felt a warm sense of pride that her mother's recipes were now about to grow wings and fly out into the wider community, to be enjoyed by other families around the town. Who knew? They might even find their way out further and further, passed on again and again, until people Cathy couldn't even imagine were baking to them in far-flung corners of the country.

Maybe even further than that, she thought with that little frisson of excitement again. After all, it was a shame for Cathy alone to be using them, and it seemed a fitting tribute to her mum's talents. She liked to think her mum would approve, or at the very least be flattered by the idea.

As the grainy twilight gloom gathered outside her kitchen window later that evening, Cathy sat at the table with a cup of tea. It was perhaps her fourth or fifth of the day already – she'd had so many top-ups from an insistent Iris that she really couldn't be certain. She probably hadn't needed to make one but it had become a habit: sitting at the kitchen table – unless it was for a meal – meant a mug of good strong tea, possibly a biscuit and, when she'd baked, more than one cake. It explained the extra few pounds of padding that had crept on in the time since her mum had died.

Comfort eating, one less tactful aunt had called it, but Cathy didn't care. Her aunt couldn't possibly understand what it was like for Cathy, and Cathy didn't think she should be judging. She'd take comfort where she could, and if that came in the form of a custard tart then so be it. It wasn't just down to the food anyway – it was also down to the fact that Cathy had a lot less running around to do these days with nobody to look after but herself. Perhaps that was about to change though.

In the meantime, she could occupy a lot of time gathering together some of the recipes that people had wanted from her and writing them down clearly so they could understand them.

In front of her now sat a brand-new exercise book embossed with pink flamingos and palm trees, ready to be filled. When all the recipes were in there, people could borrow it, pass it around, copy what they wanted from it and, when they were done, bring it back for Cathy to keep until the next time someone might want a recipe from her.

Once she'd collated them all she might even upload them to the internet as a blog. It would take time to set up (something she had more than enough of) but would make them available to the wider community. She could do that, she reasoned, but she was still going to put them all in her exercise book too, because she had a feeling quite a few of the older people who'd asked for them today – like Myrtle and Iris – didn't go online and would still need paper versions.

And as she came across new recipes she could add to it – she could even get additions from other people at the coffee mornings, new ones she could try out herself. Along with her rather sorry little fairy cakes, Myrtle had brought courgette cake. Cathy had never tasted it before and couldn't imagine it being nice, but she'd tried it anyway and found it surprisingly good. Maybe she'd get the recipe for that, tinker about with it a little, make it even better and then add it to her collection.

On the first page she wrote: 'Cathy's Cake Recipes'. Then she turned to the next clean page and stopped. Should she write a list of contents? An index? While that might make it easy for people to find a specific recipe it would soon get in a muddle when she started to add new things. She decided not to include a contents page, and maybe she'd think about an index later. She resolved to start with the more basic recipes first and then bring in the more complicated ones as the book progressed, so that people could try out the easy ones and work their way through the book as they felt more confident. Not that she was assuming a lack of baking skill on the part of anyone who might read it, but at least it would cater for the likes of Erica, who had freely admitted that baking made her nervous.

She tapped the pen against her chin, thoughtful for a moment, eyes on the darkening skies beyond the kitchen window. The sound of the radiators groaning into life broke the silence and the pipes began to creak and chug as heat started to trickle through them. Cathy looked back at her empty page. Where to start?

Banana loaf, she decided finally. Nice and simple, very hard to get wrong, universally loved and practically a health food, with all that potassium and fibre bursting from it.

Often, Cathy had very strong feelings and memories attached to certain foods and banana loaf was one of those. It made her think back to the days when her mum had still been well enough to look after her rather than the other way around, because it was one of the cakes she often baked for Cathy whenever she was recovering from an illness – like when Cathy had spent her twelfth birthday in bed with flu.

Not exactly the celebrations she'd been looking forward to – a trip to the local burger bar with her friends – but one mischievous microscopic bug had ensured that wasn't going to happen. She couldn't recall ever feeling so ill – she'd been utterly floored by it – but even as she lay in bed, she was more afraid of what effect it might have on her mum should she catch it than she was for herself. She'd noticed her mum was frailer these days, that she caught colds more easily and struggled with them for longer than she ought to, and had tried to keep her from getting too close as much as she could. Miriam had tried to nurse Cathy, of course, but Cathy had often not allowed it and had asked her to stay out of her room as much as possible. At first her mum had looked hurt and offended by the request, but then she seemed to understand what Cathy was trying to do and perhaps felt a little relieved by it too.

Thankfully, when Cathy had woken two days after her birthday, she'd felt lighter and brighter and wondered if she was finally over the worst of it. Her mum had shown no signs of infection so far and they could only hope that she'd escaped it.

So, still weak and tired, Cathy had come downstairs with an actual appetite. Small, but she could definitely eat something and that was progress.

*

'Oh, you're up!'

Cathy smiled wanly at her mum's exclamation of delight. 'I'm hungry.'

The smile blooming again, Cathy's mother took a step towards her and brushed a stray lock of hair from her face.

'That's good then… You must be out of the woods.'

'I don't know,' Cathy said, taking a step back.

'I'm sure it will be fine now. We've been careful – I won't hug you yet – how's that?'

Cathy nodded. Though she wanted that hug more than anything, she contented herself with what they had for now. She turned towards the kitchen, perfectly capable and willing to get herself a snack, but her mum following anyway.

Cathy turned to her. 'I can do it.'

'I know you can; I just want to help.'

'I'm only having soup – I'll just open a tin.'

'I'll do it for you; you've been poorly.'

'I know but I don't want you to be poorly too.'

Her mum waved a dismissive hand. 'I'll be careful.'

'Mum, I need you to stay away from me.'

'And I need to be your mum!'

Cathy paused, about to say something else, but then she closed her mouth. Something in her mum's expression was so pained, so desperate, as if she knew something bigger than this was coming for both of them, something she hadn't told Cathy – something she couldn't bring herself to tell her – that Cathy hadn't the heart to challenge her again. Her mum had obviously decided that not being able to be a mother was worse than any flu risk, no matter how hard it might hit her.

'Please,' she continued, 'let me do this for you. Let me be your mum sometimes.'

Cathy would never say outright the huge burden of responsibility she felt for her mum, even at the tender age of twelve. Perhaps it was because she could see how weak her mum's immune system was and she was often so acutely aware of the loss of her father that she didn't want to risk losing her other parent. But, whatever the reason, that burden was one she often carried. She'd never considered herself a young carer – a phrase a teacher had once used – but she understood very well how it would feel to be one. Sometimes she just wished she could be a normal girl like her friends.

In the kitchen, the scales and old stoneware mixing bowl were on the table, along with a bag of flour, caster sugar, eggs and a tiny bottle of vanilla essence.

'What are you making?' Cathy asked.

'I was going to do a banana loaf. I know it didn't seem like there was any point really because I'd be eating it alone, but it was something to do.'

Cathy sat at the table. There was no further discussion over who would make the soup – her mum simply went to the cupboard and looked inside. 'Tomato or chicken? If I'd known you were going to want soup I'd have made fresh.'

'It's alright, Mum. Even I didn't know I was going to want soup until I did. Chicken please.'

'It's funny how these things go when you're young and fit,' her mum said. 'One minute you're at death's door, the next you're craving chips. You want some bread with your soup?'

'No, I don't think I could eat bread.'

'Maybe you'll want some later. You might even be in the mood for cake later, eh? Once you've had your soup it might kick-start your appetite.'

'Can I stay up and bake with you?'

'Are you feeling up to it?' Her mum poured the soup into a small saucepan. 'Don't you think you ought to take it steady? Perhaps you ought to go back to bed after this.'

'I'm sick of being in bed.'

'You could read – you don't have to go to sleep.'

'I'd still rather be down here. It's too early to be in bed.'

Her mum nodded slowly as she stirred the soup. 'If that's what you want.'

Cathy gave a tired smile as she rested her chin on her hands and leaned on the table, already worn out from being up but determined not to succumb. 'Thanks, Mum.'

*

If Cathy closed her eyes now, she could still see her mum so clearly, standing in this very kitchen, stirring soup at the stove, chatting away, happy to see Cathy up and about and clearly appreciative of her company. The light from the window showed up the copper in her brunette curls and as she hummed something from some old musical, her voice was about the prettiest thing Cathy had ever heard.

When Cathy had finished her soup she'd helped her mum make the cake – though now that she thought about it, it was far more likely that she'd sat and watched as her mum did most of it, simply happy to be up and content to be in the bubble of love that she and her mum shared in their little cottage.

In fact, as Cathy turned her thoughts back to the task in hand, it was far harder than she'd imagined to recall everything that went into a banana loaf, and in what quantities, than it was to recall the sights of that day, how her mother's singing had sounded and how the cake had made the air of the kitchen warm and sweet as it baked. Her mum's banana loaf was one of those things Cathy had done so often she could now make it on autopilot; no conscious thought was required, and she did it almost by muscle memory. Like a typist who instinctively reached for the keys on the board but was completely stumped when asked to say where each one was, Cathy could make a banana loaf in her sleep but she couldn't tell you how.

In the end, she decided to trick her brain into thinking she was about to make one and suddenly found her hands travelling the cupboards almost of their own volition, settling on every ingredient she would need until everything was lined up on the kitchen counter. Once she was done, she could see instantly that it was all there – now all she needed to do was get the measurements down. She'd do this by eye – she'd done it for so many years she just knew when it looked right. So she put everything out, but then instead of tipping it into the stoneware bowl to mix she took it to the scales to weigh and jotted down every value. She wrote it precisely for the people who liked order, and then she added cup measurements for people who liked to play a bit faster and looser.

When she'd done all that she took her notes and turned them into something more coherent, and then she wrote it all down in the book in her best and most careful handwriting, finishing with a flourish of little sketches of bananas and eggs and mixing spoons at the corners of the page. Perhaps the doodles were overdoing it a tad, but it was her book and if she fancied doodling in it then why not? Short of some saucy, Nigella-style soft-focus photos, she didn't have much else to pretty it up.

She smiled as she inspected her handiwork and realised that she'd really enjoyed doing it – so much that she'd completely lost herself in the task. Her eyes travelled to the windows again and saw it was now dark. The tea she'd made earlier had gone cold too, almost untouched, and despite the amount of cake she'd eaten that morning, her stomach was starting to sing for its supper. She really had taken longer than she'd imagined she would, and on just one recipe. But she was happy with that one and it hadn't exactly been a chore. She'd do one more tonight, but first she'd have to make herself a little something to eat.

Going to the fridge she paused, taking in what was on offer. It was looking a bit empty really – she probably needed to shop tomorrow. But then she saw exactly the thing she fancied and to hell with the calories. She got the pack out and went to the stove.

A big fat bacon sandwich – that would do nicely.

Chapter Five

Monday morning always came around quickly, but while some would have rolled over in bed, frowning at the alarm clock as it rang in the arrival of a new working week, Cathy was always happy to be woken by hers. It meant spending the day with Fleur.

She loved her job on the flower stall. She loved the gossip and banter, the heady mixtures of floral scents that mingled with damp concrete and disinfectant and the aroma of coffee from the nearby café. She loved being busy but not stressed and not having someone's life depend on her. She loved that she could brighten the day of some lonely old lady by sparing half an hour to talk, or when Fleur congratulated her on how beautifully she'd done an arrangement or a wreath, and she loved it even more when her boss went into paroxysms of pleasure over some cake or fancy Cathy had baked and brought in for them to share with their morning tea.

It didn't matter if they were busy or quiet, whether their customers were grateful or awkward, whether it rained on the streets outside or the sun leaked in through the moss-smudged skylights of the huge old stone building that housed the market, Cathy was happiest these days when she was working. For those few hours, she could escape the loneliness of the home where she rattled around on her own night after night, where every corner reminded her of her mum, memories that were still raw for now, and that – even though Cathy looked as if she was coping – would take longer to soften than anyone could really know.

She'd once told Fleur all this, and Fleur – perhaps rather sensibly – had asked why Cathy didn't just sell up and move house. If the place she lived in held such sadness for her, why didn't she just leave it behind and move on? It would be a good idea but for the fact that it was more complicated than that. Because, while the house that Cathy had once shared with her mum held lots of sad memories, it held happy ones too, and Cathy wasn't sure she was ready to leave those behind just yet, even if sometimes it became hard to look back into her past and see the good times through the fog of the bad ones that she was still trying so hard to dispel.

Besides, she loved her pretty cottage on the outskirts of town and she was well aware that it would be hard to find anything else that lovely and how lucky she was to have inherited it. The rooms might have sometimes felt too small and the beamed ceilings too low, and the tiny sash windows might have had gaps in the frames where the wind whistled through when it was high, and the front door might have been heavy panelled wood that often swelled during the winter, but to Cathy it all felt so familiar and comfortable that she couldn't imagine living in a big bright modern house, even though she admired them in magazines and on TV.

Her mum had loved it too, and though she was no longer here, that fact was another reason not to give the place up. And even if it hadn't been quite as lovely as it was, and even if her mum hadn't loved it as much, the location and size was just about perfect for Cathy as she lived now, so why would she put herself through the stress of trying to find somewhere else that was probably not going to be as good for her?

Fleur stood in the tiny floor space of French for Flowers now, munching solemnly on a delicate pistachio macaron from a batch that

Cathy had spent the previous evening whipping up in readiness for today. They were on their first cup of tea of the day – which they always had once they'd set up the stall with all the day's fresh flower deliveries. Fleur always made the first cup of tea because she was always in far earlier than Cathy. Being single (after a particularly messy break-up) with no kids, she always said it didn't bother her to come in at the crack of dawn because her business was about all she had that really meant anything to her. Sometimes that made Cathy sad to hear, though she knew that Fleur was loved by many friends and that she had a huge family both in England and in Barbados, and she was sure that Fleur – while sometimes discontented – wasn't lonely or unhappy. From the way she talked about her ex, her boss didn't seem all that interested in another man either, and from that point of view it was easy to see why she'd devote all her energy to her business.

As they stood together waiting for the working day to kick in, Cathy was telling Fleur about the recipe book she was planning to put together for the people she'd met at St Cuthbert's.

'That's a brilliant idea,' Fleur said. 'I've always thought it a shame that such delicious recipes were only in your head and nobody else could have a go at them.'

'They were in Mum's head really,' Cathy said. 'And a lot of them I never had a chance to get out before she died. Even when she did share them with me, I can't always remember exactly what she did or how she did it, so I'm having to fill up a lot of gaps as best I can with what I know about baking.'

'Which is a lot.'

'Not as much as some. I'm just an amateur, dabbling on a Sunday for something to do.'

'Isn't that what most people who bake are doing?'

'I suppose so, when you put it like that.' Cathy paused, the welcome warmth from the tea seeping through the mug and into her numb fingers. She hadn't realised how cold it had become in the market building until she'd stopped running around. It was always cooler in winter, but today was bitter, even with the extra heater Fleur had switched on and stashed beneath the counter. 'It was only really a handful of people who wanted recipes anyway and I bet they were only being polite, even then.'

Fleur raised a pair of disbelieving eyebrows.

'I know,' Cathy said, laughing. 'I'm at it again, talking myself down.'

'And you know what I think about that.' Fleur was silent for a moment, her gaze trained on the huge double doors that marked the entrance to the old building. 'You know that printers on the high street?'

'Yes…' Cathy wondered where this sudden turn was going to take the conversation.

'They've got an offer on.'

'Have they?'

'So you could get your little book printed.'

Cathy took a sip of her tea, unsure how to reply to this. An exercise book full of scribbles was hardly worth anything to anyone, and certainly not worth getting printed.

'What for?' she asked finally.

'You could sell them on here.'

Cathy's mug stopped halfway on the journey to her mouth this time. She frowned at Fleur, whose pensive gaze hadn't moved from the entrance doors.

'On the stall?'

'Why not?'

'Who'd want them?'

'Lots of people.'

'The people on the cake stall wouldn't like it.'

'They can go hang. People are allowed to make their own cakes as well as buy from them. I can't see anyone over there tearing a strip off Mary Berry if she walked in here now, could you?'

'Well, no, but… she's a celebrity.'

Fleur turned to her now. 'Even Mary Berry had to start somewhere. I'm just saying you could make yourself a little extra and I think they'd go down well.'

'And you'd be OK with them being on the stall here?'

'Course I would! If I thought we could get away with it, I'd have you selling the cakes too.'

'I couldn't—'

'I know, but there are no food hygiene issues with selling a little recipe book, are there? You could make a killing if you got them out in time for Christmas. You could even put Christmas recipes in there. I should have thought now's the perfect time to get started on your Christmas baking. What are we now – about four, five weeks to go? Isn't that when people usually get started?'

'I'd have to find the money to get them printed first,' Cathy said thoughtfully.

She paused, letting herself absorb the idea. But then she shook her head. 'There's no time for that – it's going to take ages to put the book together as it is, and even though I have a lot, I don't think I've got enough to make a proper, decent-sized book – at least, not decent enough that people would want to pay for it. And doesn't a recipe book have to be all glossy with photographs and wipe-clean pages and stuff? Would the printers on the high street even be able to do that?'

'You could easily take photos of your cakes for them to put in. They could even put photos of you in there.'

'Me?' Cathy burst out laughing. 'We're supposed to be persuading people to bake, not putting them off their pavlovas!'

'I think you'd look lovely in there. Homely, wholesome... a domestic goddess with a secret saucy side... It works for Nigella; she's made a fortune out of it.'

'Now I know you've got something in your tea,' Cathy replied, still laughing. 'Not that I don't appreciate the compliments. It's a lovely dream, but it's just that. Pie in the sky... if you'll excuse the pun. But I might get some copies made for the next coffee morning; just a few pamphlet-sized ones.'

'I still think you're missing a trick there, but if you're determined...'

'Thanks, Fleur.'

Cathy put down her tea for a moment and gave her boss a quick hug.

Fleur laughed lightly as Cathy drew back again. 'What was all that about?'

'For having such faith in me and saying such nice things.'

'They're not nice; they're only the truth.'

'Even so.' Cathy drained the last of her tea. 'I'm going to rinse my mug out in the kitchens out back. Want me to take yours?'

'You can do.' Fleur handed hers over. There was a layer of tea at the bottom, but her boss always left one. Habit, she said, because of all the years her grandma had brewed up using tea leaves – some inevitably found their way to the bottom of the cup, so if Fleur drank down too far, she'd find herself with a mouthful of bitter leaves.

With the mugs clean, Cathy wandered back to the flower stall. As she approached, she saw that Fleur was talking to a man as she bound a lush bunch of scarlet roses. He had his back to Cathy, but he was tall and broad, well dressed with a head of thick, dark hair. Someone was going to be a lucky woman, Cathy thought as she watched the exchange with a smile. The man handed Fleur a banknote, and as she rang it through the till, he turned slightly to glance around the market, presumably waiting for his change.

Cathy froze and almost dropped the mugs she was carrying.

'Jonas!' she breathed.

Chapter Six

He recognised her almost at the same time as she did him, and the shock on his face was almost as great. But while Cathy looked as if she didn't know whether to burst into tears or run away, Jonas broke into a more relaxed smile.

'Long time no see,' he said as Cathy put down the mugs. She glanced briefly at Fleur, but not too quickly to miss a curious and questioning look on Fleur's face.

'Five years,' Cathy said.

'God, that long? That's flown.'

Not for me, Cathy thought. *I've felt every day of those five years.*

'Hasn't it just?' she said, forcing a smile. 'How are you? I thought you'd moved to Scotland with…?'

'Eleanor.'

'Ah, yes, sorry, I forgot…'

As if she could have forgotten his wife. She'd cried when she'd first heard the news that he was to be married, even though she'd resigned herself to their own split. She hadn't even known why she'd cried, but part of her suspected that it had more to do with the life she felt she was missing out on than because she was still hopelessly in love with him. She'd told herself that enough times too, though having him stand here in front of her now after all this time, she wasn't so sure it was true. All she knew at this moment was that she was forcibly reminded of how lonely she'd been and how much she'd missed the embrace of a loving partner, even if she hadn't realised it before.

'We did but… well, I missed home. We came back last week actually. For good. Took a while for us both to get new jobs down here but it was what we both wanted.'

Wordlessly – perhaps not wanting to interrupt what was clearly an exchange loaded with subtext, with history, with things unsaid that both were thinking about – Fleur handed Jonas his change. He dropped it into his jacket pocket and then took the flowers from her.

'So you work here now?' he asked, letting his gaze flit over the stall before it settled on Cathy again.

'Yes. For a couple of months now.'

'And Miriam…?'

Cathy's smile faded.

'Oh, God, I'm so sorry,' he said.

'Yes; Mum died about three months ago. But she's at peace at last and she went way longer than any of her doctors thought she would.'

'And you're OK?'

'I have to be.'

'You have people around you, don't you?' Jonas asked, firing an uncertain glance at Fleur as he did, perhaps wondering if he was giving away things he oughtn't. 'People to lean on? Family? Friends?'

'You know my family,' Cathy said, pushing that awkward, stiff smile back across her face again. 'About as useful as a chocolate teapot, and since Mum died most of them are afraid to get too close in case I actually dare ask them to do things for me. But I'm not alone so you don't need to worry about me.'

'I wasn't, I just…'

His sentence tailed off. He'd given up the right to worry about Cathy five years ago. It had taken time, but there were no hard feelings now. There couldn't be; the love they'd once shared was like a police cold case – it had happened, with drama and fireworks and when it had ended it had torn both lives apart, but it was so long in the past now that everyone had moved on and stopped railing at the injustice of it. Now there were only memories of those fireworks, growing hazier and more distant with every year that passed, until one day they'd barely remember what it had felt like at all. In the end it had been nobody's fault – not really – it had just been the only solution to a situation that was always going to cause pain for someone, no matter how it ended.

'They're lovely,' Cathy said, nodding at the roses in his arms. They were for his wife – that much was obvious – a wife who clearly meant a great deal to him. She didn't want to acknowledge it but she couldn't think of anything else to say.

'Oh, yes…' Jonas looked down at the flowers, and Cathy could have sworn he was blushing. He used to blush a lot, when he felt he'd been caught out doing something he wasn't meant to be doing or telling a little white lie. It was one of the things she'd adored about him.

'Special occasion?' Cathy asked, pursuing the line of conversation in a supreme act of self-harm. Why was she putting herself through this?

He looked up at her. 'Our wedding anniversary actually.'

'Ah. Well, happy anniversary.'

'Thanks.'

He paused, holding her in a warm gaze that felt all at once so heartachingly familiar that felt like she might stop breathing. She could so easily fall into the bottomless depths of those eyes and never resurface and she fought the sensation now, even as they tugged her under. Why did he have to do that? Why was he here now, after all this time? Was this fate? Or was this fate's idea of a joke? They'd managed perfectly well to stay out of each other's way for five years – although him being in Scotland for most of them had certainly helped with that.

She hadn't even heard he'd come back, but then, who was she going to hear that from? Mutual friends had drifted away when they'd split, and it would have been Jonas they'd kept in touch with anyway, not Cathy, who'd barely left her mother's side and certainly had no time to socialise. She hadn't really cared for social media – part of her just too afraid to see what wonderful lives everyone else was having for the resentment that might stoke up in her, resentment that her beautiful mother didn't deserve. Cathy had simply let the world move on without her, putting all her energy into making her mum's last years as good and happy as they could be. She'd known that there would be an end to this part of her own life sooner or later and when it came she could face it better knowing that she'd done all she could. For her, the light would return and the world would open up again, but her mum could never have that, and that thought alone had driven Cathy to put her own needs aside.

'I suppose...' Jonas cleared his throat, tearing his gaze away. 'I should be... you know... getting along. It's good to see you looking so well, by the way.'

Cathy paused. She almost looked down to give herself a once-over but managed to stop herself. She was fairly certain, however, that she didn't look well. Unless that was code for: *you've got fat*. She'd left the house this morning in old jeans and a chunky-knit jumper, knowing it would be cold in the market stall and that her clothes would probably get messed up, and she knew that this jumper, teamed with her lurid-green work tabard, was hardly her most flattering outfit. But she also realised that Jonas was just trying to find something nice to say.

'You too,' she finally replied, only she meant it. He looked so well, so handsome and relaxed, it was like an extra kick to the gut, just to make certain she stayed down.

'Maybe I'll see you around... now that I know where you are.'

He'd always known where she was – he knew where she lived after all – but he'd never sought her out. He'd never come to see how she was coping, to say he was missing her, to say that his life had become poorer without her in it. She'd told him not to when they'd split up, of course, and then once he'd got married later on he wouldn't have been able to. But in the beginning he could have and he hadn't. Maybe he'd thought she'd really meant it, but since when did empty words said in the heat of the moment ever mean anything? More likely than not, now that he knew where she worked, he'd do his utmost never to set foot in the market again. And he had a wife to think about, so she supposed in a strange sort of way it made him a good man, the better person of the two of them, because Cathy wasn't sure if she'd be able to stay away from him had the tables been turned.

'Bye,' Cathy said.

Jonas nodded briefly to Fleur, who'd been doing her best to look as if she wasn't listening, but the fact that she'd rearranged the same pot of daffodils four times now – the one that just happened to be in earshot – said otherwise. Then he acknowledged Cathy again with a brief, sad smile before he turned and walked away.

Cathy hardly realised how long her sigh was until she felt her lungs empty of air.

'Well, that was a bit intense,' Fleur said, her eyes following Jonas until he'd left the building. 'I take it you two were once an item.'

Cathy nodded silently, hardly trusting her voice not to crack. She turned her attention to tidying up some oddments of string that were littering the counter. Fleur would want more of an explanation than that, but she couldn't give it to her – not yet. She'd never told Fleur about Jonas during the months she'd worked for her, though she'd mentioned in passing that she'd once been engaged. She'd never really felt that she had to fill in the details – he was so far in her past that she really hadn't imagined she'd be seeing him again. However, it looked as if that was about to change and she was going to have to fill her boss in soon enough.

Seeing Jonas again when she'd least expected it had been a shock. But it had been more than that. It had opened up an old wound that Cathy had thought neatly healed. She'd been so preoccupied with her mum and then trying to rebuild her life in the wake of her mother's passing that she hadn't even noticed it was still there – or maybe she'd tried so hard to push it from her thoughts that she'd been just a little too successful. But the slightest pressure had torn it open again. It had brought memories – good and bad – flooding back, and with that torrent had come the bitter flotsam and jetsam, resentment towards her situation and her decisions, and the unfair hand life had dealt her that had meant Jonas and Cathy could never be, no matter how much they'd loved each other.

In the end, Jonas hadn't had enough patience and Cathy hadn't had enough strength, and they'd both let it go. Their parting had been amicable, full of explanations and understanding – perhaps too much understanding – and the most painful thing Cathy had ever done. But he was married now too, and Cathy had to ask herself, knowing this, would it have worked between them even without the pressures that looking after Cathy's mum had put on their relationship? Would it make her feel better to believe that they'd always been fated to split up and that he'd never been her destiny anyway?

She'd never know the answer to that and perhaps it was just as well. It was hard enough living with the regrets she already had without adding to the pile. Life had happened, Jonas had moved on and until this moment so had Cathy.

'Want to tell me about it?' Fleur asked.

Cathy leaned against the counter and sighed. Right now she could do with a customer to distract them but the market was quiet and the only stalls with customers were the butcher and the one that sold odds and ends for knitting and sewing.

'There's nothing to tell really.'

'Didn't look that way to me.'

'Remember I told you I was once engaged…?'

'Oh, I guessed that was him already by the look on your face when you saw him. So he's back in Linnetford? Is that going to cause a problem for you?'

'Of course not – why would it? He's married now. Even if I wanted to get together with him – which I don't – it wouldn't be possible.'

'Doesn't stop you from wanting it and doesn't stop it from hurting. Who broke off with who?'

'I did. Sort of. But he hardly put up a fight so I think he'd probably wanted it too.'

'So if it was mutual why do you both seem so hung up on each other?'

'Did it seem that way?'

'Certainly did to me.'

'I suppose… well, I'd never really wanted it to end that way.'

'But you did it anyway?'

'I had to. We'd been having arguments and they'd been getting worse and more frequent, and then one day we had this great big one about my mum and he said some things, and I got upset and called it a day.'

'What did he say?'

Cathy paused. It was a hard memory.

'He thought she made more of her illness because she wanted all my attention and that she hated him for taking me away from her. He thought sometimes she put on episodes so that I would have to cancel meeting him because she was scared she'd lose me. I'll admit that it did seem that way sometimes and that she definitely got worse after we got engaged. We were supposed to have a party – nothing fancy, just a meal with friends to celebrate. Mum passed out and fell down the last few stairs just as I was getting my coat to go out and I couldn't leave her then, could I? Jonas was furious when I called him to cancel and I guess he felt humiliated in front of our friends. I suppose I can understand that.'

'And then what happened?'

'We tried to carry on and I tried to make it up to him, but I guess it was something we just couldn't come back from. Every time Mum was ill he'd say I'd never be able to have a proper married life with him because she'd always need me. I hated hearing that. I could understand why he felt that way but this was my mum he was being so horrible about…'

Cathy blinked back tears and sniffed hard. 'I couldn't keep listening to that no matter how much I loved him and how much I wanted to get married. He never even put up a fight when I told him it was over – never got in touch, never tried to win me back. It made me feel that he'd wanted to leave me but just hadn't known how to do it. I suppose he must have been relieved that I'd done it so he didn't have to. Then I heard he'd started dating someone else and then the next thing they were getting married and moving away. I was OK with it.'

'Were you?'

'What else could I be? Splitting up was what we'd both wanted.'

'Did you know the woman he married?'

Cathy shook her head.

'Well at least he didn't go off with one of your friends…'

'He would never have done that.'

'Because his morals were far too good?' Fleur raised an eyebrow.

'He would never have hurt me like that.'

'Do you really think hurting you or not would have come into it?'

'Yes. He's not a bad person; he's just human.'

'You're too understanding.'

'Maybe.' Cathy gave a wry smile. 'I don't see the point in raking up all that again now and I don't see the point in blaming anyone – what's done is done.'

She said this with conviction – enough conviction to seemingly persuade Fleur, who simply nodded sagely – but she wished she could truly feel it. Because, for the first time since her mum had left her, Cathy felt not only grief, but overwhelming resentment.

It wasn't even about Jonas – not really. Seeing him today had triggered something in her, but it wasn't a longing for him. She didn't love him now – how could she after five years apart from him – but he represented all the things she'd given up or lost over the last few years, all the ways in which she'd been left behind, and seeing it so clearly for the first time stung.

She'd never admitted it until now, but she suddenly realised she wasn't faring as well as she'd imagined. She'd been strong and sure and getting on with her life, but it had all been a lie, a lie she'd told herself as well as the rest of the world. This was about more than Jonas – it had to be. If only she could figure out what it all meant and what she had to do to make it better.

Chapter Seven

Tuesday was a day off work. Usually Cathy would get up anyway, get dressed, potter around the house or go out – whatever she decided on she'd make sure she kept busy. But this morning there didn't seem any point. She'd toyed with the idea of going to the forest where her mum's ashes were scattered and walking amongst the pines, but beyond her window the rain was coming down like arrows from the leaden sky; on a day like this she'd be caked in mud before she'd walked half a mile. It was cold too, and Cathy had turned the thermostat up twice by 10 a.m. in a bid to stave off the chill that had seeped through the house. The exercise book where she'd been cataloguing her recipes was sitting on the kitchen table as she made her second mug of tea but she didn't feel much like resuming that task either. In fact, after it kept catching her eye, she took it to the sitting room with an inpatient sigh and shoved it into a drawer so she couldn't see it.

When she went back into the kitchen, she could see her phone light up from where it was plugged in to charge on a corner of the worktop.

She went over to look and saw that it was from Erica, the woman she'd met at the coffee morning at St Cuthbert's.

Hi Cathy. Hope you're ok. Just checking if you still want to get that coffee? I'm free on Thursday, just wondering if you are x

Cathy stared at the text for a moment. She'd clean forgotten that she'd given Erica her number and agreed to meet up with her. It seemed rude to say no to their meet-up and even ruder to ignore the message, but she really didn't feel like doing anything else. So because she didn't know what to do about it, she simply put the phone down and went back to sit at the table with her cup of tea, staring out of the window at the rain.

Ten minutes later, with her tea cold and barely touched, she looked at her phone again and let out a sigh. It was such a lovely message and she didn't doubt its sincerity, which made her feel like a miserable cow. She couldn't help it, but maybe she didn't have to hide away feeling like this. Maybe she ought to do something to snap out of it, however hard it might be to muster up any enthusiasm for an event that might have her snapping her out of it. In fact, she needed to force herself to do something because, even in her current mood, she recognised that to do nothing might start her on the slippery slope to a place she really wouldn't be able to get back from.

So she messaged Erica to find out what time she wanted to meet. A few more texts went back and forth and, when they'd finally agreed a time and place to meet, that was that and the date was set.

They'd agreed on a place called Ingrid's, an indie coffee shop nestled in a little cobbled, fairy-lit alleyway just off the high street. It was one of those rare gems that you wouldn't know about unless you went looking and you just knew would be worth the effort once you stepped inside. Erica didn't like chains, she'd said, and would rather support independent businesses, and Cathy hadn't tried Ingrid's before and so didn't mind either way.

It was every bit as cute and quaint on the inside as the outside had tantalisingly promised, and Cathy could see why Erica was such a fan. The floors were richly varnished wood, every wall adorned in a rambling mural of a cherry orchard in full blossom, branches snaking from the floor right up to and out across the ceiling, so vivid and lifelike you could almost hear them creaking and rustling in a spring breeze.

Cathy's first thought, once she'd finished staring in wonderment, was that it must have taken someone hours and hours – maybe even weeks or months – to paint. She later discovered that Ingrid herself (the eponymous owner) had done it. Ingrid had studied fine art at university in Oslo some years before but, finding the profession too unpredictable an income source, had decided to go into the catering business instead. It had turned out to be almost as unpredictable in the end, only a slightly more predicable kind of unpredictable and in a less glamorous way.

Cathy told her how beautiful she thought it was, and though it was clear that Ingrid heard that a lot, the compliment still made her glow with pride. Cathy had always wished she'd been more arty but, sadly, it was just another thing that she was really bad at. Her mum had always said that Cathy expressed her creativity through her baking but, although Cathy could accept that she had a certain talent with mirror glaze and sugar roses, it was hardly the same.

The meet-up had been strange at first. It was nice to see Erica, of course, but conversation had started off stilted and awkward. After all, they barely knew each other. But then in some ways that negative became a positive too, because it meant there was a lot to talk about and share.

They were sitting on chairs that looked as if they'd been hewn from still-living tree roots, the wood smooth and bleached and delicate with tables to match. At first glance they'd looked beautiful but uncomfortable and Cathy had been surprised to find they were anything but. They had to contain some magical property, because when she sat down it was like the seat had been specially carved to hold her and her alone. In fact, the whole of Ingrid's coffee house felt sort of magical, like a tea shop populated by gnomes and elves from an Enid Blyton story.

Cathy had ordered a latte, which was very good, and Erica had a flat white. They'd ordered and quickly devoured cakes too, though Erica had joked that Cathy buying cake from Ingrid was a little like selling coals to Newcastle. Cathy had to laugh at that too, but the cranberry granola flapjack she'd tried had been squidgy and moreish, and she'd have happily shipped a whole load home if she hadn't already had a tray of courgette cake made to Myrtle's recipe cooling on a wire rack in her kitchen.

The first thing Cathy learned was that Erica had worked at a restaurant which had closed around the time her dad had become really ill with his cancer and so she'd taken the time to help her mum look after him. Her husband had been happy to support them both financially and had a job at a car manufacturing plant that paid enough for him to do that. Cathy liked this about Erica straight away; even though the situation was a little different from the one she'd found herself in as sole carer for her mum, it was still something they had in common. Since then, Erica hadn't found another job, though she told Cathy she was thinking of retraining in something else – though she hadn't decided what yet – and that was why she hadn't rushed into another waiting job.

Erica also told Cathy about her two siblings – Michelle and Matthias – about losing their dad to cancer earlier that year and the ways in which they'd all coped (or not) with that. To Cathy, Erica's situation sounded utterly heartbreaking.

'Dad had just turned sixty,' Erica said. 'You hear about it all the time, don't you? Men who have always been fit as a flea but then get caught by something totally unexpected that they don't even know they've got until it's too late. He never showed any symptoms and the only reason his cancer was discovered at all was incidentally during a routine wellness check. They gave him six months. He didn't even last four. I think it was the shock – he couldn't deal with being ill, and he couldn't get his head around the diagnosis. None of us could. Matthias especially struggled, but then he'd had such a bad few years…'

Erica paused. She appeared to be weighing up how much she could say, and Cathy sensed there was something more to what she'd begun to divulge about her brother. But she seemed to think better of it and turned the conversation back to her dad.

'Anyway… Dad seemed to get ill so quickly after that it was like he disappeared in front of our eyes…'

Instinctively, Cathy reached across the table for Erica's hand and gave it a squeeze. 'I'm so sorry,' she said.

Erica gave a watery smile and shook herself. 'These things happen, don't they? We all have to go eventually.'

'Yes, but it's a shame we can't all take the nicest way out. Falling asleep at a ripe old age and going with a smile on your face – what's wrong with that? That's the way we all ought to go if we've got to.'

'My mum has always said that,' Erica replied. 'And I'm lucky – at least I still have her. Though she worries me so much at times. I don't think she's ever completely honest about how lonely she is; just tells me she's an old war horse and that I shouldn't bother myself about her.'

'She knows that's never going to happen, I'm sure,' Cathy said. 'She sounds lovely.'

Erica nodded. 'She is.'

'So, how long have you been married?' Cathy asked. 'Malcolm, isn't it?'

'You've got a good memory,' Erica replied, drying her eyes on a napkin. 'I'm sure I only mentioned him in passing at the coffee morning last week. It is Malcolm. About ten years now – second marriage. My first husband turned out to be a dick.'

Cathy burst out laughing. 'So you got rid of him?'

'Oh no,' Erica said. 'I wasn't that smart at the time. I eventually discovered he was having an affair with the neighbour – clichéd or what? It took me five years to figure it out though. How stupid did I feel? And I looked even more stupid when I gave him the "it's her or me" choice and he chose that brassy cow!'

'Is he still with her?' Cathy asked.

Erica shrugged. 'Don't know and don't care. They moved away. If he is, I hope they're very miserable together.'

'Do you have children?'

The fleeting look on Erica's face made Cathy wish she hadn't asked, but it disappeared as quickly as it had come and she shook her head. 'No – it's just me and Malc. How about you?' she asked Cathy. 'Got a man tucked away somewhere you haven't told me about?'

'No,' Cathy said. 'I lead a very boring life. It's just me and my shadow most of the time.'

'It's probably the easiest way to live,' Erica said. 'My family life is constant chaos even without kids.'

Cathy nodded silently. She could have told her how lonely she sometimes was but she liked Erica and she wanted her to ask her to coffee again, and she wouldn't do that if she thought all she did was mope and complain.

'So there's never been anyone?'

'Oh yes,' Cathy said carefully. 'I *was* engaged. It just didn't work out.'

'That must have been hard.'

'It was; I loved him a lot. But like you said, these things happen.'

Erica shot her a sympathetic smile before reaching for her mug. Cathy didn't want to talk any more about this; she was tired enough from having told Fleur and then thinking about it constantly since, going over and over moments and events in her head, things that had happened years before between her and Jonas that ought to have been well and truly forgotten. They had been, and would have stayed that way if he hadn't decided to show up and drag them out from the depths of her memory again.

'There's another coffee morning at St Cuthbert's next week,' she said, keen to change the subject so she could stop thinking about Jonas. 'Are you going?'

'Another charity one?'

'I don't think so. Just a general meeting-up thing, I think. Are you going?'

Erica shook her head. 'I don't know… I spent the last one trying to avoid getting roped into going to church on Sunday. Iris must be God's top recruiter. And they're all a bit…'

'Old?' Cathy asked, raising her eyebrows with a faint smile.

Erica grinned. 'I'm glad you said it.'

'But they are all really nice and I feel a bit bad never turning up again when they were so kind and so keen for us to go back for the next one. Besides, it would give me a good excuse to bake lots of things and force-feed them to people.'

'I don't think you'd have to force-feed them to anyone,' Erica said. 'You'd have to use force to keep me away from your cakes.'

Cathy couldn't help but laugh at this. 'Iris has been trying to persuade me to go to church too. I wouldn't mind so much once in a while, but I feel that if I go once I wouldn't be allowed to stop going, and I don't want to be tied to a promise like that.'

'I don't have time for stuff like that on a Sunday even if I wanted to go,' Erica said. 'There's just too much going on.'

'I wish I could say that,' Cathy said with a small smile.

'Oh, it's nothing exciting. Just family stuff – making sure Mum's OK and not getting lonely, keeping on top of the housework and such…'

'I might still go to the coffee morning, though,' Cathy said. 'I really enjoyed the last one, even though it was full of old folks. You've got to admit they're quite entertaining.'

'Iris and Dora certainly are. I thought at one point I was going to have to break up an actual catfight last time we were there.'

Cathy laughed. 'When was that?'

'When they both wanted the last Black Forest muffin.'

'Oh!' Cathy said. 'I thought they were joking!'

'They might have been but they definitely have a strange love–hate relationship. Like me and my sister – we can't stand the sight of each other most days but if anyone did anything to her they'd have me to answer to. She'd be the same.'

'Iris and Dora are cousins, though. I'll admit I never had that relationship with any of my cousins, but I suppose if you've been brought up close you might become like sisters.'

'I suppose so.'

'So we've agreed we're going to the next coffee morning?'

'Well if you go then I'll go,' Erica said. 'There's strength in numbers – together we'll be able to resist Iris. I'll bake this time if you let me have one of your recipes to try,' she added. 'I've been thinking about those coconut things all week – they were soooo good!'

'I've been writing them down actually,' Cathy said. 'My mum always kept them mostly in her head and I've always done the same, but I thought it was about time I made a note of them because…'

She paused. *Because I don't have anyone to teach them to and no daughter to pass them on to and that might never happen. If I don't write them down now they might be lost forever…*

'Well,' she continued brightly – perhaps a little too brightly – 'because I did wonder whether the people who'd said they'd like them might actually want a copy. I mean, I know people asked for recipes but maybe they were just being polite.'

'I don't know about that,' Erica said. 'They could have just said the cakes were nice and left it at that. Everyone told Myrtle her fairy cakes were nice but nobody wanted the recipe because who would want to replicate those little disasters in their own kitchen – what a waste of food!'

'Oh but the courgette cake was lovely,' Cathy said, rushing to Myrtle's defence, despite the old lady being completely oblivious to anything being said about her. 'I took the recipe from her for that.'

'Courgette has no business being in any kind of cake. It has no business in anything if you ask me – it's just ugly cucumber.'

Cathy laughed. 'I don't mind it so much,' she said.

'Hmm.' Erica peered at Cathy over the rim of her cup as she took a sip. Which led Cathy to believe that her views on courgettes were ones that Erica disagreed with most profoundly.

'So it's a date!'

'The church coffee morning – the hottest date I've been on in a long time,' Erica said. 'How depressing is that?'

Cathy started to laugh again, but even as she did, she realised that it actually *was* the hottest date she'd been on in years – and that was no joke.

Chapter Eight

Cathy had settled on baking a batch of chocolate brownies (half with hazelnuts and half without), some vanilla cupcakes, egg custard tarts and shortbread, and she'd whipped everything up so quickly that she felt almost guilty that she was putting in very little effort. In fact, she nearly brought in a whole load of new ingredients to make a few more complicated things, but when she'd sent a photo of her spread to Erica and asked whether it was enough of a contribution to the coffee morning, Erica told her not to be mental and that she'd already baked enough to feed half the population of Greater Manchester, let alone their tiny gathering, and to remember that others might be bringing food too. So she'd taken Erica's advice and left it at that.

'Oh, here she is!'

Iris clapped her hands together with a broad smile as Cathy lugged her plastic tubs in. 'And if I'm not mistaken she's got some of her divine goodies with her!'

'Anyone would think you were more pleased to see the cakes than her,' Dora said, unfolding from her chair to come over and take some of the containers from Cathy.

'You're the one grabbing them before her coat's come off,' Iris fired back.

'I'm just helping the woman!' Dora snapped. 'Unlike some, who just stand and watch her struggle.'

Iris threw her cousin a sour look but said nothing. Instead she turned to Cathy again, her face instantly transforming into a bright smile.

'I'm so glad you came back. So you enjoyed the last one?'

'Very much,' Cathy said.

'How wonderful. So does this mean we might see you in church soon too?'

Cathy hesitated. She was about to offer some awkward, bumbling and non-committal reply when Dora jumped in to save her.

'Don't hassle the woman!' she said. 'You're obsessed with people coming to church; you're not recruiting for the Moonies, you know! Leave her alone – if she wants to come she will, and if she doesn't she'll still be welcome at other events.' She gave Cathy a sideways look. 'All this is because she fancies the vicar, you know.'

'I do not!' Iris cried, a look of utter outrage on her face.

'Oh you do!' Dora laughed. 'There's no point in denying it – everyone knows!'

Cathy wasn't sure what sort of reply she was meant to give so she smiled uncertainly and glanced around the room. There were definitely fewer people today than there had been for the last coffee morning. Erica hadn't arrived yet, though she'd said she was still coming when Cathy had messaged her to double-check the previous evening. It was a little disappointing to see she wasn't there yet and Cathy hoped she hadn't changed her mind about it. Colin was in the corner arranging cups around a large steel tea urn. Myrtle was talking to him and one or two other people Cathy recognised but couldn't put names to.

Just as Cathy was doing a quick mental rundown of the faces she knew and the ones she didn't, Iris uttered an exclamation of satisfaction, turning to the door with a smile, and Cathy looked to see Erica had arrived, carrying a plastic container of her own. She waved at Cathy as she walked in before handing her tub to Iris.

'How lovely to see you!' Iris said. She held the box up to her face, as if trying to see through the opaque plastic. 'What have you got for us?'

'I had a go at those madeleine things,' Erica said, smiling at Cathy as she continued. 'I've no idea what they'll taste like but if they're no good it'll be totally my fault because your recipe was so easy to follow.'

Cathy beamed at her. 'I'm sure they'll be lovely. I'm glad you got on alright with it.'

'I actually enjoyed myself.' Erica unfastened her coat. 'I've never considered myself a real cook before – neither has Malc, come to think of it – but I can see now why people like to do it. I found it so therapeutic to ignore the news and my phone and everything else and just concentrate on something completely different. And you do get quite a buzz when they come out of the oven looking at least a little bit like they're supposed to. At least eventually. The first lot were so overdone they looked as if they'd been baked on the surface of the sun. I think my oven temperature's a bit out of whack so I kept checking the second batch and they came out much better.'

'It's the most peaceful time for me,' Cathy said. 'I'm never as calm and content as I am when I'm baking and I love feeling like I'm creating something, even if it is only food. I can imagine if baking makes me feel that happy, artists and sculptors who make fantastic works of art must feel delirious when they look at what they've done.'

'I don't know about that,' Dora piped up. 'I knew a painter once. The most miserable old bastard I've ever met.'

'Dora!' Iris squeaked.

'You knew him too,' Dora said. 'Marcel… you must remember him. He used to threaten to kill himself every time he finished a painting because he said he'd never be able to create anything that beautiful again and so what was the point in going on? And you know, he wasn't even that good. I mean, there's a few hanging up in the church but he's hardly Turner.'

Iris looked as if she might contradict Dora's assertion for a moment. But then an expression of illumination lit her face, as did a slightly wicked grin of the kind Cathy had never imagined she'd see on someone who spent so much time in a church.

She clicked her fingers. 'Marcel! Didn't he move to Doncaster?'

'Yes; lucky Doncaster!'

Erica looked almost as bemused as Cathy as she followed the conversation, but then took the opportunity of a brief lull in Iris and Dora's stream-of-consciousness recollections of the infamous Marcel to gently guide the conversation away from it.

'Well, I think your cakes are works of art, Cathy,' she said. 'Mine, I'm not so sure about but I enjoyed giving it a go and I do sort of see what you mean. They don't look as pretty as yours did but I'm quite proud of them for a first attempt. Malcolm ate one and he hasn't had to go to the hospital yet so I'm fairly confident they're not going to kill anyone either.'

'What they taste like is all that matters,' Cathy said, laughing.

'Well,' Erica returned with a grin, 'I can't say Malcolm has the best taste – he eats so fast he barely tastes anything – so they might not taste all that pretty either.'

'Why don't you find a seat?' Iris said to Cathy and Erica. 'Colin!' she shouted over to where he was wrestling the tea urn onto a trolley. 'How are we doing with those hot drinks?'

'I've been ready for ages. I was just waiting for you lot to stop nattering.'

'We weren't nattering,' Iris said, looking indignant.

'What do you call it then?' Dora replied, rolling her eyes. 'We weren't doing the hundred metres sprint!'

'Yes, but Colin is saying it in a way that makes us sound like chatterboxes.'

'We *are* chatterboxes,' Dora said. 'Well, you are anyway. The rest of us would like the opportunity to be chatterboxes but we can't get a word in when you're talking.'

'You were the one going on about that Marcel fellow!' Iris squeaked.

'Only because you mentioned artists.'

'It was Cathy who mentioned artists.'

Cathy looked vaguely alarmed at being dragged back into this as she popped her handbag on a seat next to Erica's. She was about to respond when Erica laid a hand on her arm and winked.

'I wouldn't bother,' she said in a low voice. 'Easier to let it go.'

Cathy relaxed. She was beginning to realise that this coffee morning had the potential to turn into the Mad Hatter's tea party, and while she wasn't sure how she felt about that, at least it would be entertaining. As long as she didn't become Alice, dragged into an utterly bewildering exchange that she had no chance of understanding. At least she had Erica there. The more time she spent with her, the more she liked her, and she was beginning to hope that this might be the start of a very good friendship.

She glanced up to see that Colin had brought the drinks trolley over to the seating area, while Iris and Dora were busy unwrapping and uncovering the treats people had brought in.

'Help yourselves, folks!' Colin said cheerily, and nobody needed telling twice as they fell on the offerings. Along with cakes from Cathy, Erica and Dora, there was a huge selection pack of biscuits that Myrtle had brought in – fancy ones from Waitrose, she'd said, because she hadn't had time to bake and felt a bit guilty about it.

Once everyone was settled, conversation turned to various subjects as diverse as the never-ending roadworks outside the town hall to how much Baxter Pippington's new moustache suited him (whoever Baxter Pippington was). And then, inevitably, it turned to cake appreciation. So much fuss was made over Cathy's cakes, once again, that it was becoming almost embarrassing for her.

'Anyone could do it,' she protested, her face burning. 'I mean, Erica's have turned out lovely. It's all down to following the recipe really.'

'Don't be so modest,' Erica said. 'Mine might be alright but they're not a patch on yours.'

'That's only down to practice,' Cathy insisted. 'The more you do it, the better you'll be.'

'But it's instinctive with you – anyone can see that.' Erica looked around the room and a few people nodded agreement.

'Well,' Cathy said, her face growing even hotter. 'That's from practice too. After a while you can see straight away what looks and even smells right. But the basic principle of following a recipe is the same point we all start at.'

'Really?' Erica looked sceptical. 'But you bake without a recipe. You told us that you do it all from memory and I doubt any of us could do that.'

'Only because I've done it so often.'

'You know what,' Dora put in as she chewed on a brownie (with hazelnuts, because as far as she was concerned all this nut allergy business was a fad and nobody had nut allergies in her day), looking slightly like a contented cow with a cud, 'you should give lessons.'

Cathy looked blankly at her. 'Lessons?'

'You could use our kitchen here... couldn't she, Iris?'

It was Iris's turn to look blank. 'Our kitchen? Here? At St Cuthbert's?'

Dora took another bite of her brownie. 'I'm sure Reverend Lovely Locks would say yes if you asked him nicely,' she said, not worried at all by the fact that her mouth was rather full of chocolate as she spoke.

'He's got a lot on already,' Iris said stiffly. 'I couldn't ask him to use the kitchen just because a few people want to make better cakes.'

Dora shrugged carelessly. 'Make it some kind of community thing for the needy and he would.'

'But that would be lying to him!'

Dora rolled her eyes. 'Not if it *was* some kind of community thing for the needy.'

'Yes, but what needy person needs cookery lessons?' Iris asked, looking confused. 'Surely they have more pressing needs than that?'

'You know,' Colin said thoughtfully, 'that's not actually a bad idea, Dora. You could charge a pound or two a head, get people to bring their own ingredients in, and the admission money could go to the church fund. Or, if you wanted to make it more community-spirited, you could make it free for people in need of a little extra support – lonely pensioners, people with nobody to fall back on or who have particular emotional needs... that sort of thing. The more vulnerable members of society that could do with the monotony of their week breaking up – let's face it, there are plenty of them.'

Cathy suspected that quite a few of them might be in the room now and, judging by his meaningful look at Iris, Colin knew for sure they were.

Iris said nothing for a moment. She sipped at her tea and a strange silence fell over the room. But then she looked up. 'I think the vicar might go for that.'

'I think so too,' Colin said.

'I think he'd love it,' Dora agreed, and Myrtle made an enthusiastic noise through her mouthful of jammy dodger to show her support too.

Cathy looked at Erica, Dora, Iris and Colin in turn. Then she looked at everyone else, slightly gobsmacked that nobody had yet pointed out what a stupid idea it was and how obvious it was to anyone that she would be rubbish at leading any sort of class. And at what point was anyone going to ask her if she even wanted to teach cookery classes – whether the students were needy or not?

Almost as if she'd read her mind, Erica turned to Cathy. 'What do you think? Would you fancy it?'

Cathy's frown deepened. 'I don't know. It would depend on so much.'

'It's all hypothetical, of course,' Iris said. 'Very much up in the air and the vicar may well say no. It may prove to be quite impractical too, even if he says yes, but is the idea of it something that appeals to you?'

Cathy formed the word: *no.*

But she stopped herself from saying it. Apart from working a couple of days with Fleur she was quite bored day to day and she couldn't rely on social events like this to fill the gap, or expect that new friends would always be available to meet up. The way she'd reacted to meeting Jonas again was currently playing a part in her thought processes too. Seeing him and the way his life had moved on had thrown her – not only in the way it had shocked her but in that it had called into question everything about her life as it currently was, whether there was any point to it and certainly whether there was any point to her. But today... being here today with this lovely bunch of people she felt more hopeful, more optimistic. Perhaps she could try again to turn things around and, with the support of the St Cuthbert's coffee gang (which was what she was going to call them from now on), she could do that.

Feeling useful to someone in some capacity would certainly go some way to doing that, surely? Maybe something like this could be the answer, the thing she'd been searching for all along. And she did love baking so much that it couldn't be that much of a hardship to share her passion with others, could it? Would it be so bad to give it a try?

Anyway, she reasoned, these thoughts flying through her head faster than she could keep up with, the vicar was probably going to say no anyway.

'I'm not sure I'd be any good at teaching people,' she said.

'You wouldn't have to make it that formal,' Colin replied. 'You would only have to supply the recipe, maybe do a quick demonstration… Everyone will simply get on with it. You'd go round giving help and guidance when they need it. It would really be a social thing more than anything else.'

'And there are plenty of people who would benefit from knowing how to cook from scratch,' Dora said. 'Too many eating things from packets and tins these days – good home cooking is a fast-disappearing skill.'

Cathy wasn't sure that was completely true – the number of cookery programmes on TV would argue against that – but she did see where Dora was coming from. If someone had grown up in a house where nobody cooked or they'd never been shown how to do anything, they'd have grown up with a relationship with food that was sadly lacking in real love or appreciation.

With every second that passed she was warming to the idea.

'I suppose it might be alright. I might learn a thing or two as well – I don't imagine everyone who'd come wouldn't be able to cook at all.'

'Exactly,' Dora said. 'They might just fancy a meet-up with other people who like cooking, or they might just want to get better, but even the worst cooks can have the odd trick or two up their sleeve…'

Dora's glance rested on Myrtle for a moment. Luckily, she was preoccupied trying to wrestle the last custard cream from the bottom of the Waitrose selection pack and hadn't noticed Dora looking at her. Cathy had to admit that she sort of saw what Dora was trying to say, though Myrtle seemed like a rather unkind example – after all, her courgette cake had been pretty good, even if Cathy had had to tinker with the recipe a bit as she'd gone along.

'I'll talk to the vicar,' Iris said.

'I thought you might,' Dora said.

Iris looked sharply at her, but if Dora had meant any sarcasm, her expression of absolute innocence was giving nothing away.

'I can't promise anything though,' Iris added.

'I think it's brilliant,' Erica said warmly. 'I think he'll say yes – he's got to. I'll come; I'd love to learn how to make more cakes.'

'Me too,' Myrtle said.

'Count me in,' Colin added with a broad smile. 'I'm one of your folks who've spent their lives eating from packets and tins, Dora. I've never so much as held a spatula but I'm willing to learn.'

Cathy blew out a breath as she surveyed the faces around her. She'd been expecting many things from her visit this morning, maybe even hoped for one or two, but this certainly hadn't been one of them. Surprise plans and spontaneous decisions weren't things that had featured highly in her life over the last few years, and she wasn't quite sure how she felt about them. *It's alright*, she told herself, *the vicar will probably say no.*

But what if he said yes?

Chapter Nine

'And…?'

'He said yes – we can go ahead and do the class.'

'I can see you're excited too.'

'Is it that obvious?'

'Yes, you're glowing!'

Fleur smiled fondly at Cathy, who put a self-conscious hand to her face. It didn't feel hot.

'Am I?'

'I haven't seen you look so happy since… Well, I'm not sure I've ever seen you look so happy.'

'I've been happy,' Cathy said, a slight defensive note creeping into her tone. 'I'm not that miserable, am I?'

'You smile, but that's not the same.'

'Isn't it?'

Fleur folded her arms and leaned against the counter, regarding Cathy for the longest moment. Then she shook her head slowly. 'We can all smile and pretend there's no pain going on behind it, and some of the time we can even fool everyone else into believing that too. But I can see it. From what you've told me you haven't had an easy few years, love, so don't feel bad for me pointing it out; nobody would blame you for faking that smile with what you've been through. Hell, I'm sure a lot of people wouldn't even try to smile. But today… today it's real enough. Whatever happens at your new class I think it's good news that it's got the go-ahead. It'll be good for you, regardless of whether it's good for anyone else.'

'I suppose it will,' Cathy said thoughtfully. She hadn't really considered it that way until Fleur had said it, but now it seemed so obvious that this class was probably going to do more to help Cathy than it was anyone else. She couldn't deny that she was excited too. Since the phone call from Iris her head had been buzzing with ideas for her first session – wondering who would come, what they'd be like, what they might need and want from her, how she could make certain everyone was included, what they could make that would keep the more skilled cooks challenged but not be too difficult for the less skilled ones, and what wouldn't put off complete beginners.

'Do you have any idea of numbers yet?' Fleur wound a scarlet ribbon around the stems of a bunch of snow-white roses before pinning it in place so that it didn't slip down when they were handled. They were part of an order for a winter wedding, and Cathy half wished she'd been invited to it because, if the choice of flowers was anything to go by, the wedding itself was going to be stunning. Fleur put the bouquet to one side and began work on another, smaller version where the white roses were broken up with carnations – presumably for one of the bridesmaids. She worked quickly and confidently, swapping the flowers with such dexterity that Cathy marvelled, distracted into silence as she always was, no matter how many times she'd seen it before. In a few short moments her boss flicked out a hand and Cathy placed another ribbon into it.

'Not really,' she said, remembering now that Fleur had just asked her a question.

'What will you cook?'

'I'm not sure about that either – I need to think about it. I'll go through the recipes I've already written down to see if there's something in there.'

'I'm sure it would be easier to use something you've already got in your book,' Fleur agreed. 'Did you think any more about getting it printed?'

'I haven't really had time to think about it,' Cathy said, cutting off another length of ribbon and placing it in Fleur's waiting hand. 'There's just been too much going on.'

'That sounds like an excuse if ever I heard one. Are you sure it's not just you being overly modest as usual? Now would seem like the ideal time to me.' Fleur took a pin from her mouth to fasten the stems of the posy she was currently constructing. 'You could take copies to your class so that everyone would have the recipes to hand. And if you're thinking nobody will want your book I'm sure that's not the case. If they're interested enough to sign up for the session then it stands to reason they would want a recipe book to accompany it.'

'Oh,' Cathy said. 'I was just going to write it on the whiteboard.'

'But then how would anyone make it again when they got home?'

'I thought they might write it down if they wanted to do it again.'

'Aren't you going to send them an ingredient list before the class so they know what to bring?'

'Well, probably, but that's only ingredients.'

Fleur shook her head. 'Why not send the method out too? You can't rely on people getting it down right – you only have to play Chinese whispers to see how easily people can mess things up. I'd give them exact copies if I were you.'

'But if they have a whole book of recipes at the first class they might not come back. Or if I send out the method then they might just do it at home anyway.'

'Of course they'd still come. They can get recipes on the internet if they want to stay home; there's hundreds of them out there. You said yourself it's about socialising more than it's about cooking. They'll come back to see their friends again. They'd come back for you too; people want to be shown how to do things. Why do you think the TV schedules are full of programmes telling us how to make omelettes? Everyone knows omelette is basically a smashed egg, but we still want to be shown how to do it properly.'

'You think so?'

'I do. You worry too much.'

Cathy was about to reply when her attention was caught by a figure walking in through the double doors of the market hall. Her forehead creased into a vague frown, and much as she hated the treachery of a heart that shouldn't have reacted as she recognised him, it began to beat that little bit faster anyway.

Fleur, noticing that the conversation had stopped mid-flow, turned to see what Cathy was staring at, and then her forehead creased into a frown too.

'Isn't that your old boyfriend? The one that bought flowers for his wife last week?'

'Yes,' Cathy said. And as she continued to watch, she realised with horror that he was coming to French for Flowers again.

'I've got this,' Fleur said in a low voice. 'Make yourself scarce if you feel the need to.'

But Cathy didn't have time to get away, and it would have looked too obvious anyway. She stood, rooted to the spot, unable to stop staring as Jonas walked towards them. He had his hands deep in the pockets of his expensively tailored woollen coat as he stopped at the stall and smiled.

A vague and fleeting thought crossed Cathy's mind as she noted it. When they'd been together he'd been working as a delivery driver for a local warehouse, but during the five years they'd been apart much had changed. At least it looked that way, because the clothes he was wearing suggested that he didn't drive delivery trucks these days.

Since the day he'd unexpectedly come back into her life she hadn't been able to help thinking of him, even though she wished she could, and she'd even searched for him on an old Facebook account that she hadn't logged into for so long she'd had to get a new password for it. Given her aversion to social media, that was significant in itself. But he'd either taken himself off there or else made himself invisible to the public, because she hadn't been able to find him. And if she had – what would she have done anyway? Tortured herself with photos of him and his lovely wife and his perfect new life without her – the life she might have been gifted had her own fortunes been different?

In the end she'd decided she was better off not knowing and letting the past lie – it wasn't like she was going to see him again anyway. So why did he have to go and ruin her one comforting thought by turning up again now? Why couldn't he just stay away? Did he know what this was doing to her? Did he take some perverse pleasure in making her suffer, because he must have known that his coming here would make her suffer? How could he not know? Was he really that clueless?

'Hello,' Fleur said smoothly. 'What can I do for you?'

His eyes went to Cathy, who was now behind Fleur, desperately wishing she could look like she didn't care that he was there but knowing that her face said anything but. She began to tidy away the ribbons, even though they hadn't finished using them. Anything to save having to talk to him.

Jonas scanned the pre-made bouquets and picked one carelessly from its display pot. He handed it to Fleur.

'I'll take these.'

While Fleur wrapped them for him, he spoke again, and this time Cathy couldn't ignore it.

'I was sorry to hear about your mum,' he said.

She looked up.

'I should have said that when I was last here,' he added.

'I think you did,' Cathy replied, trying but failing to smile.

'I should have said it like I meant it. Afterwards I realised that I'd been insensitive. I was too busy thinking about getting home for my anniversary dinner but that was selfish – it wouldn't have hurt to take thirty more seconds to say that I was really sorry, and that I know how hard it must have been on you.'

For a second she was back in the hallway of her home, her mum struggling for breath at the bottom of their stairs and nursing a twisted ankle, Cathy dressed to the nines and sobbing into the phone as she apologised to a clearly fuming Jonas that she was going to have to stand him up on what should have been their engagement celebration. Afterwards he'd said he was sorry for being angry and that he understood why she'd had to put her mum first, and he'd told her he was sorry for overreacting, and she'd wanted to believe him but she couldn't – not quite. It had been the beginning of the end for them and they'd never really come back from that moment.

Cathy shook her head now to clear the unwanted memory. 'It doesn't matter.'

'It does.'

'Well… thank you then.'

'You look well,' he said. 'Really well.'

That was a lie, but she didn't say so. She looked about as well as she had the first time he'd said it – which was dressed in her scruffy work clothes with a snot-green tabard and a greasy fringe completing the look.

'You're obviously doing OK,' he continued.

Another lie, or was he just blind?

'You too,' she said. 'Nice coat.'

Was it just her or were they going round in circles? Hadn't they had a very similar conversation to this the last time he'd come to the stall? What did he really want? And why did Cathy have to feel as if there was any agenda at all? Why did she have to be so full of suspicion? She shook the thought. He was here as an old friend, and why would there be anything else in it? And while she appreciated the gesture, she wished he wouldn't bother. She'd been fine without him for five years, and even if she hadn't been, this was hardly going to help – even he must be able to see that.

'Five pounds please,' Fleur cut in, shoving the bouquet at Jonas with rather more force, Cathy thought, than she usually would.

'Oh, right…'

He fumbled in his pocket for a moment before pulling out his wallet and handing the note over. Fleur took it and he took the flowers.

'Thank you.'

'You're very welcome,' she said. And added in a pointed tone: 'Is there anything else we can do for you, sir? Or will that be all?'

'Oh, yes… I guess… that's all.'

'Goodbye then, sir,' Fleur said, still in that very deliberate tone that told him it was time to leave rather than asking him to. 'Thank you for your custom.'

She might have added *please call again*, but Cathy knew that even her boss wasn't so desperate for business that she'd put Cathy through that.

Jonas looked up at Cathy, and there was something in his eyes that she hadn't seen for a long time. It was that look he'd sometimes get when he knew something was a lost cause but he wasn't quite ready to let go of it, even though he knew he should. He'd worn it the night they'd split up. She'd probably worn it too, but still they'd split up. It had been inevitable, an outcome as irresistible as the earth turning, and neither of them would have been able to stop it no matter how much they might have wanted to.

'It was good to see you again,' he said.

Cathy nodded mutely. What could she say that wouldn't be a lie? It wasn't good to see him; it was a hard, exquisite sort of pain. She didn't want to see him at all, and yet when he was there in front of her she couldn't stop looking. He'd changed in the past five years, but he was still the man she'd once loved.

She kept her eyes fixed on his back as he walked away and out of the market, and only once he was gone did she allow herself a heaving breath of relief. Had she been anywhere else instead of with Fleur, she might even have allowed herself a few tears, but now wasn't the time and this was definitely not the place.

'Well,' her boss said, turning to Cathy. 'That was a bit funny, wasn't it?'

'Was it?' Cathy said, trying to sound careless.

'Why do you think he would come here again?'

'He wanted flowers, I suppose.'

'Hmm. And there are no other florists around here he could get them from?'

'I suppose we have nice bunches… affordable, you know.'

'Yes, because he really looked as if he was poverty-stricken so I guess price would be an issue for a man like that…'

Fleur held Cathy in a measured gaze, and Cathy eventually quailed under it. She shrugged.

'I don't know why he came here but I wish he wouldn't.'

'I wonder what his wife would say if she knew.'

Cathy stared at her. 'What do you mean?'

'Oh, come on! You'd have to be blind not to see the man still cares for you.'

Cathy shook her head. 'He might care for me but not in the way you think. I care for him too but only as someone I was once engaged to.'

Fleur went back to her bouquets, but the loaded silence of her non-reply was almost as unbearable as any reply might have been. What did she think of what she'd seen? What did she make of all this?

'None of it matters now anyway,' Cathy said at last, the silence forcing her to fill it with something that might make it weigh less heavily.

'I'd say it does to you.'

'Even if it did it wouldn't change the fact that he's married and we've both moved on. It's just sentimentality, that's all. For him too – that's why he came back today.'

'You just keep telling yourself that,' Fleur said with a small smile.

Cathy tried to ignore it. Instead, she collected their mugs and headed for the kitchens so that she wouldn't have to say anything at all, because, for the first time since Cathy had started working with her, she felt like telling her lovely boss to shut up and mind her own business.

Chapter Ten

Her hands were knotted together as she sat on a high stool at the worktop and waited, while her knees jigged a staccato rhythm as she tried to calm her nerves. She really wished she could sit still because it was kind of exhausting. Iris placed a mug of tea down in front of her.

'I'm really looking forward to it,' she said.

Cathy wished she could say the same. For a few days she'd been excited for her first class, but as it had drawn closer she'd started to wish she'd said no to the idea. The nerves had begun to build a few days before, and by this morning she was about ready to throw up what little breakfast she'd managed to force down. It would be fine once they got started – she knew that – and it wasn't like anyone was expecting anything spectacular. She hadn't pretended to be a qualified teacher, or that anyone would be a professional-standard baker by the time they'd finished, but the idea of standing in front of a bunch of people giving advice and tuition, like she knew more than them, still made her feel like a fraud. It was too late to run away now – the first participants would be arriving at any moment – but Lord, did Cathy want to.

She'd got there an hour early to find only Iris around to let her in and had taken her time to set up, hoping that feeling utterly prepared would help to calm her nerves, but she'd finished all that with time to spare and, in the end, the sitting around waiting with nothing to take her mind off it had only made things worse.

At least the kitchen at St Cuthbert's church hall was big and surprisingly modern and well equipped. It was bright and clean, the walls painted a simple cream and the sunlight from the windows filtered by neutral-coloured vertical blinds, and fitted to a standard that any restaurant would be proud of. There were stainless-steel worktops and sinks, one of those stretchy shower nozzle things to rinse dishes (Cathy had never known what they were called) and a bank of four ovens, as well as numerous hobs and cupboards crammed with utensils, crockery, pots and pans. It was almost like whoever had stocked it had been waiting for something like Cathy's class. Iris had told her that they had quite a lot of equipment, but Cathy had been a little sceptical about it until she'd seen the impressive inventory for herself. She supposed they must do a lot of catering for various events, but she hadn't really considered it before. Iris had shown Cathy around first thing and, though ordinarily the chance to use a space like this would have been heaven for Cathy, today it was wasted on her because she just couldn't think about that.

'Do you have everything you need?' Iris asked.

'I think so.'

Cathy gave the worktop a vague sweep. She could well have needed lots of things, but she couldn't make her brain work right now to figure out what might be missing. However, she'd made meticulous plans during the days leading up to this one so she had to assume that she probably had everything covered. Even if she hadn't, whatever was missing would be a thing so minor they could probably manage without it. She just wished that everyone would get here so they could make a start and then, perhaps, her nerves might calm a little. It wasn't like she was waiting to be shot at dawn and she knew it was irrational to be so stressed about something so insignificant, but still, the worst thing about all of this was the waiting.

'Oh, look,' Iris said, her gaze going to the door. 'Here's Dora. Why she's come I don't know – it's hardly aimed at her.'

Cathy couldn't think why it wouldn't be aimed at Dora – if she wanted to learn how to bake or get better at it or simply socialise, then why wouldn't she come? That had been the main idea behind setting these classes up after all. She suspected that it had more to do with Iris being annoyed that Dora was going to be here, baiting her all morning, which, if Cathy had been in a less stressed mood, would have been quite funny. They were such an odd pair – half the time best friends and half the time mortal enemies – but Cathy liked them both.

'Hello, Dora.' Cathy slid off her stool and went to take some of Dora's bags while she got her coat off and hung it up.

'I've come because it was my idea,' Dora said pointedly as she glared at Iris, who – to her credit – blushed; she'd clearly thought her cousin hadn't heard her comment and was mortified to discover she had.

'It wasn't your idea; it was mine,' Iris said sulkily, not to be beaten anyway.

'You wouldn't know a good idea if it bit you on the nose,' Dora said. She looked at Cathy. 'Wasn't it my idea?'

Cathy glanced from one to the other. 'Um…'

If only someone else would arrive to take the heat off her.

Perhaps someone up there was listening, because just as she was thinking this, Myrtle arrived, dragging a wheeled shopping basket behind her. Cathy almost launched herself at the newcomer.

'Myrtle! I'm so glad you could come!'

'I wouldn't have missed it for anything,' Myrtle replied, taking off her gloves and reaching into her shopper. She pulled out a plastic tub and took the lid off before placing it on the worktop. Cathy peered inside, expecting it to be the first of the ingredients they'd need for the Madeira loaf she was planning to get them all to bake, but to her surprise it was full of mints.

'Oh, you've brought mint imperials!' Dora exclaimed, marching over and popping one into her mouth. 'Are they in stock again at the pound store?'

'I bought twelve bags,' Myrtle said, 'just in case they run out again.'

Cathy suspected they'd be running out very quickly if everyone was buying twelve bags at a time just in case, but she thought better of saying so.

Myrtle shook the tub at her. 'Would you like one?'

'Maybe later,' Cathy replied with a faintly bemused smile. 'Thank you.'

Myrtle gave a solemn nod as she took one for herself and then placed the tub back on the worktop. 'I'll just leave them out here so people can help themselves.'

'Have you got all your ingredients, Myrtle?' Iris asked with a slight tinge of impatience in her tone. 'Because we don't have any to spare if you don't have what you need, you know.'

'Actually, I do,' Cathy put in, and Iris shot her such a withering look that she wished she hadn't.

'People,' Iris replied, with great emphasis on the word, as if *people* were somehow the great unwashed, 'need to come prepared otherwise we'll spend half the lesson sorting them out with things they haven't brought. Isn't having all your ingredients ready the first rule of cookery?'

'Well, yes,' Cathy replied, wondering when Iris had morphed into a mini dictator. If it had happened this morning she'd somehow missed it. Was this what a bit of responsibility did to her? 'But this is such an informal morning that it doesn't really matter. For the first lesson, at least, I thought I'd bring a bit spare because people might not realise they have to bring their own.'

'There were specific instructions on the posters,' Iris said. 'And we gave out ingredient lists in advance to everyone who signed up.'

'What if someone just decides to come along today who hasn't signed up?' Dora asked. 'They won't have seen the ingredient list?'

Iris pursed her lips, but much as she might have wanted to give an answer she didn't have one.

'Exactly,' Myrtle said. 'So Cathy is right to have extra with her.'

'They'll have to pay for it if they have it from us,' Iris said, for want of something to say that didn't admit Dora was right.

'I'm sure we can sort something out,' Cathy said.

The rest of her reply was cut short by two more arrivals – two young women in their twenties. She hadn't seen them at St Cuthbert's before. Iris raced over to greet them, and if there had been two of her they would have formed a distinct pincer movement to make sure the newcomers didn't escape, because for a moment, as they looked around at the mostly octogenarian occupants of the room, they looked as if they might try to.

'Welcome!' Iris said. 'Have you come for the class?'

'Yes,' one of them said uncertainly. 'Is this the right place? The cookery class?'

'It is.' Cathy went over with a warm smile. 'I'm Cathy and I'll be on hand to help you out while you bake. I'm terrible with names and I might struggle today, so I'll apologise in advance, but tell me yours anyway.'

'I'm Lindsey,' one of the young women said. She pointed to her friend. 'And this is Beth.'

'Brilliant!' Cathy said. 'You're a few minutes early but that's good – plenty of time to get settled before we begin. How about you find yourself a space at the worktop and get your stuff out? As soon as we've got everyone here I'll introduce myself properly and we'll make a start.'

The women went off to a corner of the kitchen, talking to each other in hushed tones as they did.

A few minutes later more people arrived. And Cathy greeted them as she'd greeted everyone else. She was beginning to feel pleased at the turnout. It wasn't huge but, if she'd been honest, she'd been a little terrified that nobody would bother to come at all. Briefly, she raised her eyes to the ceiling and wondered what her mum would say if she could see her now. Would she be proud? Cathy hadn't actually done anything yet, but even getting this far felt like an achievement. If she'd been told six months before that she'd be organising and delivering something like this, she wouldn't have believed it.

As Cathy was explaining one or two things about what to expect from the class to the newcomers, Erica arrived. She had a young girl with her. Erica didn't have children of her own, but this girl couldn't have been older than sixteen or seventeen and she looked remarkably like Erica, with the same mid-brown shade of hair, the same hazel eyes and the same button nose. But whereas Erica's expression was open and friendly, the girl's couldn't have been further from that. She looked thoroughly bored already, giving the kitchen and its occupants a sneering once-over. Erica looked her way and, seeing it, turned the smile she'd worn for Cathy into a warning glare.

'Don't!' Cathy heard her say.

The girl's lip curled a little more. 'I don't know what you're expecting me to do.'

'Whatever it is,' Erica replied, 'I know it won't be good.'

Cathy made her way over. 'I'm so glad you could come,' she said. She had a smile for Erica, and a rather more reserved one for Erica's young companion, who clearly didn't want to be there. Cathy wondered what the deal was, but she guessed that explanations might have to wait.

'Of course we were going to come!' Erica said. 'We wouldn't miss your first class!'

'I would,' the girl muttered, and Cathy saw Erica give her another warning glare.

'I think it's more of a club than a class, really,' Cathy said. 'I'm hardly a proper teacher.'

'Well,' Erica said, 'you'll know more than both of us. This is my niece, Tansy,' she added, angling her head at the girl who'd come with her.

'Hello, Tansy,' Cathy said. 'That's a lovely name.'

Tansy broke into a fake smile that was gone as quickly as it had appeared.

'Well,' Cathy continued uncertainly. 'It's nice to see you here. Have you done much baking?'

'About as much as me, I'm afraid,' Erica answered for her. 'So you've got your work cut out.'

'It's much easier than you might think,' Cathy said to Tansy. 'You'll pick it up in no time.'

Tansy gave the distinct impression that all she wanted to pick up was her pace as she left the building, but she said nothing and, as Erica gave her yet another warning look, smoothed her expression into something that – if not friendly – at least now didn't look as if she wanted to kill everyone in the room.

Cathy let a few more minutes pass. It meant the lesson would start a little late, but she didn't mind that because she wanted to make certain nobody else was due to come before she started. The last thing she wanted was to keep explaining the beginning bit over and over again for new arrivals – not only would she find it frustrating but it would annoy the other participants too.

As she checked a few things off with Iris everyone chatted, those who knew each other already catching up and those who didn't getting to know the others. All apart from Tansy, who stood next to Erica with a scowl that could have been set in stone. Why had Erica brought someone who so clearly didn't want to be there?

Cathy's nerves had settled more and more as everyone arrived, but now that the session was about to begin they were back with a vengeance. She looked up at the clock to see it was five past the hour, and then once more at the doorway, before deciding that if she didn't make a start she was going to pass out with fear. If anyone else turned up now they'd just have to catch up as best they could.

Chapter Eleven

Iris had offered to stay behind to help Cathy clean St Cuthbert's kitchen, and then Dora had offered too; Cathy had to laugh because it was clear from her face that Iris didn't know whether to be grateful or annoyed. But Cathy was grateful because the vicar had stipulated that his agreement to the classes going ahead was on the proviso that the kitchen was left spotless every time they used it. Although people had cleaned their own stations, Cathy had decided that the best way to comply with this request was probably to go over everything again once everyone had left, so that way she'd know the place was definitely clean. Right now, Dora was running a damp cloth over the doors of the ovens.

'I didn't care much for that young girl,' she said.

Cathy turned to her. 'Which one?' she asked, though she knew exactly who Dora meant. Partly because nobody had really taken to Tansy (as far as Cathy could tell), and partly because Erica's niece was probably the only person in that room who could have been confidently referred to as a young girl.

'The one who came with Erica. Face like a bulldog chewing a wasp.' Dora scrubbed so vigorously at a burned-on grease spot that Cathy was tempted to run and take the cloth from her, certain that such violent exercise couldn't end well in a woman of Dora's advanced age. 'Never stopped complaining and hardly an expression that wasn't a sneer. If she was mine she'd get a smack round the ear.'

'Good thing she's not then,' Iris put in. 'Because that sort of thing has been banned by the government, you know.'

'Ridiculous.' Dora sniffed. 'I had many a cuff round the ear as a young girl and it did me no harm. Most of the time I deserved it too.'

Iris rolled her eyes. 'Things were different back then.'

'Yes they were,' Dora agreed vehemently, perhaps not seeing quite what Iris was getting at. 'And that's what's wrong with society today – no discipline. Treated like little princes and princesses these kids are – they need a few life lessons, a bit of hardship. Wouldn't do them any harm to have no said to them once in a while.'

'Oh, I think Erica's niece has had plenty of life lessons,' Iris said darkly, and now Cathy – who had been letting their bickering wash over her to some extent as she mopped the floor – whipped round to face her, noting that Dora also looked keen to know more.

'What do you mean by that?' Dora asked.

Iris shrugged. 'Erica said a few things in passing.'

'Like what?'

'It's not my place to say,' Iris said sanctimoniously, though she had a gleam in her eye and Cathy knew she was enjoying the fact that she had information they didn't. More particularly, information that her cousin didn't have. It was obvious she was going to milk the situation for all it was worth.

Dora turned back to her task. 'Suit yourself then.'

A few minutes passed and then: 'Erica says she hates her mother's new boyfriend!' Iris blurted out.

Cathy smiled to herself. So much for Iris's impeccable discretion.

'What new boyfriend?' Dora asked.

'What's her name…?' Iris's brow creased.

'Who?' Dora asked, her tone becoming ever more impatient.

'The girl…'

'Tansy?' Cathy offered.

'Yes,' Iris said. 'Tansy hates her mum's new boyfriend.'

'Well,' Cathy said, 'that's hardly a novel situation. I'll bet there are thousands of teenagers who hate their parents' new partners. So her mum and dad are divorced?'

'I don't think she knows who her dad is,' Iris said.

Cathy frowned slightly. 'Erica told you this?'

'Not exactly,' Iris said. 'But I think so.'

Cathy wasn't going to give too much credence to a statement like that, with very little to back it up. But she pushed on anyway. 'Is she close to her mum?'

'And another thing,' Iris said, ignoring Cathy's question. 'What was Tansy doing here today?'

'She came to join in,' Cathy said, a little puzzled by the question.

'But why wasn't she at school?'

'Isn't she too old to be at school?' Cathy asked.

'Well…' Iris folded her arms and regarded Cathy with a look of triumph. 'If she's too old for school then she ought to be working.'

'Maybe it was a day off,' Cathy said.

'Or maybe she's a benefits scrounger,' Dora said. 'You see them on the telly.'

Cathy turned to her. 'Dora!'

At this, Dora at least had the decency to look ashamed.

'She didn't exactly endear herself to me,' Cathy said, recalling how more than once she'd tried to start a conversation with Tansy only to receive stony silence in return or a sneer or some other look that said:

I can hardly be bothered to acknowledge your existence because you're really quite pathetic. 'But I don't think we should be judging her just because she's not whistling a happy tune all the time. Some people just don't have happy faces.'

'She didn't have a happy anything,' Iris said, and Dora nodded.

'OK,' Cathy said slowly. 'Did Erica say anything else?'

'I overheard Erica telling her more than once that she'd have to go home sooner or later and that she'd have to talk to her mother properly and she couldn't keep running to her or her uncle every time she had a spat with her mum.'

'She's running to Erica a lot then? Is that what you mean?'

Iris nodded. 'And her uncle.'

'Erica did tell me she had a brother,' Cathy said thoughtfully. 'Matthias I think his name is.'

'I hope she doesn't bring her niece again,' Dora said. 'Brings down the whole mood of the room.'

'She wasn't that bad,' Cathy said, though she couldn't help but agree a little with Dora. Erica's niece certainly had been difficult to engage with. Even as she tried not to think this, Cathy's mind flashed back to a number of incidents that reinforced everything Dora was saying, like Tansy's sneer at poor Myrtle's offer of a mint, how she'd marched in front of Colin to put her cake on the oven shelf he'd been planning to use and how she'd smirked when someone's cake had burned.

'They're all the same at that age,' Iris said sagely. 'Hormones.'

In one breath, Iris was telling them that she thought Tansy was having a difficult home life, and in the next she was blaming it on hormones. Cathy resisted the urge to shake her head in bewilderment. She couldn't help but think that there might be something in what Iris had originally said, though she wondered why Erica hadn't volunteered that information to her. Not that they were close, of course – they'd only just started getting to know one another – but Erica had told her so many other things about her family life, and had alluded to the fact that she found her sister frustrating at times, that it seemed strange she'd have kept this from them. Unless she somehow felt that it wasn't her story to tell. Perhaps she wanted to respect Tansy's privacy and her right to share her problems with the people only she chose to. Still, Cathy thought she'd call Erica later. She wouldn't ask outright, but maybe Erica would bring it up and then at least if Tansy came to the class with her again, Cathy would have some background.

She shook herself as Iris turned on the tap to refill her bowl.

'Sewing club will be here in half an hour,' she said briskly. 'Better get cleaned up and be out before they arrive or someone will be running to the vicar to complain.'

Dora made a noise of agreement.

'We should be nearly done,' Cathy said. 'Thanks for helping me out.'

'It's our pleasure,' Dora said. 'Isn't it, Iris?'

Iris smiled at Cathy. 'It is. I've only known you for a couple of weeks and already I feel as if we've been friends for a hundred years.'

'Really?' Cathy blushed. She couldn't imagine making that kind of impression on anyone, and perhaps it was a bit of an exaggeration on Iris's part, but it was a lovely thing for her to say nonetheless.

'I know,' Dora said. 'I feel exactly the same way.'

'Well…' Cathy began, blushing harder than ever. 'Thank you!'

She turned back to her mopping, not knowing what else to say but with a smile broader than any she'd worn in a long, long time.

Chapter Twelve

Cathy wrestled with the idea of phoning Erica for a while before she did it. She didn't want to bother her if Erica didn't want to talk and she'd thought perhaps that Erica might call her, but when it got to 8 p.m. and that hadn't happened she gave in.

To her relief, Erica sounded pleased to hear from her.

'I was going to phone you but I just got so busy,' she said. 'Did you enjoy today? I thought it went really well and your students seemed to enjoy it.'

'Did you?' Cathy asked.

Erica laughed. 'Of course I did! Tansy did too.'

'That's good,' Cathy said, though according to what Iris, Dora and Cathy herself had seen, Tansy hadn't looked very much like she was enjoying being alive, let alone anything about the class. 'I thought… well, I suppose Tansy felt it a bit – being there with such a lot of older people.'

'A little bit, but I don't think it bothered her all that much. She's usually just happy to be out of the house for a while.'

There was no tone in Erica's voice that suggested anything other than a relaxed attitude to her niece, which was completely at odds with what Iris had said earlier. Cathy wasn't going to push a conversation about it if Erica didn't want to have one, but she couldn't deny that she was curious.

'Did her mum enjoy the cake?' Cathy asked.

'Oh, Tansy hasn't been home yet – she's still here with me and Malc,' Erica said. 'I think she's planning on staying over but she hasn't said either way yet.'

'Right...'

'So you're going to carry on with the classes?' Erica asked.

'Yes. Did you think I wouldn't?'

'Not in a bad way – I just know you were a bit anxious about it beforehand.'

Cathy laughed. 'I'm still anxious about it. I don't think that will ever stop, but I did enjoy it, and it was nice to see that everyone else seemed to get a lot out of it too.'

'Oh, they did!' Erica agreed. 'Especially me and Tans. I can't wait for the next one.'

'Will Tansy come again?'

'It depends whether she's with me or if she's at college that day. She isn't there every day – she has some gaps in her timetable where there are no lessons and that usually includes Friday.'

'Doesn't she meet up with her friends and things?'

'The thing about Tans is she doesn't suffer fools gladly and I think that makes it hard for her to keep friends. You know what most teenagers are like – it's all boyfriend dramas and selfies. She hates all that and she's not afraid to tell anyone when she thinks they're being stupid.'

'Oh,' Cathy said. 'So she doesn't have friends?'

'I'm sure she has, but I don't know that it's a wide circle.'

There was a pause.

'It's good to see her voluntarily going out and doing something other than being hunched over her phone actually,' Erica said into the gap. 'It drives Malc mad; he thinks she ought to be at her own house anyway so they just wind each other up.'

'Well, she's always welcome if she wants to come back,' Cathy said, feeling terribly guilty about the fact that she was really hoping Tansy would decide not to bother next week.

Overnight it had snowed. It was a little early in the season, and Cathy hadn't checked the weather forecast before she'd gone to bed, so it had come as a surprise when she'd opened the curtains to get ready for work to see the street outside buried beneath a glinting, sugary blanket. It looked pretty – like a Christmas card – another bittersweet reminder that Christmas was fast approaching; a Christmas that Cathy would more than likely be spending alone. She supposed she'd get invites from relatives to have lunch with them, but that would only make her feel worse, because sitting there, she'd recall that she and her mum had never been invited, and that she was only there this year because she was alone. Whichever way she chose to spend the season, it was going to be painful.

Shaking her melancholy, she turned her thoughts to the day ahead. At least she'd be at French for Flowers today and work days were always good days. And as it had stopped snowing now and the winter sun was throwing kind rays across the snowy landscape, it might be a good day to take the longer walk into work to make the most of it. That meant walking the canal path, past the old textile factory that had since been turned into an industrial museum where crowds of bored schoolchildren were regularly ferried in and out to learn about a past that most of them probably didn't care about and could never imagine. Cathy liked the museum though. She'd taken her mum around it once. Hardly an adventure to the other side of the world, but Miriam had loved it and had talked about it for days afterwards. Cathy had been meaning to take her again – not straight away, because what would have been the point of that? She'd been waiting for some suitable exhibition or event that her mum would enjoy, that would make her visit different from the last one…

Of course that hadn't happened. Miriam had died before the perfect event had come round.

Cathy wrapped herself up and headed out in plenty of time to get to the town centre via the canal. The frosted air curled away from her as she walked in the bright sunlight, like the clouds of a Van Gogh painting. Fresh snow creaked under her boots, stretching ahead on the path, pristine and glistening and just begging for footprints. A field of new snow was like the first page of a new notebook – it left you itching to make your mark so you could say to the world: look, I'm here. Cathy had never been able to resist either – perhaps because she didn't often feel she'd made much of a mark on the world in any other respect.

As she contemplated this in the vaguest of ways, she was suddenly aware of panting behind her. She whipped round to see a shaggy-looking Alsatian bounding towards her.

'Hello, handsome,' she said with a smile. The dog looked up at her for a moment, as if to acknowledge the compliment, before circling back the way it had come and heading towards a man on the path. Cathy hadn't noticed him before, so he must have been striding at quite a pace to be there now. But he was tall, she noted, though still too far away to be able to tell much else about him, so she supposed he probably would walk quite fast.

She watched for a moment as the dog raced up and down the path, kicking up snow as it went, clearly delighted at the way it filled the air and snapping playfully at the clumps as they came back down. She could hear the low chuckle of the owner, but then blushed as he looked right at her.

Had she been staring? Maybe, but now she felt like a toddler caught with their hand in the sweetie box. She faced forward again and quickened her step.

But before she'd gone six feet, the dog was back, and this time it decided to try to make friends, coming right up to Cathy and sniffing at her.

'Guin!' the man shouted.

Cathy turned again to see him racing up the path now.

'Guin!' he repeated. 'Leave the poor lady alone!'

'Oh, it's alright,' Cathy said. 'He's not bothering me... It's a he?'

'Yes,' the man said. He'd stopped running now and was striding the last few feet to try to retrieve his dog, who didn't seem to want retrieving and had already hared off again, down the path ahead of them. 'I sometimes wonder who's taking who for a walk when we're out.'

Cathy gave him a shy smile before lowering her gaze. 'He's a beautiful dog.'

'You want him?' the man said.

Cathy looked up to see him grin. It was hard not to notice that he had a lovely grin – sort of naughty; not the bad-boy kind of naughty, but an old-fashioned kind of naughty. Fun, harmless, a bit cheeky. He was probably about her age – maybe more mid-thirties than late – and had brown hair and hazel eyes. Even though she knew they'd never met, Cathy couldn't help thinking he looked vaguely familiar.

'I don't think I'd be able to control him,' Cathy said.

'Neither can I,' the man replied with that naughty grin again. His gaze lingered on her for a moment. But then he turned to the path again and let out a shrill whistle.

'Guin! Come here!'

She watched as he suddenly gave chase. Guin was edging rather too close to the water's edge and Cathy didn't blame the man for wanting to make sure he didn't fall in. She saw him finally catch up and put the dog back on his leash, and continued to watch as they strode off together, so briskly that they'd soon disappeared beyond a curve on the path.

Cathy walked on for another ten minutes, lost in thought, until it suddenly occurred to her that the snowy landscape and the muffled calm of the canal had been forgotten, and that for the last ten minutes her thoughts had been almost entirely taken up by the man she'd just met. She shook herself. It was one thing to be lonely from time to time but quite another to fantasise about a stranger she'd probably never meet again. Unless…

Inwardly she chastised herself with a little embarrassed laugh. Walk the canal path every day just in case she saw him there again? How ridiculous! Perhaps there was a part of her that now wished she had a man in her life just so she wouldn't be quite so alone, but that kind of behaviour seemed a bit desperate, even to her. Love would come in its own sweet time. At least, that's what she'd been telling herself ever since she and Jonas had gone their separate ways. And perhaps it was coming, but God, was it taking its time!

By the time Cathy got to the market building her toes were numb, despite the thick socks inside her boots, as were her fingers and the end of her nose. But her cheeks had a rosy glow and she felt as if her lungs had been given a good spring clean.

'Morning,' Fleur said. 'You got here OK, then? Radio says traffic is terrible on the ring road.'

'I didn't get the bus so I didn't get caught in it,' Cathy said, taking her coat off and storing it in a cubbyhole beneath the counter, along with her handbag.

'Wise choice,' Fleur replied. She'd already made two mugs of tea and handed one to Cathy. 'You walked then? Nice morning for it.'

'I thought so.' Cathy took the tea from her, fingers tingling as the heat spread through them. 'How's it going?'

'Can't complain.' Fleur pulled a hanky from her pocket and gave her nose a gentle blow. 'How was your class?'

'Oh, it was lovely!' Cathy said.

Fleur smiled. 'I told you it would be.'

'I mean, I was nervous but everyone was so nice and encouraging and they all seemed to enjoy it. Lots of them took the photocopies of the recipes I gave them too, and they're all going to try some of them at home, even before next week's lesson. I told them to take photos if they could and to let me know how they got on with them – you know, if they were straightforward enough, easy enough to do.'

'I'm sure they'll be fine…'

Fleur stopped and looked expectantly at her.

'What?' Cathy asked.

'Where's our cake? I've made you tea… now you have to uphold your end of the bargain.'

Cathy laughed and reached beneath the counter for her bag. She took out a smallish Tupperware container.

'Bloody hell – is that all we're getting?' Fleur asked.

'Sorry, but everything else got eaten or taken home,' Cathy said.

Fleur gave a sigh of mock impatience. 'Alright then, so I'm an afterthought. Soon forgotten for all your new friends. Let's see then, what have you managed to salvage for me? I'm so hungry I'd eat dog biscuits if that's what you'd brought.'

The mention of dog biscuits briefly brought to mind Cathy's encounter with Guin, the handsome Alsatian, and his rather more handsome owner, but she dismissed it instantly, that little voice in her head chastising her once again.

'It's only banana loaf,' Cathy said.

'Only banana loaf? That's my favourite! OK, so you're forgiven.'

Cathy opened the tub and Fleur reached in for a slice.

'You want to know what *did* happen yesterday?' Fleur asked as she munched.

Cathy frowned. 'What?'

'That man came to the stall again for more flowers. Either his wife is the best wife on the planet or he's having an affair.'

'Jonas?'

'The one you used to go out with?'

'Yes. He came again?'

'Uh-huh. Not that I'm complaining – it's all money to me. But he did look very disappointed that you weren't here.'

'Did he?'

Fleur reached into the tub that Cathy had completely forgotten she was still holding for another slice of cake. 'Oh, there's two left after this – I'll let you have those.'

Cathy gave a vague nod, though she wasn't really listening and she didn't really care about the cake after all, even though she'd worked up enough of an appetite during her walk in that she'd really been looking forward to it.

Don't be stupid, she told herself sternly. *Expecting there to be anything in this is even more ridiculous than fantasising about a man you've just met walking his dog.* But even so, she had to wonder just what – if anything – Jonas was up to. Why come in again? Hadn't they said everything that needed saying already? Cathy had felt their previous two encounters to be nothing but awkward, only stirring up unwanted feelings and bittersweet memories that she was perhaps better off without. Surely he must have felt the same way – and he had a wife now too, of course, which was even more reason to stay away. So why come back?

And then Cathy was struck by a sudden horrible epiphany.

'Don't worry,' Fleur said, popping the last of her cake into her mouth and fixing Cathy with a shrewd gaze. 'If he comes in today I'll serve him, and if you want to scoot off I won't mind.'

Cathy nodded. She didn't entirely know how she felt about this new development but she knew that no good could come of developing feelings for Jonas again. To that end, the best course of action was probably to avoid him. If she'd felt more comfortable with him – as she once had – she might have taken him to one side and explained all this, but that wasn't going to be possible now their relationship had changed so much. No, she decided, the best course of action here was to stay out of his way. Which was fine and right and would be a lot easier if he would only stop coming to the stall. Cathy wanted to stay out of his way, but it was beginning to look as if – for whatever reason – he didn't want to stay out of hers.

Chapter Thirteen

When Erica had messaged to see if Cathy wanted to meet up at Ingrid's again, Cathy had jumped at the chance. They were sitting in there now, amongst the fairy-tale décor, Cathy sipping at a creamy mocha.

'Why don't you join a dating site?' Erica asked, looking over the rim of her cup at Cathy.

Cathy shook her head. 'I thought about it and others have suggested it too. But I'm not comfortable with the idea – you never know what kind of weirdos you're going to meet if you put yourself on one of those.'

'You shouldn't believe everything you read in the papers.' Erica reached for her drink and used the biscotti at the side to swirl the cream round before taking a bite of it. 'Everyone on Tinder isn't an axe murderer.'

'But you don't know anything about them,' Cathy said. 'They might not be telling you the truth about themselves and you'd have no way to know until it was too late.'

'You could say that about everyone you meet in real life though,' Erica said. She raised her eyebrows. 'You sound like my brother; that's the sort of thing he's always saying. I ought to get you two together.'

Cathy didn't know how to reply to that so she took a mouthful of her drink instead. She was beginning to wish this particular conversation hadn't begun. But it had, and it was her own fault for bringing up

Jonas. But she'd needed to get it off her chest, and even though she'd talked at length about the situation to Fleur, she still didn't feel as if she'd fully explored it enough to put it to bed. The fact that Jonas kept coming to the stall troubled her and she didn't know what to make of it – she'd hoped Erica might have some insights that would help. But so far, she'd just called him a stupid bastard and said that he ought to concentrate on his wife, and then proceeded to tell Cathy that she deserved better than that.

'I think he must be the unluckiest bloke alive when it comes to women,' Erica continued. 'And there's nothing wrong with him; I know he's my brother and I'm bound to say so, but he's a really lovely bloke. It doesn't seem right to me. He's about your age too.'

Cathy gave a nervous smile. How was she going to get out of this without offending Erica? While she had started to feel the lack of a man in her life and thought it might be time to start dating, she wasn't about to get railroaded into dates with her friend's brother, especially considering the damage it might do to her friendship with Erica if things ended badly.

But then Erica glanced at Cathy and perhaps realised her mistake because her expression was troubled for a moment.

'Not that I'd want to tell you who to go out with of course,' she said.

'I'm sure your brother is nice,' Cathy said. 'I mean, I'm sure we'd get along just fine – at least, if he's like you then we would—'

'Don't worry about it,' Erica said, smiling. 'I wouldn't fix you up on a blind date or anything. In fact, I don't think either of you would thank me for meddling. Matthias would probably just tell me to mind my own business if I mentioned it to him. And, come to think of it, last time I did fix him up with a woman I worked with, she ended up two-timing him, so…'

Cathy gave a tight smile and dipped her head to her drink.

'Going back to your problem, though,' Erica said. 'I wouldn't give Jonas the satisfaction of thinking you cared. Pretend that it really doesn't bother you that he keeps coming to your stall. He'll get fed up soon enough and stop – they always do. He probably just wants to know that he can still have an effect on you.'

Erica fiddled with her teaspoon. 'Maybe he's a bit bored and seeing you has reminded him of a time before he was bored. Don't think for a minute he'd be leaving his wife to come back to you.'

'Oh, I never thought that,' Cathy said fervently. 'I was just confused – I mean, that's exactly it, isn't it? He's married now, and he says he's really happy, but he keeps turning up. I'm sure it's probably just what you said. I expect if nothing more happens he will stop. Anyway, I don't know why he'd be bothering himself about me – I don't look like I used to when we were together... I've put on a load of weight for a start.'

'So? You're still pretty.'

'I don't think—' Cathy began, but Erica cut across her.

'Don't you dare say you're not because you're too fat! What's that got to do with anything? Bigger women can be just as attractive – sometimes even more so! You're lovely... Repeat after me: *I am lovely*!'

Cathy gave a self-conscious laugh. 'Maybe not just now,' she said. 'But thank you – that's kind of you to say.'

'It's not kindness; it's just stating a fact. Anyway, whatever's going on, have you thought about just telling him to back off if it bothers you that much?'

'Oh, I couldn't do that,' Cathy said. 'It seems so arrogant for a start; assuming that he's coming to the stall just to see me. He might actually be coming for flowers.'

Erica raised her eyebrows so high there was a danger they might shoot off her forehead. 'You really think that? There are plenty of other florists in Linnetford!'

'Of course there are, but he might just like ours now that he's been there.'

'If anything – given your history – I'd have thought just knowing you were working there would be a reason to stay away, regardless of how nice your flowers might be.'

'I had thought that to be honest,' Cathy conceded. 'And most men don't notice any difference,' she added. 'A flower's a flower to a bloke. Most who come to our stall wouldn't know a carnation from an aspidistra if their life depended on it. They just point at what they want and call it all flowers!'

'Ah, now that's where I have to disagree,' Erica said. 'Matt would know.'

'Matt?'

'Matthias. My brother. He'd know that sort of thing. Into art and everything.'

'Is that what he does? Is he an artist?' Cathy asked.

'Actually, he's a physiotherapist. He works mostly with cardiac patients – you know, getting them back on their feet after heart attacks and that sort of thing,' Erica said with real pride in her voice.

Cathy found herself staring at Erica. Maybe she'd been too hasty with her earlier dismissal of him. Maybe he was exactly the sort of man she'd like to go out with. He certainly sounded like a bit of a hero – and sensitive and intelligent too.

She shook the thought away. Her original judgement was the most sensible one. There was no telling the awkwardness that a disastrous date with a friend's brother might cause, and she was beginning to value Erica's friendship too much for that to happen.

'His job sounds amazing.'

Erica nodded. 'I think so… though I'd never tell him that because his head might get big and we already have one troublesome sibling in the family without creating another one.'

'That's your sister?' Cathy asked.

'Michelle – Tansy's mum. I feel for that girl because God knows she gets no attention from her mother.'

'Is that why she was staying with you the other day?' Cathy asked.

'She stays with me a lot. The trouble is, Malc's not so keen so that causes friction.'

Cathy remembered her mentioning something about that before. 'Why isn't he keen?'

Erica shrugged. 'Personality clash, I suppose. He used to be alright with her, when she was little, but the last few years he's got more and more impatient. Thinks she has an attitude.'

Cathy thought Tansy had an attitude too, as had plenty of others at the cookery club, but she wasn't about to say so to Erica, who was clearly fond of the girl.

'So they don't get on at all?'

'Tans doesn't exactly help herself. Malc's fairly easy-going, but she just knows how to push his buttons. Like the other day, she left the bathroom light on in the middle of the night so we didn't know it had been burning for hours until we got up the next day. Now, we're all guilty of the odd lapse, but the fact is it's not the first time and he's asked her umpteen times to make sure she doesn't do it. Not only does she keep doing it, but she doesn't even apologise when he brings it up. If anything, she makes him sound unreasonable. I think he's perfectly entitled to be pissed off if I'm completely honest but I can't come down on his side.'

'Why not? If he's right, why can't you come down on his side? Surely you can explain it to her?'

'I can and I do.'

'So what does she say?'

'She says she's not doing any of it deliberately.'

'I suppose you can't say a lot to that.'

'Exactly. I'm sure it's just a difficult phase.'

'For Tansy or Malc?'

Erica gave a quick grin. 'Both of them. I can only hope they get it out of their systems and become grown-ups soon so they can start to get along again – it would certainly make my life easier.'

'I can imagine. Poor you.'

'Poor Tansy really. I'm alright – it's Tans who has all the real problems.'

'Like what?'

Erica paused. But then she shook her head. 'You don't want to hear all that right now... So, what are we making next class?'

It was obvious that Erica didn't want to discuss it any further and although Cathy was burning to know what Tansy's real problems were she didn't push it. While they were becoming good friends, they weren't quite at that point yet.

'I thought we might make Victoria sponge.' But then Cathy clapped a hand over her mouth. 'I didn't tell anyone that, did I? They won't know what ingredients to buy!'

'What do you need for a Victoria sponge?' Erica asked. 'Can't be that much, can it?'

'Well, no, it's pretty basic actually... Flour, butter, eggs, jam...' Cathy was thoughtful for a moment. 'Maybe I could buy enough for everyone to use. It probably wouldn't cost that much.'

'Put a notice out on social media to let people know what they have to bring rather than footing the bill yourself. You are starting a Facebook group for it, aren't you?' Erica asked, as if that was the most obvious thing in the world.

It wasn't that obvious, because Cathy hadn't thought of it at all.

'Why don't I start one for you?' Erica added, guessing by the look on Cathy's face that her question was going to get a negative answer.

'Oh, would you?'

'It'd be too late to do anything about it for this week but if we let everyone know at the next lesson they can join then. That way you'll be able to give out essential information in plenty of time. It'd be a nice way for everyone to keep in touch outside the lessons too.'

'I can't imagine Dora or Iris using it,' Cathy said doubtfully. 'Or Myrtle.'

'You'd be surprised,' Erica said. 'Some of the older folks spend more time on social media than the youngsters these days. Let me deal with all that and I'll have a word with everyone next time. If the regular church ladies don't want to join it won't matter – they're pretty easy to find. We can always just leave messages at the church for them – Iris is there almost every day as far as I can tell.'

'That would be brilliant!' Cathy said. 'Thank you!'

'Not a problem. Glad to be pitching in and it's really not such a big deal.'

Cathy beamed. It might not have been a big deal to Erica but she appreciated it more than she could say. Whether it was a big task or not, it was the sentiment behind it that meant the most. If only she'd found a friend like Erica when she'd been caring for her mother, it might not have been such a hard and lonely road.

Chapter Fourteen

Cathy was thrilled to see everyone from the first session turn up again to cookery club, even the two younger women, Lindsey and Beth, who'd seemed so uncertain about being there at first. In fact, when Cathy went over to greet them, Beth was excited to tell her that she'd tried out at least three of the recipes Cathy had given them photocopies of and she'd been delighted when they'd all been delicious.

Erica had brought Tansy again, and though the teenager was as sullen and unlikeable as she'd been the week before, Cathy couldn't help but feel that perhaps this might be an unfair representation of the girl – after all, why would she come again if she really didn't want to be there? Tansy had free will and Cathy didn't imagine Erica was the sort of woman to order her to attend something she didn't want to, so she must have wanted to be there, even if it really didn't look that way.

Still, Cathy caught the exchange of a significant look between Iris and Dora and guessed what they might say amongst themselves about it later. They'd obviously decided that they didn't like Tansy and nothing anyone did or said would persuade them otherwise. And when Cathy went over to talk to Erica and her niece, it was difficult not to agree with them a little, because the way Tansy looked at everyone in the room as Cathy spoke gave the distinct impression that she'd be quite happy to blow them all up.

'I'm so glad you've come back,' Cathy said, trying to ignore the girl's look of contempt.

'We loved it last week, didn't we, Tans?' Erica said.

Tansy didn't reply.

'We've got plenty of ingredients too, if anyone doesn't have what they need,' Erica continued. 'Tansy ran to the shop to get extra this morning. I know we've got the Facebook group set up now but not everyone has signed up yet.'

'I've got some extra too,' Cathy said. 'I think Iris got the word out to the church ladies so there shouldn't be too many people who still need ingredients. If anything, we might find we've got too much extra today.'

'Well, it just means we'll have to use it to make more cake at home, eh, Tans?' Erica said, and Tansy nodded sullenly, but at least it was an acknowledgement, which was more than Cathy had ever got from her. If that was all her aunt got, then Cathy couldn't imagine how much more she'd ever get from her. But she was here, and perhaps that was validation enough.

'Right...' Cathy said, suddenly feeling awkward and a little bit stupid. 'I'll just go and... I think Iris might want me...'

Cathy hurried away. She could hear Erica's cheery tones as she continued to talk to her niece, and Tansy's monosyllabic replies, and she had to wonder how even Erica could like her enough to spend so much time with her. She must have been hard work, even for a blood relative. But there was no time to dwell on that, and perhaps it was just as well, because the last of the participants arrived en masse and Cathy had to rush over to brief them so that they could begin on time. Then, as she was finishing up, she noticed the door open again and the vicar walk in. He waved a hand in greeting, and then nodded at Iris.

'Just need a quick word if that's OK?' he said.

'Of course!' Cathy said, going to her workstation at the head of the room while everyone tied their aprons and got equipment out.

After a few minutes with Iris the vicar came to find Cathy.

'It's kind of you to teach everyone – Iris says you're doing it without pay.'

'I'm not really teaching anyone,' Cathy replied. 'We're all just sort of cooking together. I give everyone the recipe and I offer help and guidance as we go along; some people haven't baked before and they're not sure what some of the more technical things mean. But anyone can make a cake if they've got a good-enough recipe and all the bits they need.'

'Well, if your cakes are anything to go by then the recipes are very good indeed. Iris says they're yours too – that you wrote them.'

'I didn't really write them,' Cathy said. 'My mum wrote a lot of them… well, she sort of just did them and I learned them from her and then I wrote them down for this. I usually just do it by eye – when it's something I've made a lot anyway.'

The vicar nodded slowly, regarding Cathy with a thoughtful look as he did. 'You've a natural talent then.'

'No.' Cathy smiled. 'I've just got a good memory.'

He smiled too now, but Cathy had the distinct feeling that there was something going on behind it – cogs whirring, ideas being formulated.

'Maybe I'll join in next time,' he said.

'Here?' Cathy asked.

'If you've room for one more.'

'Of course!' Cathy said. 'There's always room for one more.'

The vicar nodded. 'I'd better get on; lots to do… there always is, isn't there?'

'Right… Hang on.'

Cathy reached into her bag and took out a spare photocopy of her recipes.

'I've been adding to it,' she said, 'but I think we'll be doing flapjacks next week so, if you are coming, what you'd need is on here.'

He took the stapled pages and flicked through. 'I like the little doodles,' he said.

Cathy blushed; she didn't know whether he was poking gentle fun at her or not, but there was no malice in it and she knew none would be intended. But she did feel a little silly now.

'No, I really like them,' he said, perhaps guessing that what he'd said could be misinterpreted. 'It's a nice flourish – looks sort of Arts and Crafts, you know.'

He waved it briefly in the air and nodded. 'Thanks for this.'

'No problem. See you next week hopefully.'

There was a lot of good-natured chatter, banter and laughter in the room as everyone worked. Unlike the first week, Cathy didn't bake anything herself, because so many people had needed to ask for her advice that she'd quickly realised how impractical that was. So this time she only wandered the room, making herself available for encouragement or guidance, and she found that she really enjoyed how much she was getting to know everyone.

Every so often her gaze would stray over to where Erica and Tansy were baking together. She'd been over a couple of times and Erica had assured her they had it under control while Tansy, as usual, had hardly acknowledged Cathy at all. But whenever Cathy looked, Tansy was diligently poring over the recipe or screwing up her face in concentration as she checked measurements. Sometimes she'd be comparing her mixture to what Erica had in her bowl and she'd either frown, or look vaguely satisfied as she turned back to her own. And when it finally went in the oven, Tansy guarded the door, staring in at her cake as if she could will it to perfection using some kind of thought waves, so that nobody could get near to check their own, and Erica had to issue a gentle reminder of that fact. Looking mutinous, Tansy moved out of the way to let Beth take a look at how her own was doing, but when Beth looked as if she might open the oven, Tansy moved in to stop her.

'She's like a pit bull,' Iris said to Dora as she watched. Cathy had caught the comment so it had been loud enough to carry that far. She just hoped that nobody else – especially Tansy – had heard it. She wondered if she'd have to talk to Iris about discretion, though that might prove to be a difficult conversation. She didn't want to appear patronising. Iris was, after all, a grown woman with a perfectly good sense of what was socially acceptable and what was not. That she might choose to ignore that was another matter, of course…

Apart from that, the class went well and everyone seemed very proud of their Victoria sponges, even though there was some disparity in success. While some had sunken middles, and some had clearly put the jam and cream in before the sponges had cooled sufficiently so that they had little pink waterfalls oozing from the sides, and some had one fat sponge and one thin sponge, at least they all resembled what they were supposed to be and you couldn't have perfection straight away.

As they were clearing up, Myrtle came over to Cathy.

'I've got this recipe,' she said, seeming almost shy as she showed Cathy a mildewed exercise book. She opened it at a yellowing book-marked page. The book had to be decades old. Cathy looked to see it was for Christmas cake. 'I've been looking all over the house for it, ever since you started your class. It's my mother-in-law's book – it came to me when she passed on. It makes a lovely Christmas cake, though I haven't done it for years. I thought people here might like to try it.'

'It does look lovely,' Cathy said, scanning the page. 'But you have to do quite a lot of preparation and I don't know that it's practical to do in the time we have here.'

Myrtle looked crestfallen and Cathy couldn't bear it.

'I would imagine this book is quite precious to you?' she asked gently.

'A bit,' Myrtle said.

'If Iris doesn't mind, could I take it to the office to photocopy the page? I could add it to my own recipe book and distribute it to the class so they could have a go at making it in their own time. And I would say it's a good time to make a Christmas cake, isn't it? It should be perfect by Christmas Day if you started it about now.'

'Oh it would!' Myrtle said, beaming. 'I'll ask Iris now!'

Before Cathy could reply, she'd rushed off to Iris's station. Cathy smiled as she went. It had looked like a lovely recipe, and not only would it make a great addition to her little book, but mostly she couldn't wait to give it a try herself.

Chapter Fifteen

The snow had all but melted, with only glassy patches on paths less trodden and a bitter wind to make sure they stayed put. Despite this, Cathy decided to leave the house early for work again so she could take the canal path into the town. She'd left a mixing bowl of Myrtle's Christmas cake steeping in the cupboard at home. Full of spices and rum, it had smelled divine and Cathy knew that the whole house would be filled with the same sweet, welcoming aroma by the time she got home. It smelled like Christmas, like warm evenings in front of the fire with eggnog or pudding wine and a wedge of rich fruit cake while snowflakes fluttered past the window. Of course, Cathy's Christmas evenings would be nothing like that, but she wasn't going to let that melancholy thought stop her from making the cake anyway. She might not have a family or husband to share it at home with, but she could take it to give out to her friends and that was almost as good.

The skies were leaden as she walked the path to work, and what was left of the foliage on trees was shaken loose by a brisk, freezing wind, carried off across the fields, or otherwise dumped into the black canal whenever there was a lull. At the far side of the canal, the fields were scrubby, stretching out to meet the outskirts of the town, and on her side, there was a narrow strip of greener land that bordered the grounds of the old textile mill, which seemed to stretch away for miles. Perhaps the people who had once owned the mill had planted the vast oaks and horse chestnuts that dotted the land now, or perhaps they'd just ended up there in the natural way of things, but there was far more tree coverage on this side of the canal than on the other.

Occasionally, Cathy would see the odd narrowboat, bright flowers painted on its side, moored up with little wreaths of smoke coming from stubby chimneys. Sometimes the occupants would be out on deck and they'd give a friendly smile or wave, and sometimes Cathy would see them warm and snug inside, sitting by their tiny windows. The canal wandered sedately through the outskirts of Linnetford and out into the countryside proper, sometimes beautiful and sometimes grimy, its banks dotted with pubs and locks, until it reached Manchester. At least that was where Cathy thought it stopped, though she didn't know all that much about it other than what she'd learned at school – and even she had to accept that school was a very long way in her own past now.

She turned into a gentle bend and, as she saw a new vista open up ahead, noted a figure standing stock-still, seemingly gazing out across the canal and towards the town. He was bundled in a heavy woollen coat, Wellington boots and a charcoal-grey newsboy cap. A few feet away, a large black and tan dog raced up and down. Cathy smiled. She hadn't planned her route into work this morning thinking that she might see him again, but she couldn't deny that a small part of her had hoped for it. Yet it had seemed unlikely, because she'd walked this way so many times and never met him before. And here he was, as if it was meant to be.

Don't be silly, she told herself. *Things aren't meant to be, not in real life.*

But her step quickened anyway, even though she didn't know what she was going to say when she got there or whether he'd even remember her from their brief interaction the other day.

He turned to look as she got closer.

'Hello again,' he said warmly.

'Your dog looks like he doesn't mind the cold,' Cathy said.

'With that much fur he could pull sledges,' the man said. 'Nothing bothers him – it's me who has to stand here shivering while I wait for him to finish sniffing out rabbits.'

'Oh,' Cathy said, and she must have looked distressed at this because he quickly added: 'Not that he ever catches any. He just likes to have a nosey. Wouldn't hurt a fly. Well, actually... he does try to catch them mid-air and eat them, but that's another story.'

Cathy felt herself relax. He was joking with her; that was good, wasn't it? And he was looking as if he liked what he saw... wasn't he?

She chased the thought away. She was being utterly ridiculous – she didn't know the first thing about him. For all she knew he was married, deliriously happy with ten kids. He was probably this friendly to everyone. Regardless, she only knew that she liked the way he looked at her, and that, try as she might, she couldn't help but fall into his soft hazel eyes as soon as she gazed into them. There was something comforting rather than intimidating about his height and his broad shoulders, and even the way he was dressed did something to her that it shouldn't.

She could allow herself a little fantasy, right? She didn't know him but that didn't stop her having a little indulgence, did it? She could pretend a handsome man was interested in her and who was that hurting?

'You come this way every day?' he asked.

'Um, no, just to work. Only three days a week.'

'So you work Mondays every week?'

'Yes.'

He nodded. 'I've only just started to bring Guinness here.'

Cathy frowned.

'The dog,' he added with a chuckle. 'Daft name, I know, but it suits him.'

'Oh, I thought he was called Guin?'

'That's because I can't be bothered to shout out the entire thing. I have to call out his name so often to fetch him back from where he's not supposed to be.'

Cathy smiled. 'So where did you go before?'

'We used to go to the fields at the back of the new Morrisons but they've started to build a car park there now. I was a bit nervous about coming down here with him – thought the daft beggar might jump into the canal – but he doesn't seem that bothered about it after all. It's a bit more of a walk for me but it's good to have somewhere he can come off his leash for a while.'

'Does he need a lot of exercise?'

'He does. I work funny hours too so it's hard sometimes to give him enough. My sister says I shouldn't have got a dog in the first place if I couldn't be there all the time. She's probably right, but I couldn't part with him now for anything.'

'I suppose there are walking services and such?' Cathy asked. 'You could use one of those?'

'I like to walk him myself – he's a handful.'

Cathy glanced across at where Guin was digging, flinging clumps of earth up into the air behind him. There must have been some strength in those massive paws because the earth was frozen solid right now, but it didn't seem to be troubling him at all.

'He's beautiful,' she said.

'Do you have a dog?'

Cathy shook her head. 'I always wanted one but... well, it was a bit awkward to have one.'

'Ah,' he said. 'It's not always easy for everyone. I'm lucky I've got no one to answer to so I can do what I please.'

Cathy smiled and filed the information into a compartment labelled: figure out later what that means and if it's good news for me.

'I'd better get going,' she said, wanting nothing more than to stay here all day and get to know him. But that might look weird, be unwanted, and it would definitely make her very late for work.

'It was nice talking to you,' he said, and Cathy couldn't have controlled the little flutter in her stomach if she'd tried.

'You too,' she said. 'Have a good day.'

'I'll do my best,' he said. 'See you around maybe.'

Cathy nodded, grinning from ear to ear as she walked away, leaving him on the path to return to his contemplation of the grey skyline of the town.

'You look like the cat that got the cream,' Fleur said as Cathy arrived at the stall.

'Do I?'

'I don't know what you had for breakfast this morning but I want some,' Fleur replied with a wry smile. 'I take it the cookery club went well again?'

'Oh, yes,' Cathy replied, realising that all thoughts of the cookery club had completely left her head since she'd met the man with the dog again. She really needed to get this under control – there was a difference between a little harmless fantasy and unhealthy infatuation.

'Did you make anything for me?'

'We did Victoria sponge but I didn't bake one,' Cathy said.

'So I don't have cake this morning?' Fleur asked with mock horror. 'And I've made you a cup of tea – I've a good mind to pour it away!'

'Don't worry, I've got cupcakes that I did the night before – they're still good.'

'Well, that's alright,' Fleur said, handing Cathy a mug. 'I'll let you off this time.'

Cathy took out her usual Tupperware container and peeled back the lid to reveal half a dozen pink iced cakes.

'Do you ever spend a day not baking?' Fleur asked as she took one. 'Not that I'm complaining, just curious.'

'Of course,' Cathy said with a laugh. 'Not often, I'll admit. I don't know… I just find it relaxing.'

'I like your relaxing,' Fleur said, munching on a mouthful. 'I find it relaxing to eat the results of your relaxing.'

Cathy laughed again as she stowed her bag and coat in the cubbyhole beneath the counter. 'How was Friday here? Busy?'

'Not too bad.'

'Nothing… I don't know… eventful happen?'

'You mean did your fella come in?' Fleur asked.

Cathy looked suitably sheepish and Fleur grinned. 'No, he didn't. Does that make you happy or disappointed?'

'I suppose it ought to make me relieved.'

'But it doesn't?'

'Oh, it does. But I can't help but think about what he might want.'

'Flowers, judging by how many he's bought recently.'

Cathy gave another light laugh as she reached for her mug of tea. 'You're probably right about that – I'm just reading too much into it.'

'Hey, I'd read too much into it as well, but if he wants to spend his money with me then who am I to complain? As long as it isn't causing too much upset for you.'

Cathy sipped at her tea before she answered. 'You know what, a few days ago I might have said it was, but today I feel strangely alright about it.'

'And what's happened to change your mind?'

Cathy's mind went back to her walk that morning, a slow smile creeping across her face. 'Oh, just something and nothing.'

'Hmm, and I'm not getting any more than that?'

'I don't know that there is any more than that,' Cathy said. Putting down her mug, she reached for her tabard, dropped it over her head and fastened it in place.

Fleur narrowed her eyes. 'I'm not buying that for a minute, and as soon as we're set up here I'm going to get some answers from you.'

Cathy's laughter was louder still as she replied. 'You can try, but don't bank on it.'

Chapter Sixteen

Just over an hour earlier, Cathy had finished eating the quick jacket potato she'd done for supper in the microwave and then turned her attention to the Christmas cake mixture she'd left to steep that morning. It had smelled gorgeous as she took the cover from the bowl, but it was even better now it was cooking. She'd leave it to cool once it was done and then store it somewhere until closer to Christmas, keeping it moist with regular drizzles of rum. She might even cut off a little piece today to test it, and if it was as good as she thought it would be, she'd make some more to give as gifts to her new friends.

After clearing down the surfaces and washing up, she turned her attention to the photocopy of Myrtle's page. The handwriting showed a light touch, a style that seemed so much more formal than the handwriting Cathy saw nowadays. Fleur's was almost indecipherable, she wrote so fast and loose – though Cathy had got used to her spidery notes by now. Her mum's had been a bit more like this, but even that was nowhere near as beautiful. But Myrtle's mother-in-law had probably been educated a long, long time ago, maybe even during the early part of the twentieth century, and schooling had been a lot more formal back then.

It was funny to look at it now and imagine that young woman making these notes for the very first time, having no inkling that her recipe would survive across the years and that now a woman she would never meet was using it. The idea had always been one that fascinated Cathy, that recipes could be like heirlooms, gifts handed down the generations, that such a humble thing could connect people in such a tangible way, whether they were still living or not. It was almost like archaeology – and, in fact, Cathy had once watched a programme about Tudor baking and the way the well-educated presenter had explained how the recipes for these dishes had been unearthed suggested that he thought so too. They were an important link, a social commentary on how people had once lived, and they were worth preserving.

It got Cathy thinking now about her own recipe book, how she was trying to keep her mother's knowledge alive, and how perhaps she might be able to do the same for other people too. She was hardly in the same league as the scholars who had put together that programme, but she felt as if what she was doing was important in a small way nonetheless.

To that end, she wondered if she ought to ask for more recipes. There were bound to be more people like Myrtle who had old notes passed down, or even people who had invented their own that were so good they ought to be preserved for posterity. They didn't have to be old to be worth saving – Myrtle's courgette cake was proof of that.

Cathy made herself a cup of tea, got out her own book and sat at the kitchen table, while the delicious aroma of her Christmas cake wrapped her in its warm, richly spiced embrace. She opened up to the next clean page and began to copy Myrtle's mother-in-law's recipe. Every so often she'd take a sip of her tea, but soon she was so preoccupied with her task that she forgot about it until she reached to take some and realised it was cold. Her mother had been a zero-waste type of woman, and Cathy had inherited that trait, so she gulped down the rest with a grimace and put the cup in the sink before returning to her task.

When she was done she made her usual embellishments, drawing some sprigs of holly and a parcel with a bow in the corners. It might be silly, and the vicar's comments made her wonder whether she ought to redo the book without the sketches, but she liked them – they made it feel personal to her – so she did them anyway. Besides, it was something to do.

'What do you think, Mum?' she asked, leaning back in her chair and holding the finished page to the light. 'I bet you would have loved this recipe.'

She gave a small smile. Her mum would have tried Myrtle's offering every which way; she'd have baked dozens of them with different variations until she had one she liked and then she would have continued to make that from memory for years. At least, she might have if she hadn't been so unwell for the last decade of her life. But at least Cathy could have talked about it with her and they would have shared ideas and suggestions on how to make it better and they would have eaten the results together with the telly on in the background and a hot cup of tea. Small pleasures, but Cathy often thought it was strange that it was the smallest things she missed the most.

There was a few days until the next cookery club, but once the Facebook group was up and running and everyone who was likely to sign up had done so, she could ask people if they had recipes like Myrtle's that they wanted to see preserved for posterity. Well, as much posterity as her little book offered. But it was an opportunity to share them and for others to get enjoyment from cooking them. For anyone not on the Facebook group, she could always ask Iris to put the word out, or else talk to them about it at the next class.

And then she started to think about Fleur's idea of getting the finished recipe book printed by professionals, and the thought of seeing all those precious heirlooms on glossy pages made her more enthusiastic still.

She looked down again at her copy of Myrtle's Christmas cake recipe and smiled. She couldn't wait to see what gems might come her way in the next couple of weeks.

Strike while the iron's hot, she thought, and went to fetch her phone from the living room to send Erica a text.

Just had a thought – I'd like to collect recipes from other people. Like people at the cookery club. I was thinking of adding them to my book so that they can share with others… if they want to, of course. What do you think? Do you think you can post about it in the new Facebook group?

Putting the phone to one side while she waited for Erica's reply, she went to fill the kettle for a fresh cup of tea. She'd only just flicked the switch when her phone pinged.

Sounds like a lovely idea. Don't you want to be on the Facebook group yourself? You could explain what you want better than me.

Cathy read the message again. Erica was probably right – she ought to do it herself. She'd withdrawn from social media to escape from the constant reminders that others were having a life denied her, but perhaps there was no need for that now.

Ok; I'll do that. Thanks for setting it up x

It's not that I don't want to help, of course… x

I know that! Honestly you're right and it's fine. See you soon x

Goodnight, Cathy, see you soon x

Cathy put her phone down and went to get her old laptop. It was slow and clunky, but it would do for what she needed. Maybe if this took off and she started to use it a lot more, she'd treat herself to a newer one, as long as it wasn't too expensive.

Once she was in she left a post on the group page explaining what she wanted to do and asking if anyone had recipes they wanted to bring in. Almost immediately replies began to appear. Most shocking was the fact that Myrtle was on Facebook – Cathy just hadn't imagined her embracing technology in that way – and she replied first. She was thrilled that her Christmas cake had been a source of inspiration to Cathy and she said she could contribute lots more of her mother-in-law's recipes. Beth replied saying she'd ask her mum, and Lindsey said she thought her grandma might have something.

Cathy was pleased to see that people were on board with her idea, but as she read through posts and comments on the relatively new group page, what warmed her heart even more was seeing people's messages about how much they were loving the cookery club. They'd posted photos too, of family members enjoying the fruits of their labours or new things that they'd baked at home, having been inspired to try some of Cathy's other dishes. She didn't think she'd ever feel so valued and appreciated again. She'd often thought that one of the greatest gifts her was her love of baking because it had brought them so much pleasure as mother and daughter. But now she was beginning to realise that gift could keep on giving, even with her mother gone, through things like the cookery club and her recipe book, and the notion made her happier than she could have ever thought possible.

Chapter Seventeen

Cathy had stored the number for St Cuthbert's office phone in her own contacts list, really just in case there ever came a time when she needed to let someone know last minute that she might not make a session of cookery club, fully expecting never to have to use it. So she was surprised when she was woken the next morning by her phone ringing on the bedside table and the number showing on caller ID. So much for having a rare sleep-in.

'Hello?' she answered, her voice still groggy and strange from having just woken.

'Oh, Cathy… I haven't woken you, have I?'

'No, no… of course not. I was about to get up anyway.' Cathy pushed herself to sit and leaned against the headboard. 'What's wrong, Iris?'

'Well,' Iris began, her tone becoming suddenly officious, 'it's just that we usually have two handheld blenders…'

'Right…'

'And because we were doing the cookery club we used petty cash to buy two more…'

'OK…'

'But today there are only three in the cupboard.'

'Oh.' Cathy frowned. Was Iris insinuating that Cathy had something to do with this? 'Didn't you check they were all there when we cleaned up after cookery club?'

'I thought Dora had done that.'

'Have you asked Dora?'

'I phoned her before I phoned you. She wasn't very helpful, to be honest – a bit rude.'

Cathy glanced at the clock by her bed. It had just gone seven thirty and if Iris had called Dora before she'd called Cathy, then it was no wonder Dora hadn't been very happy about it. 'But she hadn't counted the blenders?'

'She thought you or I had done it.'

'And I thought one of you would have done it. Sorry, Iris.'

'So you don't know where the missing one might be?'

'Sorry, but I haven't a clue.'

'Oh dear,' Iris said, sounding stricken. 'Oh dear…'

'I could come down to help you look.'

'Oh, would you? The vicar won't be happy if he finds out we've lost it – petty cash is hard to come by, you know, and we can't be seen to be frittering it away on things that we're going to lose.'

'No, I understand that. Listen, I'll come to help you find it – I can't see that it can be far away – maybe it's just been put in the wrong cupboard or something.'

'I've looked in all the cupboards,' Iris said.

'Well, sometimes a fresh pair of eyes makes all the difference,' Cathy said. 'And if we don't find it, I'll buy another to replace it.'

'Oh, we couldn't let you do that.'

'I wouldn't mind – after all, it would be sort of my fault it was missing; I should have done an inventory of everything before and after class but I never thought of that.'

'I didn't either. I'm at the church hall now; I'll leave the door open for you.'

'Oh… right…'

It looked as if Cathy was going to have to get up and get dressed right away, whether she wanted to or not.

Cathy skipped breakfast but she did take a few minutes to put on a little make-up, clip back her hair and spritz it with a glossing spray she'd bought for special occasions (there hadn't been many and the bottle was quite old now, but the stuff inside was still OK). She also pulled out a more fitted coat she'd usually reserve for less muddy locations before leaving the house for the canal path. It would take a little longer to get to St Cuthbert's this way but she'd walk fast to make up the time. The skies were dark and threatening but at least it wasn't windy, and she hoped that if it was going to rain it would hold off long enough to keep her hair looking this way until she got where she was going.

She felt good and happy as she strode along the path, despite having been rudely awakened at an hour not of her choosing, and even though she didn't know what mood she'd find Iris in when she got to St Cuthbert's. She couldn't even say why, but perhaps, if she was completely honest, it had a lot to do with hope – the same hope that had made her decide that she didn't have time for breakfast that morning, but did have time to do her make-up and hair and search for her best coat.

As she walked she eagerly scanned the path ahead. What would she do if she saw him today? All sorts of conversation starters and ice-breakers ran through her head, all of them a lot cooler than what would inevitably come out if she did run into him. One of her more dubious talents had always been to completely forget what she'd meant to say in situations like this, leaving something far sillier to come out of her mouth. Jonas used to rib her constantly about her first meeting with him. They'd been introduced by a mutual friend (one of the many who'd drifted out of Cathy's life once looking after her mother had taken over it) in a bar in town and, as Cathy had said hello, dazzled by him and certain that he was far too good-looking to be interested in her, he'd taken her hand in his to shake. She'd looked at his drink on the bar and said, 'That's a lovely pint of lager.'

What she'd meant to say was something like 'I see you're already settled in here.' Or 'Mind if I join you for one of those?' or even 'Pleased to meet you.'

He'd laughed and she'd blushed. It had been one of the things he'd liked about her straight away, or so he'd said afterwards, though he'd taken great delight in ribbing her about it every so often just the same.

She'd been lost in those memories for maybe ten minutes when she saw a dog bounding across the field. Her stomach did a flip, but then hurtled down the slope again as she realised that it was a completely different dog. Some way ahead, she saw a young woman with a toddler and then watched as the dog – it looked like a collie from here – raced towards them and gave the child a big lick, sending the little one into spasms of laughter while the woman complained and tried to wipe the child's face with her sleeve.

Cute, Cathy thought as she watched, though she couldn't help but be disappointed that it wasn't who she'd hoped to see. She and the woman exchanged a brief good morning as Cathy squeezed past and marched on, the dog walking after her for a few metres until it decided she wasn't worth pursuing after all and went off to sniff at a tree.

Up ahead, the path now forked into two, one that led further along the canal and the other that would take Cathy into town. The second was the one she needed to take, although she looked longingly at the other one for a moment before she veered off. How far along did the man walk when he went out with Guin? And it was strange, she thought, that right now she knew more about his dog than she did him, including his name.

She cast a last look along the route that continued down the canal. He might be further down but was it worth taking the time to hurry down there to check? And if she did, what would she do? A brief hello and a few comments about the weather? Was there any point? Perhaps he hadn't come out today, or perhaps he'd found somewhere else to walk his dog. Perhaps he hadn't given her a second thought since their last meeting and all the signals she thought she'd seen were in her head.

Cathy suddenly felt a bit pathetic. All this for a man she knew nothing about. If someone she knew had told her they were doing this she'd have thought them a bit weird, maybe even slightly scary. And yet, inexplicably, here was Cathy herself doing just that and she didn't know why. She only knew there was something about him that kept drawing her here, that kept her wanting to see more and know more. And she couldn't have told anyone what that was if they'd asked.

Maybe she'd been on her own too long. One thing was certain: she wasn't going to see him today and, besides, she had more important things to worry about right now. Iris was waiting, probably ready to write her resignation to the vicar because she couldn't find the offending blender, and Cathy had promised to go straight up there to help look. Thoughts of handsome, mysterious dog walkers would have to be put away for the time being.

The heat in the office of St Cuthbert's church hall was almost tropical, forcing Cathy to strip off her coat as soon as she walked in. The central heating was on – or at least the radiator Cathy had walked past felt as if it was pumping out a fair amount of heat – but Iris had an electric fire going in the corner anyway.

'I don't understand it,' she said. 'I've looked everywhere and when I came off the phone to you I looked again.'

'It can't be far away,' Cathy said. She draped her coat over a chair back and placed her handbag next to it. Iris had locked the front doors again after she'd come in so there was no worry that anyone could get in to take it. So Cathy followed Iris out of the office and in the direction of the kitchen, glad to be away from the overbearing heat. 'Could you have taken it somewhere strange and left it there?' she continued.

Iris turned to her looking confused.

'I mean, like been preoccupied thinking about something else and have it in your hand as you went into another room? I do it all the time, walk around the house with something, not thinking what I'm doing and end up putting it down in a really random place without realising I've left it there. Once I found the tea caddy in the bathroom and I had no idea how it had got there, but as there was only me in the house I must have taken it there without remembering it at all.'

'I don't do things like that,' Iris said firmly, and Cathy realised that, knowing what she did about Iris so far, that was probably true.

'Right. It was just a suggestion. If you didn't do that, is it possible that someone else did?'

'Like you?' Iris said.

'Or Dora, as we were the three people cleaning up after we last used the kitchen.'

'I don't think so,' Iris said. 'You'd have thought someone would have come across it by now. We have a cleaner in three times a week and she hasn't said she's found anything.' She paused for a moment, key in the lock of the kitchen door, before she twisted to open it. 'I ought to have a word with her anyway, just to be certain she hasn't found it and not said.'

'How much did it cost?' Cathy asked as Iris flicked the lights on to illuminate what was becoming one of Cathy's favourite places. The sight of all those gleaming chrome worktops and beautiful ovens made her want to roll her sleeves up and get started on something so she could fill that space with warm, sugary aromas. 'You can get them fairly cheap, can't you?'

'It wasn't expensive but that's beside the point. It's the principle of the matter. I won't be able to rest knowing it's lying around somewhere going to waste. Or…' Iris said, her tone darkening now, 'that we have a thief in our midst.'

Cathy paused, her hand almost unconsciously caressing a wooden spoon in a drawer she'd just opened to check.

'Thief?' Cathy stared at Iris. 'Who do you think would do that? Nobody in our cookery club as far as I can see. I mean, why would they? For a start, they'd be taking the one bit of equipment they'd be needing when they came here. Even if they wanted it for themselves, that would be a bit daft.'

'Who knows what motives drive people to crime,' Iris said grimly, and Cathy had to wonder vaguely whether she'd just accidentally wandered onto the set of Silent Witness. They were talking about what was probably no more than twenty pounds' worth of hand blender, not the Brink's-Mat gold.

'Look, it'll turn up,' Cathy said. 'We just need to keep looking. And if it doesn't, I'll go and buy one today and that will be case closed.'

They searched the kitchen for half an hour in relative silence, one of them uttering only a few words to announce that there was no sign of it in the place they'd just looked or to ask how the other was getting on.

'I'm beginning to doubt my own sanity,' Cathy said eventually, slamming a cupboard door shut with a sigh of frustration. 'I wonder if I've taken the bloody thing home with me without realising.'

'I'm beginning to think the same,' Iris said. 'I ought to check with Dora again.'

'Do you think she might have it?'

'Probably not but I just don't know what else to do.'

'Iris, let's just forget it. I'll go and buy another one, because this is just not worth the stress.'

Iris opened her mouth to reply, but a voice from the kitchen doorway made them both spin round.

'Hello, ladies.'

'Vicar!' Iris exclaimed, looking very flustered. If she'd been a toddler he would be asking her what she'd done with the sweetie jar right about now. 'We're just doing an inventory,' she added, and Cathy didn't offer any contradiction, understanding immediately that this was something Iris probably didn't want to bother him with. More to the point, she probably didn't want him to think that it was something she didn't have under control.

'Oh, you carry on,' he said warmly, and with that Iris relaxed. Perhaps a bit too much, because she swung from guilty to resembling a star-struck teen. Her voice rose at least an octave while she batted her eyelashes and a hand crept up to tease out her grey curls.

'And are we all present and correct?' he continued, smiling good-naturedly. If the vicar had noticed the obvious effect he was having on Iris then he was at least discreet enough not to let it show.

'I think so,' Iris said. 'Actually, yes… yes, we are.'

'Glad to hear it.' He smiled at Cathy again.

'Are you still thinking of joining us next week?' she asked.

'Oh, not next week, I'm afraid – meeting with the big boss. Not the very big boss, you understand… he's far too busy for the likes of me. I'll have to make do with the Archbishop for now.'

His smile widened to a grin that seemed overly pleased with his joke. Maybe it was very funny in church circles. Cathy managed to acknowledge it with a polite smile of her own.

'But if there is spare cake at the end of the lesson you can be sure if you leave a slice on my desk it would be very much appreciated.'

'I'll remember to make a spare one for you next week,' Iris said fervently.

'I'll look forward to it,' he said. 'Well, as we're not currently getting burgled, I'll leave you two to get on with it.'

'Oh no,' Iris said. 'Is that what you thought? I should have phoned you to tell you what we'd be doing.'

'Oh, don't worry,' he said. 'I had to go to the office to pick something up and I saw the light was on in the kitchens; that's all. I knew there'd be a perfectly good explanation. After all, if I can't trust you with the keys, Iris, then who can I trust? You're the best caretaker I could ask for.'

Iris looked as if she might burst with pride, smiling all over her face. 'Thank you!'

'I don't know what I'd do if you ever retired,' he said as he raked a hand through his impressively untamed hair. There was an audible gasp from Iris's direction and Cathy glanced across, filled with a vague alarm that she might have to catch her mid-swoon. But Iris was wearing that same soppy smile that she'd had – more or less – since he'd arrived.

'I'll be in later to look over the accounts, Vicar,' she said.

'That would be great; thanks, Iris. Oh, and if you could check what we have to spare, we could do with some new Christmas decorations – the ones we've been using for the last few years are beginning to look a bit tatty and I thought we might invest in a few new bits and pieces to pep everything up.'

'I thought so too,' Iris said. 'I was looking at what we've got with Dora only the other day and I said just that. I'm sure I'll be able to find something spare in the coffers.'

'I know I can rely on you,' he said. 'If ever there was a woman who could magic funds out of thin air, it's you.'

With a last smile, he sauntered out again, hands in his pockets.

From the kitchen doorway they could see straight across the hall to where the office was. Iris watched and waited for the vicar to go in and close the door behind him before turning to Cathy again, her expression completely back to its normal shrewish self.

'I do hope he doesn't find out that something we've only just paid for has gone missing already.'

'Relax,' Cathy said. 'Like I said, I'll go and buy a replacement and nobody needs to be any the wiser. Next time, we'll do a thorough check of the equipment as people are clearing down so that if anything else goes missing we can ask people while they're here if they know where it is. There could be a very simple explanation for this that we just haven't considered – there usually is.'

Iris didn't look convinced but, as they couldn't locate the missing item and nobody had time to spend hours looking for it, even she had to admit that Cathy's proposal made the most sense. Judging by how long they'd already spent on the task, it didn't look as if it would turn up even if they did. The easiest thing was to cut their losses and simply get another and hope something like this didn't happen again.

Chapter Eighteen

Cathy took the box out from the bag and looked at it. In the end, she'd been able to pick up a comparable blender quite cheaply; though it wasn't quite the same as the one that had gone missing, she hoped it would be good enough for Iris.

By the time she'd finished at the shops – having got a few bits and pieces for herself and stopped for a quick coffee and a chat at Ingrid's – dusk had been falling and so Cathy had forgone her plan to walk back home along the canal path. It probably wouldn't have made any difference anyway. She'd caught sight of herself in the mirror as she'd come through the front door and by now her hair was windswept, her make-up had worn off and she looked tired. It was probably just as well she hadn't met anyone *interesting* on her way home.

She shrugged off her coat and left it on the bed to put back in the wardrobe later, and then took off her boots, going back downstairs barefoot. By now, the heating had come on and the house was warm.

It was as she was putting the kettle on for a well-earned brew that her phone began to ring. She smiled to see it was Erica.

'Hello… how are you?'

'I'm alright,' Erica said. 'I'll be better when Malc goes to work and he's out of my hair. He's on the noon shift and he's driving me mad.

When he's on the day shift he's normally out of the house before I get up… God, I wish he was on day shifts all the time!'

'Poor Malc,' Cathy said. 'Did you call for anything in particular or just a chat? Not that I mind a chat, of course, as long as you don't mind the sound of the kettle boiling and me clanging around. I've just got in and I'm parched. Which reminds me, I went into Ingrid's today. She had a new coffee cake on the menu; you'll have to try some next time.'

'Sounds good,' Erica said, but now her breezy tone seemed to have disappeared. 'I did actually call for something in particular. It's going to sound a bit weird but… well, I seem to have taken a blender home from St Cuthbert's kitchen…'

Cathy frowned. How did someone take something like that home by accident? She'd admit to putting things in weird places before now, but to take something like that home from someone else's kitchen by accident? And Cathy knew Erica wouldn't have done it on purpose… It didn't seem to make any sense.

Unless it wasn't Erica. Tansy? Would Tansy have done something like that? If so why? And why would Erica feel the need to cover for her? Why not just admit what had happened and have a good laugh about the silliness of it?

'I'm glad you've called me about it,' Cathy said. 'Iris was stressing a bit when she couldn't find it so I went to the shops to get another. Now that it's turned up I can take this one back for a refund. Thanks for letting me know before I opened it.'

'I'm really sorry,' Erica said. 'I feel like a total idiot.'

'Why?' Cathy put Erica on the loudspeaker and sat the phone on the counter while she went to fill the kettle.

'I just do. It's a really stupid thing to happen, isn't it? I have no idea how it got in my bag – it was just there when I looked this morning.'

Cathy frowned again. Something about this didn't stack up at all. 'It probably just fell in. It's funny how these things can happen. Maybe you walked past it on the way out and knocked it into your open bag or something. Or you were having a senior moment and dropped it in. It is a bit strange but it doesn't matter – at least we've found it.'

'I can get it to you first thing if you like.'

'There's no need to make a special trip. I'll call Iris and let her know we've got it and then I'll take this other one back to the shop. We won't need it until next cookery club so just keep hold of it and bring it when you come… You *are* coming to the next one, aren't you?'

Cathy didn't know what made her ask that; she could only say there was something in Erica's tone that didn't sound happy at all, and it was definitely more than Malcolm driving her mad.

'I think so,' Erica said, confirming Cathy's suspicions, because she didn't sound very certain.

'Of course,' Cathy said, trying to sound casual, 'I'll understand if you're busy. I can't expect everyone to be free every week…'

'I'll come,' Erica said. 'I'm not sure about Tansy for next time but count me in.'

Cathy gave a half smile as she dropped a teabag into a mug. She couldn't say she was particularly gutted at the thought of no Tansy next time and she didn't think anyone else would be either. 'I understand. It's full of people much older than her, isn't it? I'm quite surprised she's done the two weeks she has if I'm honest – not sure I would have been up for a club full of old folks at her age.'

'Oh, it's not that. I think she's enjoying the baking – she actually loves cooking. She used to say, when she was little, that she wanted to be a chef. It's just... well, I think she's a bit busy, that's all.'

Cathy recalled now the look of intense concentration on Tansy's face when they finally got down to baking, and she could see what Erica meant because it had looked as if her niece had been deadly serious about the cookery aspect of the session, even if she appeared to hate everything about the socialising. But hadn't Erica said once before that Tansy had very few friends? Still, it didn't seem the time to point that out.

'College or something, I suppose?' she said instead, gifting Erica an excuse.

'Something like that, yes.'

'It'll be a shame to lose her from the numbers but it's OK. Maybe she'll give it another go when she's less busy?'

'Maybe,' Erica said, though she sounded unconvinced.

'OK. So I'll see you there if I don't see you before?'

'It'll probably be there; I've got quite a lot on this week – family stuff, you know...'

'Oh. Well, that's OK. I hope you get whatever it is sorted.'

'Thanks. And I'm sorry again about the blender.'

'Don't give it another thought,' Cathy said, now thoroughly convinced that Erica hadn't taken the blender at all and that it was most likely Tansy. But if that was the case, it was a puzzle Cathy was sure she'd end up giving a lot of thought to.

Chapter Nineteen

It was nearing the end of November, and with Christmas now feeling closer, Fleur had bought bundles of sturdy mistletoe sprigs, dotted with pearly berries, to sell on the stall. Cathy thought them gorgeous, though she couldn't help but feel a little sad about the fact that she had no reason to have a sprig up in her house. As Fleur unpacked them to display, she bound up the odds and ends that had come free and gave them to Cathy.

'What am I supposed to do with them?' Cathy asked, laughing. 'Who am I going to be kissing?'

'They're not just for kissing under, you know,' Fleur replied. 'That's some nonsense that Charles Dickens came up with.'

'I wouldn't tell your customers that if you want to sell it,' Cathy replied with a smile.

'I'd rather have it for the original use anyway,' Fleur said. 'Far more valuable.'

'Which is?'

'To protect against evil spirits and bring luck.'

'God, give me that whole delivery then!'

Fleur chuckled. 'So you can hang it in your house and not worry about that kissing rubbish.'

'Hmm, kissing is overrated – at least, that's what I keep telling myself so I'll feel better about not getting any.'

'You and me both, my love,' Fleur said. 'Not that I'm bothered right now. Best thing I did was kick that no-good loser out of my house.'

'You mean Gavin?' Cathy asked.

'Don't!' Fleur held up a hand. 'Don't utter that name in my presence!'

'Sorry,' Cathy said, though she could see that while Fleur meant it, she wasn't angry at Cathy. She was angry at her ex, of course, who'd moved in all charm and good looks and, once he'd got his feet under Fleur's table, had systematically gone about trying to take her for every penny she had. In subtle ways at first, so that nobody had realised it was happening – least of all Fleur. But Fleur was no gullible fool and it hadn't taken her long to realise she was being taken for a mug. She'd booted him out, no fuss, no tears, though Cathy also knew that was a front. She'd been hurt, no doubt about that, and she'd felt stupid too, but she wasn't going to let anyone see that.

'Sometimes I think there's not a one of them worth having,' Fleur continued. 'Here's me, single at forty-eight, still not able to find a good man worth my effort.'

'I'm sure it's not like that,' Cathy said.

Fleur looked unconvinced. And the conversation had turned Cathy's thoughts to another man, one who she had thought she'd known well but was turning out to be someone else entirely.

'I don't suppose Jonas has been to the stall again?' she asked, almost dreading to hear the answer, whatever it was.

'No. Perhaps he's got the message.'

'I didn't realise I was sending one,' Cathy said.

'You weren't really; you're far too nice for that. I was doing my best to get it over loud and clear though. A man like that shouldn't be messing around, especially not with the feelings of a woman like you.'

A woman like me? Cathy held back a frown. What did that mean? Did Fleur view her as fragile? Someone who was damaged, vulnerable, gullible… even desperate? Cathy wasn't sure what to say in reply to that. She'd always felt she looked as if she was coping, even when she wasn't. But did Fleur see it differently? Did everyone see it as her boss did? Did something about her scream pity case?

'Enough of that anyway,' Fleur said, sparing Cathy the need to respond. 'I expect you'll be going to see your mum's ashes soon, as it's getting nearer to Christmas. If you are, you can take this…' She produced a wreath from beneath the counter, fashioned from glossy holly studded with scarlet berries. 'I made one too many for an order. I could sell it, of course, but I wondered if you might want it.'

'How much is it?' Cathy asked.

Fleur chuckled. 'For you? A cake! What have you got for me today?'

'Really?' Cathy asked, touched at Fleur's kindness. 'Are you sure?'

'Of course I am! It's like bartering, isn't it? I swap something that I've made for something that you've made. Now, come on, don't tease – I know you've baked something. The day you stop baking is the day the earth will stop turning.'

Cathy grinned. 'You know me too well. I thought, as it's almost December, it was time for mince pies.'

Fleur clapped her hands together. 'Perfect!'

Cathy smiled as she pulled the plastic tub from her bag and offered it to Fleur. It was full of perfect circles of frilled pastry, dusted with icing sugar, and the rich smell of Cathy's home-made, brandy-laced mincemeat wafted out. Fleur grabbed one and bit into it, looking rapturous as the flavours exploded onto her tongue.

'Worth every scratch from those blasted holly leaves,' she said. 'Seriously, woman, I think you were put on this earth to make me fat.'

Cathy giggled. 'Maybe I should give the baking a rest for a while then.'

'No way!' Fleur said, laughing as she popped the last morsel into her mouth. 'The minute you stop bringing me cakes you're fired!'

Fleur's wreath really was beautiful. Cathy was sitting on the bus out of town, the wreath in a thick, padded plastic bag on her knee. Every so often she'd open it to have a look at the leathery leaves and bright berries, and it would give her a warm feeling. It was more than just an arrangement; it was a heartfelt gift. Cathy wouldn't have been a bit surprised to learn that Fleur hadn't made it by accident at all and that she'd made it especially for Cathy and had just told her that to make her feel OK about taking it. Fleur liked to give the impression she didn't care about anything or anyone, when really she probably cared too much. While Cathy might not be certain if Fleur's extra wreath had been purposely crafted or not, she was sure that if her mum could have seen it she'd have thought it beautiful too. Her mum loved Christmas and everything that came with it, and by now she'd have had the house decorated with holly and mistletoe, and a new poinsettia would have appeared on the windowsill too, scarlet leaves against a grey sky. Before she'd been too ill to get around she would have been cooking and baking for weeks, the air of the kitchen constantly warm and sweet.

As the bus rocked and rolled, climbing the hill out of Linnetford and towards the forest where Cathy's mum now rested, Cathy let her mind wander back to the last Christmas she could remember her mum being well enough to bake. It had been non-stop for the week before – fruit cake, mince pies, sausage rolls, ham and egg pies, yule logs dusted with sugar and plain old fairy cakes made fancy with iced

Christmas scenes – and there'd been far too much for the two of them to eat. They'd taken some to relatives and some to the homeless shelter and even then her mum hadn't been able to stop. Cathy hadn't minded. Miriam had been ill for a few weeks and had hardly bothered to move from the sofa, so it was good to see her feel like doing anything and even better to work alongside her. They'd sang along to the Phantom of the Opera soundtrack – her mum's favourite. Hardly festive, Cathy had pointed out, so Miriam had fetched an old Santa hat from a box in the loft and put it on.

'Festive enough for you?' she'd laughed, before launching into the chorus of 'The Music of the Night'.

Cathy had been more of a pop music girl at that age and she hadn't appreciated her mum's music taste, though she'd always loved to hear her sing and these days loved to listen to those old soundtracks herself. But even back then she'd joined in, laughing at the absurdity of it as they both got louder and louder to sing over the sounds of the food processor as they made breadcrumbs for far too many Scotch eggs for them to eat in a year, let alone a week. They'd been so happy that day and they'd had the loveliest Christmas that year – not full of parties or lavish three-course dinners dressed in their finest like some of her friends were having with their families, but humble and quiet, cosy and full of love.

Twenty minutes later Cathy got off the bus with tears in her eyes. Hastily, she dried them and hoped nobody would notice. She had another ten-minute walk to the edge of the forest where her mum's ashes were scattered but she had a day off work, another five or six hours of daylight and nowhere better to be. The weather was bright and brisk today, and even from this distance she could hear the snapping and creaking of branches as the wind snatched at them in the forest ahead, a sort of low collective grumbling. To the west, her home town of Linnetford lay in a valley, a far-off jumble of grey roofs and brown bricks, shot through by black roads like threads on a loom. The sound of its traffic was now too far away to be heard and Cathy took in a long breath of cold, clear air. Even though the town was right there, in plain sight, it felt a million miles away up here. Everything looked different and smelled different, and if you closed your eyes it wasn't hard to imagine yourself in some Nordic wilderness rather than on the edge of an old town in the north of England that was still trying to shake off the grime of its industrial past.

Cathy began to walk.

It was quite difficult to identify the exact spot where her mum's ashes had been scattered so Cathy had given up trying long ago. Once she felt certain she was in the general area she stopped. Under her feet was a carpet of soft, fragrant pine needles, some browning and brittle, others fresher, and overhead the sky had all but disappeared behind the boughs of the huge trees that towered above her, only visible in flashes of blue and white here and there. All was peaceful and Cathy closed her eyes for a moment to soak it up. Her mum could hardly have picked a more perfect place to take up her final rest. Cathy loved it here, and she had a feeling that her mum's decision to have her ashes spread here was almost as much a recognition of that as it was her own wishes. It was just the sort of thing she would have done, to give Cathy somewhere lovely to come and visit rather than some dreary cemetery that she'd know her daughter would feel it was her duty to go to but would hate.

When Cathy opened them again she went to the nearest sturdy trunk and laid her hand against it, taking a minute to visualise her mum's face, to recall the sound of her voice. Already it seemed to be harder and harder each time she came, but she had to remember – she had to do at least that one small thing for her mum now that there was nothing else she could do for her. She thought about the way her mum laughed at things that weren't funny, when Cathy would roll her eyes and pretend to be annoyed. She thought about her fussing over the silliest things while being stoical about the hard stuff, about how she rarely complained even when Cathy knew she was suffering, how she tried to stay bright and positive even at the end when her lungs had all but buckled beneath the weight of the disease that would kill her. She was never hurt or offended at Cathy's frustrated outbursts, though Cathy suspected she often felt guilty about the burden she'd placed on her daughter.

Perhaps she felt guilty about the lack of a father in Cathy's life too; though that wasn't her fault, Cathy wondered if she'd felt like it was. Cathy's dad had been missing for a long time and Cathy could barely remember him. She only knew that one day he'd kissed her goodbye, and the next he was gone. A congenital heart defect. They'd said the attack he'd had aged thirty would have killed him instantly and he probably wouldn't have known anything about it. Miriam had never exactly got on well with his family, even less so once he'd gone, and although they tried to get along for Cathy's sake while she'd been little, as soon as Cathy stopped being a cute little kid and began to come with adult burdens of her own, they'd abandoned her.

Cathy often struggled to recall the details of the time around her father's death but one thing had always stood out clearly. Her mum had insisted on doing much of the catering for the wake herself. Cathy recalled now that she'd been like a machine in the way she'd tackled it, like someone Cathy hadn't recognised. Even now, Cathy was struck with that same sense of how strange it had felt to see this completely new person inhabit her mother – how the usually bright smile had disappeared, how she'd stopped singing songs from shows and her beautiful eyes had become dull hollows. Cathy remembered that she'd been scared by this woman she no longer knew and that she hadn't known what to do or how to behave around her. She'd watched as her mother whizzed feverishly around the kitchen making hot-water crust pies and flaky sausage rolls and sponges and rich Madeira cakes. She didn't stop, didn't tire and barely showed any emotion other than grim determination.

But it had all been a lie and later that night, the night before her father's funeral, after Cathy had been sent to bed, she'd cracked. Cathy hadn't been in bed when it happened. She'd been sitting on the top stair in her flannelette nightgown, listening to the sounds from downstairs and wishing she could have her mother back. She had no idea how long she'd been there but something had given her the courage to venture down and that's when she'd found her mum slumped over the old stoneware mixing bowl that had been in the family longer than Cathy herself, sobbing uncontrollably.

*

'Mummy...?'

A tentative hand found her mother's shoulder, a tiny uncertain voice issuing from little Cathy's throat, barely loud enough to trouble the sound of her mother's crying. Cathy understood so little of what was happening but she felt it, so powerfully that she began to cry herself, barely knowing why except that her daddy had gone somewhere he wasn't coming back from and her mummy was very unhappy about it. She didn't understand it and yet there was something instinctive that made her understand more than she realised, more than any five-year-old should ever have to comprehend.

'Mummy… Please don't cry.'

But she kept on crying, floodgates of emotion now open and the torrent they had unleashed too powerful to let them close again.

Cathy stood at her side, hand resting on her mother's shoulder, helpless and afraid to speak again for the fear she'd make it all worse, that her simply being there was making it worse, but powerless to leave. Perhaps her being there was making it worse, but not for the reasons Cathy would have imagined – never for those reasons. Years later the moment would come up in a candid yet painful conversation and Cathy would discover that hearing her daughter's voice had only served to remind Miriam of how terrified she'd been at the thought of bringing her up alone, how she felt she'd ultimately fail and had already been blaming herself for a failure that was yet to happen.

After what seemed like hours, Cathy's mum looked up. Her face was streaked with tears, her sobs stuttering to whimpers and then to a final heaving breath that stopped them in their tracks.

'Mummy…?' Cathy whispered.

'I'm alright,' her mum replied, though she could have had no idea what Cathy's question had really meant. Even Cathy didn't know what her one-word question was asking. It was so much more than a direct question, more of a vague but desperate plea for reassurance, for her mum to do more than say she was alright but to really be alright. She dried her eyes and pulled Cathy onto her knee, hugging her tightly – almost too tightly so that Cathy gave a little squeak.

'I love you,' she said.

Cathy burrowed further into her mum's arms and let those words wash over her. It was almost enough to make her feel better, almost enough to make her believe that perhaps the mum she thought she'd lost to an emotional vacuum had finally found her way home. But not quite. What she needed to truly believe it was for something normal to happen, something that the real mummy would have done.

After a few moments of silence in her arms, Cathy's mum peeled away to look down at her. She'd stopped crying now, though her face was puffy and her eyes red and swollen. 'You ought to be in bed – you'll be exhausted tomorrow and it's going to be a long day.'

'Can't I stay with you?'

'No – I have too much to do here.'

'Please, Mummy.'

'No; it's bedtime. Don't make life hard for me right now, Catherine; I've got enough people trying to do that.'

Cathy stared at her mother. She rarely called her Catherine. The strangeness of it started her bottom lip trembling. 'I don't want to go to bed. Please can I stay with you?'

'Why don't you want to go to bed?' her mother asked wearily. 'I wish I could.'

Cathy shook her head, eyes wide. 'I'm scared.'

'What are you scared of?'

Cathy paused. She was scared but she couldn't understand what she was scared of, let alone articulate it. Had she been thirty years older perhaps she still wouldn't have been able to. She shook her head again. 'I don't know.'

Cathy's mother studied her for a moment. But then she gave her head a firm shake, as if coming to a decision.

'Alright,' she said in a voice steeled with determination once again, all trace of the emotional wreckage she'd been only moments before gone. 'If you're staying up you can make yourself useful and help me. I have to roll some pastry for cheese puffs – do you think you can do that?'

Cathy gave a mute nod. As long as she was close to her mum she didn't care. She was handed the rolling pin and together they got back to work.

*

Cathy's mind returned to the forest of here and now, her eyes glazed with tears that she sniffed hastily back. She'd often felt guilty herself since her mum's death, even if she could have felt no more than helpless over her dad's, for all the times she'd complained or been less than patient. Her mother had been cursed with a hard life and Cathy had rarely appreciated that as fully as she ought to have. If she'd had to do it all again she would have, only this time, knowing what the aftermath would feel like, she'd have done it willingly, without complaint, always with a smile on her face. She'd have told her mum more often that she loved her, that she was grateful for the years she'd spent bringing her up, that it was now her turn to care and that there was no reason to feel like a burden. Cathy had felt those things, of course, but sometimes articulating them had been much harder to do.

She thought back now to what Fleur had said the day before, how it had been laden with subtext. Did everyone see Cathy as fragile or vulnerable? She didn't feel it – if anything she felt strong, she felt like a survivor; after all, look at what she'd survived so far in her life. She didn't want people to see her that way or feel sorry for her.

Her eyes stubbornly filling with tears again, she took Fleur's wreath from the carrier bag and laid it at the foot of the tree.

'Hope you like it, Mum,' she said.

She lingered a moment longer, and then turned to find the path out.

*

Cathy got off the bus a few stops early. It had been a last-minute decision, a sudden urge to walk home via the canal path, even though the sky was darkening and it would soon be dusk. If she hurried, though, she'd make it back long before then, and you never knew who you might meet on the way. It had been a strange and melancholy day of reflection and she really needed something to cheer her up; something to give her hope. But almost as soon as she'd watched her bus drive on she regretted her decision. It started to rain, heavy and freezing, and she still had a good thirty minutes' walk before she could get out of it. It was at times like this she wished she'd kept the car she'd sold; after her mother's death she'd decided that she didn't go far enough to warrant keeping it on.

Pulling the hood of her coat up and fastening the top button, she shoved her hands deep in her pockets and did her best to stay dry as she began the trek home. She allowed herself a wry smile, despite the cold and wet. There was only one reason she was adding this extra time to her journey and, when she really looked at it, it was a very silly reason. She looked for him anyway as she walked the path, even though it had always been morning when she'd seen him before with his dog, and even though she had no reason to believe that he was always going to walk his dog in exactly the same place every day.

As she walked she scanned the path. The rain smashed into the water of the canal, the surface a mess of tiny solar systems radiating from each drop. If she hadn't been so cold Cathy might have taken a moment to appreciate how pretty it looked, or how the town was shrouded in a heavy grey blanket of cloud that somehow softened its hard edges, or how the clouds whipped across the horizon, throwing the landscape into a fast-moving patchwork of light and dark.

But she was cold and she barely gave these things a second thought, and she was soon annoyed at herself because it was clear that nobody else was stupid enough to be out on an afternoon like this. By the time she'd reached the turn-off, where the path led back to a housing estate that led to her own home, she'd seen not another living soul.

Stupid, she thought as she looked down at the mud on her boots.

Still, at least she hadn't spent the day sitting in the house waiting for life to happen to her.

Chapter Twenty

Even though the rain had cleared overnight and the morning was brighter, Cathy made a conscious decision not to walk the canal path today. She had a lot to carry for cookery club, for one thing, and if she was going just to try to bump into her mystery man, it was silly, and maybe a little bit desperate too. So she walked through her estate and on to town, and in a funny way she was glad she did, because some of her neighbours had started to put up their Christmas decorations and the road looked bright and cheery.

As for her own decorations, it hardly seemed worth getting them down from the loft this year, not just for her to look at and be reminded that it was Christmas but that this year she was looking at them alone. Her mum would have wanted them putting up around now, and she'd have been tapping her foot along to Christmas songs as she told Cathy where she wanted streamers and plaques and wreaths to hang.

What Cathy could get excited about, as she walked to St Cuthbert's, was her recipe book. She'd had replies to her post on Facebook and she was looking forward to seeing what recipes people had brought in to contribute. She'd also had a message from Beth saying she was bringing her older sister to give it a go, and Cathy was looking forward to welcoming a new member to the club. She knew the vicar wouldn't make his appearance this week – although, that might be a good thing because him being there would make Iris so star-struck that she'd be absolutely useless, and Cathy still relied a great deal on her assistance when it came to things like knowing where keys and switches and pieces of equipment were. Cathy liked him, of course; the problem was, Iris liked him just a bit too much. And goodness only knew what sort of mischief it would provoke in Dora, who loved to tease Iris almost as much as Iris loved to follow the vicar round.

As she arrived at the front doors of the church hall, Iris was waiting for her outside.

'You could have gone in,' Cathy said. 'You must have been freezing out here.'

'I've only just arrived myself,' Iris said. 'And I knew you'd be here any minute – I thought I'd wait as it would save me walking back across the hall to let you in.'

It was hardly a marathon, but Cathy just smiled. 'Thanks. How are you this morning?'

'Same as always,' Iris said, as if that was enough information for anyone. As she unlocked the old wooden doors, Cathy's attention was drawn to a car, slowing to a halt on the kerb close by. Erica got out.

'You're early,' Cathy said, going to meet her. 'Raring to go?'

'Oh, the car's broken down. Malc had already left the house for work so I've had to grab a lift with my brother before he went into work himself. It was better than fighting for a seat on the bus in rush hour.'

Cathy glanced at the car. She couldn't see anyone in the driver's seat, but the boot was open and she could only assume that Erica's brother was round there getting something out. She looked closer to see if Tansy was in there, but the back seats were empty too. She couldn't say she was all that disappointed, despite the effect Tansy's absence would have on her numbers – she'd feel a lot more relaxed today without that sneering presence.

The sound of the boot slamming echoed down the street and Erica's brother emerged from the back of the car with a bag. He strode towards Erica, holding it out for her but, as he looked up, whatever he'd been about to say to her died on his lips. He stared at Cathy, and then, with a sudden realisation of her own, Cathy's mouth dropped open.

A huge grin split his face.

'Well, talk about a small world!' he said.

'You're Erica's brother?' Cathy looked from him to Erica, as if expecting some kind of explanation. But that was silly, because how was her new friend to know that Cathy had already met her brother on the path that ran alongside the canal? How was she to know that this was the same man Cathy had been hoping to run into again, the reason that Cathy had got soaked the day before as she'd walked that way in the rain?

And, with a jolt of excitement, Cathy was suddenly reminded of one very important detail that Erica had given her about her brother: he was single.

'I am,' he said. 'So you must be Cathy?'

He glanced at Iris briefly before turning back to Cathy, perhaps doubting himself for a millisecond before deciding that his original guess was the right one. Cathy didn't know what Erica might have told him about her, but she was pleased that her friend had at least felt her important enough to mention to him. And that he'd remembered her name at all.

'And you must be Matthias?'

'Call me Matt,' he said, his grin spreading wider still. 'I don't know what my mum was thinking giving me a name like Matthias.'

'I like it,' Cathy said. 'It's unusual.'

Erica cleared her throat and Cathy turned to her now, realising that neither she nor Matthias had yet explained how they already knew each other 'Would someone like to tell me what's going on?'

'My thoughts exactly,' Iris put in. 'And is anyone actually entering this building or not, because I'm standing here like chips with these keys and we've got a kitchen to set up.'

'We've bumped into each other a couple of times already,' Matthias said, holding Cathy in a steady gaze as he did. She liked the way he looked at her. She could have been mistaken, of course, but it felt as if he was as interested in her as she was in him. What to do about that was a different matter entirely, especially now that it was complicated by the fact that he was Erica's brother and Cathy had already decided that it would be a bad idea to date someone so close to her friend… but for now she was ignoring that little thorn in her side and enjoying the moment. 'While I was walking Guin on the canal path.'

Now it was Erica's turn to show a wide grin. 'On the canal path… really? Well, isn't that interesting?'

At this, Matthias shot a brief look of warning at his sister. Cathy was pretty sure she hadn't mentioned their short meetings by the canal to Erica – though she'd been tempted a few times, something had always stopped her – so she could only assume, from Erica's reaction, that he had. And if he had, what had he said about her? It must have been good because Erica looked pleased, and also a little bit smug, like she was party to a fun secret and she was enjoying, for the moment, being the only person who knew it.

'Only to say good morning,' Cathy added. 'Of course, if I'd known that you were Erica's brother…'

'Well, it's not the first thing you think to ask when you meet someone out walking their dog, is it?' he said, laughing.

'No,' Cathy said, laughing herself now. 'But how strange...'

'The world is full of the most wonderful coincidences, isn't it?' Erica said.

Iris let out a sigh. 'I'll go and get started, shall I?'

She went inside, but although they all watched her go, nobody made a move to follow. Cathy wanted to get as much as she could from this meeting, and maybe Matthias did too. Erica seemed content to watch and grin and feel smug about it. There was no way she could fail to see how interested Cathy was, and after trying to matchmake and having her attempts rejected, Cathy fully expected an *I told you so* later that morning.

Matthias looked again at his sister. 'I expect you want to go in and get started.'

'There's no point in going in until Cathy does,' Erica said.

Cathy wanted to say something to him but she didn't know what. The situation had caught her completely off-guard and, as usual, all her cool lines had deserted her. Not that they would have been that cool, even if she'd been able to think of any of them.

'I suppose I'd better go in,' she said.

'Oh, right... of course,' he replied. 'I suppose I'd better get to work anyway – don't want to get stuck in traffic. See you around, maybe?'

'I hope so,' Cathy said. 'Bye, Mattias.'

'Matt,' he said, grinning at her and opening his car door.

'Matt,' Cathy repeated, smiling. 'Sorry; it didn't take me long to forget, did it?'

'I'll let you off this once.' He shot her a last grin before getting into his car.

They watched for a moment as he started the engine and began to pull away from the kerb. Then Cathy turned to see Erica wearing a huge naughty grin that made her look disconcertingly like her brother.

'Don't worry,' she said. 'He's got a late shift tomorrow. I've got a feeling if you take a walk by the canal tomorrow morning, you'll definitely find him there.'

On any other day, Cathy might have been disappointed to see that Tansy, the vicar and one or two others were missing from class, but her head was spinning from the strange but wonderful coincidence that had come to light that morning and her mood was just too good for disappointment. Erica kept giving her knowing looks, and Cathy caught her whispering to Iris and Dora more than once while angling her head in Cathy's direction. Cathy didn't want to assume that she was interesting enough to be the subject of their gossiping but was finding it hard to think anything else.

Because Fleur had got so excited about them, and because they hadn't actually tackled pastry yet at cookery club, Cathy had decided that they'd have a go at mince pies together. Everyone had been happy about that, even though some had said they didn't actually like mince pies. In fact, the number of people who'd told her that had worried her at first, and initially Cathy had been all for suggesting something else. However, almost all of those people had said that everyone they knew did like mince pies and they'd happily bake them to give away, especially as it was getting closer to Christmas.

If Cathy was honest, she had a love–hate relationship with mince pies herself. They were another one of those things her mum would bake every Christmas just because it was Christmas and you couldn't have Christmas without mince pies. Cathy smiled as the scene unfolded in her mind.

*

She'd have been perhaps six or seven when she'd first helped her mum to make them. Cutting the shapes out was her favourite bit. She stood on a chair to reach the table and it wobbled on an uneven bit of floor tile every time she pressed down. The pies were always wonky, either too thin or too thick, with edges that wouldn't fasten together once the mincemeat was in there. Still, Cathy's mum had smiled with pride and pulled her in for a hug once they were all cut.

'You're a natural,' she said. And little Cathy could have burst with pride. She hugged her mum tighter still. Miriam laughed lightly. 'You can let go now, sweetie; lovely as they look right now, we need to put them in the oven and make them even lovelier.'

'Can I put them in?'

'We need to brush them first and sprinkle some sugar over them and then they'll be ready. You think you can do that?'

Cathy nodded eagerly, and then followed a flurry of splattered milk and spilled sugar before the pies were ready to bake. And when they were done was the bit Cathy usually liked best – tasting.

'Ready?' her mum asked once they'd cooled enough to eat and she had two cups of tea on the table – one for her in a big mug the colour of amber, and one in a smaller mug that was more milk than tea for Cathy.

'Yes.'

Cathy grabbed for the mince pie and bit into it. Instantly, her face went from excited expectation to serious disappointment. Her mum laughed loudly.

'They take some getting used to, sweetie. You don't have to eat it if you don't like it.'

Cathy wanted to eat it to make her mum happy, and so she shoved the rest in and chewed rapidly until it went down, and the sight of it made her mum laugh more loudly than ever.

*

Right now, as Cathy wandered around, the air filling with flour as it puffed up from workstations in little clouds, the memory was still fresh in her mind and making her smile. Some were handling pastry better than others and her expertise had been called on a lot more than in previous weeks. Most of the time the fault was that people were just too diligent, overworking it so that it was like plasticine or rolling it too thick or too thin. Cathy tried to explain that sometimes it was all about having the confidence to leave well alone when it looked like it might be mixed; with pastry, less was often more, but many just didn't seem to get it, and she'd been greeted with some blank looks. She hoped that less than perfect pastry wouldn't put them off trying it again at home, because she felt certain that it wouldn't take long for people to get the hang of it and good home-made pastry really was worth the effort.

'Tansy would have this nailed by now,' Erica said as Cathy went over to see how she was getting on. 'She's really good at stuff like this.'

'It's a shame she couldn't come today,' Cathy said.

'I expect she'll come over to ours later,' Erica said. 'I might let her have a go at these in our kitchen if Malc doesn't object too much.'

'They're still not getting along?' Cathy asked.

'I can't see it changing any time soon to be honest. He's too middle-aged and Tansy is too much of a teenager; not an ideal combination for harmony.'

'But she still likes to spend time at your house?'

'It's either that or her own…' Erica shrugged. 'Now's not the time to go into that.'

Cathy knew when a conversation was done with, so she moved on. Erica kept on putting this information off; every time Cathy got close to hearing it her friend moved the conversation on. She knew she'd hear it sooner or later, but couldn't help feeling sooner might be more useful because she was beginning to worry that later might lead to her putting her foot in it.

As everyone cleaned down the counters, Cathy took great care to check all the equipment before they went. As Erica had handed in the missing blender with another sheepish apology earlier, it meant everything was accounted for and Cathy allowed herself to relax. She hadn't worried unduly about the blender incident, but she had been a little nervous that if things like that kept going wrong she'd be told she could no longer use the kitchen at St Cuthbert's for the cookery club. She was beginning to look forward to their weekly meet-ups so much that she'd miss them terribly if they had to come to an end.

She'd just finished counting everything when two of the youngest members of the club, twenty-something Beth and her sister Alicia, came over. Beth held out a sheet of lined paper with spidery writing on it.

'We only managed to get this last night,' she said. 'It's our great-grandma's recipe for barmbrack. We had to go and visit her in the old people's home so she could write it down for us.'

Cathy read down the list. 'I've never made this before.'

'It's Irish,' Alicia said. 'You don't see it in shops. We had a go at it last night, actually, after we got back from the home. I thought it was disgusting but Mum started to cry when she tasted it because she said she remembered our great-grandma making it for her when she was young and it tasted just the same, so I'm guessing that means it was like it ought to be.'

'We thought… maybe you might want it for your book?' Beth said. 'It's not exactly a Christmas recipe but people used to eat it in the winter apparently.'

'They don't have to be Christmas recipes,' Cathy said, 'although that is a good idea! This looks lovely – I can't wait to have a go. Quite simple ingredients too – they're often the best ones.'

'So it could go in?' Beth asked.

'Oh, definitely,' Cathy said.

Beth and Alicia both beamed at her. 'Great-Grandma will be really pleased when we tell her.'

'I'm really glad you brought it in. Can I keep hold of this sheet?'

'Yes,' Alicia said. 'We can have a copy when you put the book together, can't we? With all the other recipes?'

'That's what I was planning to do,' Cathy said. She looked at Alicia. 'How have you found today?'

'Oh, I loved it,' she replied. 'I'm definitely coming again next week if I can get the day off work. I work as a waitress and I usually get my hours about a week ahead so I'll know better tomorrow. But if I'm not on the rota I'll definitely come.'

'I'm glad to hear it,' Cathy said. She was about to say more when Iris called her over. 'I'm sorry… it looks as though I'm needed. Thanks so much for your recipe and hopefully I'll see you next week.'

Cathy went over to Iris, who lowered her voice as she glanced at Erica, currently wiping down the worktop where she'd been rolling her pastry. 'Have you checked nothing is missing today?'

'Yes,' Cathy said patiently.

'So… no more strange incidents?'

'No,' Cathy said, beginning to wish that she hadn't told Iris where the missing blender had ended up and how she'd got it back.

Iris looked satisfied, and Cathy left it at that. Even if there had been anything missing, she wasn't about to start demanding to search everyone's bags before they left – that was one sure-fire way to make sure people didn't come back again.

Chapter Twenty-One

Cathy had a few slices of the barmbrack wrapped up in her bag for Fleur to taste. She was on her way to do an extra shift at French for Flowers. She was sure Fleur would enjoy it – Fleur often said herself she'd never met a cake she didn't like – and Cathy thought it had turned out pretty well for a first try; well enough to give out.

As she'd baked the previous evening she'd been filled with a great sense of contentment. Life was looking up – she felt certain of it. Cookery club was going well and everyone seemed to be enjoying it (even if they didn't always make it), her little book was coming together, she had lots of new friends and then there was Matthias…

Of course, Matthias was an unknown quantity, but Cathy allowed herself the luxury to imagine that it could go somewhere. He'd definitely been interested, and her hunch had been borne out by the barrage of not-so-subtle hints that Erica kept throwing at her. It might have been that her friend was excited, or just happy to be proven right about how perfect their pairing might be, and she said a lot of things that Cathy took with a pinch of salt, but the one bit of advice that she had given, about being certain Cathy would find her brother on the canal path this morning with his dog, was one that Cathy was certainly going to heed today.

Her hair had been left down today and the glossing spray liberally applied. She'd put on some make-up again too, enough to make it worth the effort but natural enough to look as if she wasn't trying too hard. The best coat had come out, as had some little diamond stud earrings that she hadn't worn since the last wedding she'd been to, which had been at least five years ago, if not longer. It was a lot of effort for a walk to work, but unlike other days when she felt it might have been a bit wasted, today she enjoyed the process and hadn't minded getting up a bit earlier to do it. Today, she felt as if it might just be appreciated.

She held on to that hope as she walked the canal path. The weather was being kind to her too; though it was cold, the sun was out and the ground had dried so she wasn't constantly slipping on hidden patches of mud. She walked with the sun on her face and a spring in her step, the frosty air of the morning filling her lungs, her eyes on the path ahead, constantly searching, bursting with nervous anticipation. However, it was almost twenty minutes later before she was rewarded. She'd just about given up, Matthias and his dog nowhere in sight, before she heard panting from behind and turned to see Guin racing towards her. Just as he reached her, he veered from the path and went haring across the scrubland with the sort of joyful abandon that only a dog could display. Cathy stopped and broke into a broad smile as Matthias strode in his wake.

'Good morning,' he said, catching up with her.

'It's a nice one,' Cathy replied, immediately groaning inwardly once again at her boring response.

'It is,' he said. 'Where are you off to?'

'Work,' she said.

'Ah. Erica says you work at the market.'

'French for Flowers…'

He looked blank.

'Clearly you don't buy many flowers,' she said with a laugh. 'It's the name of the florist.'

'Not for a while,' he admitted with a sheepish look. 'Nobody to buy them for.'

'You could get them for your mum.'

'I could, but if she can't eat it she doesn't usually want it,' he said.

Cathy giggled.

He gave a suddenly awkward smile. What would he have said, she wondered, if she'd told him that she'd walked this path hoping to see him even when she hadn't had to go to work? Or that there was a far shorter route into work and she could have taken that too, only she'd wanted to see him here? Would that have sounded a bit desperate?

Maybe, she decided, and left her original reply to stand on its own.

'So she'd love you,' he added.

'Your mum? Would she?'

'Well, you can bake. Erica says you're pretty good too, like Bake Off standard.'

Cathy blushed. 'Oh, I don't think I'm anywhere near that good. I do enjoy it, though. I suppose that makes me sound a bit boring.'

'Not at all. I've often thought I'd like to take cookery lessons but I think I might be one of those people who are unteachable. I can open a tin of beans or set the timer on a microwave as well as anyone, but that's about my limit.'

'Nobody is unteachable,' Cathy said.

He smiled, holding her in a gaze that made her legs suddenly feel like jelly. 'Would you put money on that? I think I might be the man to prove your theory wrong.'

'I bet I could teach you,' she said, feeling all at once incredibly shy and uncharacteristically bold.

'Now, there's a challenge,' he said, laughing again. 'You may live to regret that.'

'I don't think so,' she said with a coquettish look, feeling bolder by the second.

'So you walk this route every day?' he asked.

'Sometimes I come this way for a change,' she said. 'There is a quicker route. If I've got time I prefer to come along here, though. The other way is through the estate and it's not as nice.'

God, Cathy wanted to punch herself right now. She was so bloody boring she was even boring herself, but she couldn't think of anything interesting to say now that she needed to.

'Weird, isn't it?' he asked, shoving his hands in his pockets. 'How things turn out. Us chatting out here and then it turning out that you've known my sister all along. What are the chances…?'

'It is,' Cathy said. 'I really like Erica. I've only just got to know her, really. She came to a charity coffee morning at St Cuthbert's – that's how we met.'

'Oh yeah, she's always doing stuff like that. A sucker for a charity event is Erica. Not that I think that's a bad thing, of course. It's just nice if you have time for that sort of thing.' He paused, and suddenly looked mortified. 'Not that I'm insinuating you have nothing better to do, or anything…'

'I can't say that I do, to be honest,' Cathy said, smiling. 'I wasn't offended – I didn't even think anything of your comment. I do have a lot of time on my hands – at least, I did. Less so these days with the cookery club and other things.'

He gave her a warm smile, and then his gaze searched the field for a moment. Cathy realised that he was checking where Guin was, though she'd completely forgotten about him. It was a good job she didn't have a dog to walk right now.

When he found the handsome figure of his dog, he seemed satisfied and turned back to her.

'Look, this might be forward and if you say no I won't be offended, but… oh, you know what, it doesn't matter.'

'You want a cookery lesson?' Cathy asked with a grin, knowing full well that he wasn't talking about cookery lessons.

'I was thinking more of a drink,' he said. 'You drink, don't you?'

Cathy resisted the impulse to ask if she somehow looked like the sort of person who didn't drink. The fact was, she didn't, but that was only because she had nobody worth drinking with and drinking alone at home was just no fun at all.

'Yes,' she said, 'I drink. And yes, I'd love to have one with you.'

He broke into a broad grin, his hazel eyes alive with humour. With the sun on him now, his hair looked more gold than brown. Cathy could still see that resemblance to his sister, but less so today. Today he looked more like himself and no one else. Perhaps that was a good thing, because he wasn't just Erica's brother anymore; he was Matthias, the man Cathy was going to have a drink with, the man she'd probably be dreaming about tonight, the man who'd got her more excited than she'd been in years.

'I guess you'll need my number,' she said.

At this he looked sheepish. 'Actually… oh, God, this sounds weird now but it's not meant to be. I wanted to call you last night and I phoned Erica and… well, she gave me your number. But she also said you'd be here this morning and she thought this might be an easier way to ask you out.'

'And was it?' Cathy asked, smiling; she didn't find it weird at all.

'No,' he said, laughing. 'It was so much harder in person. That's the first and last time I take advice from my sister.'

Cathy giggled. 'Then I'd better get your number,' she said.

He pulled out his phone and dialled her number. When the call came through she answered with another giggle. 'Hello.'

He grinned as he spoke into his own phone, a second's delay on the line making him come through in stereo as Cathy heard his natural voice too. 'Hello, Cathy. Can I take you out tonight?'

'Yes, you can,' she said.

'Then I'll pick you up at seven.'

'Ooh, decisive and direct, I like it,' she replied, still talking to him through her phone. 'I'll be ready.'

'Great.'

He put his phone away and Cathy quickly stored his number in her contacts. She looked up to find him gazing at her. For a second she wondered if he'd kiss her – he looked as if he wanted to. *She* wanted him to.

'Shall I walk the rest of the way with you?' he asked instead. 'I mean, you don't mind?'

'I don't mind at all if it doesn't take you out of your way.'

'It does, but I'd love to.'

Cathy smiled. 'Then I'd love it too.'

But by the time they'd reached the end of their walk together and Matthias turned to take Guin home, Cathy realised with a faint sense of panic that she was going to be late for work. She'd completely lost track of the time and had no idea how it had taken them so long to walk a path that ought to have got her there in plenty of time, but somehow it had happened. Perhaps it was a good sign for the date they'd arranged, but that didn't stop her being a little worried about what Fleur might say.

She needn't have fretted. Instead of waiting for an apology from Cathy for being late (only ten minutes but Cathy hated to be tardy),

Fleur had many apologies for Cathy. First, that the tea she usually made in readiness for her arrival had gone cold. She wanted to make Cathy another but Cathy wouldn't hear of it. Second, that they'd had a rather large delivery of poinsettias and that she'd need Cathy to do a bit of heavy lifting for her. Third, that Jonas had come by again the day before and that Fleur felt she ought to have confronted him but hadn't. Cathy was glad that she hadn't, because if it had been perfectly innocent on his part (and it was conceivable, knowing the Jonas she'd once been with, that he really was just trying to give his business to Fleur as a favour to Cathy), then that would have been a very awkward way to lose a customer. Fourth, that, for the first time ever, Fleur didn't love the thing that Cathy had baked for her.

'It's a bit bready,' she said. She didn't exactly spit it across the room but she swallowed it with an apologetic grimace. 'You know, not really a cake.'

'Not to worry,' Cathy said cheerfully as she wrapped the rest back up and put it away. She rather liked it and she'd happily eat the rest herself later with her lunch.

'I'm sorry.'

'Don't be daft,' Cathy said, laughing. 'I'm not going to be upset every time I make something you don't like. You can't like it all.'

'That's the thing, I usually do. It's just this…'

Fleur pulled a comical face and Cathy had to laugh again. 'Maybe Irish food just doesn't do it for you.'

'Is that what it is?'

'Two of my cookery club girls gave me the recipe from their Irish great-grandma. I thought it sounded interesting.'

'It's interesting alright.'

'Anyway, I'm going to take it as a good thing that you didn't like it.'

'Why would you do that?'

'Well, now I know that when you say you like something—'

'—which is everything else—'

'—yes; now I know that when you say you like it you really mean it.'

'Did you think I didn't mean it?'

'Well, I had wondered if you were just being kind.'

'Honestly…' Fleur frowned. 'When have you ever known me do anything just to be kind?'

'All the time!' Cathy said with another laugh. 'You pretend to be scary and tough but underneath it you're just a cuddly toy rabbit.'

'Hmm,' Fleur said, trying to keep the frown up but grinning through it.

And there was a fifth apology, one that made Cathy laugh like a giddy schoolgirl. Cathy explained why she was late, and she told her all about Matthias and how he'd asked her out, and Fleur squealed so loudly with excitement that all the nearby traders whipped their heads round to look, causing Fleur to issue an immediate request for forgiveness.

'There's no need,' Cathy said, a smile that could have powered the heating in the market building. 'I'm pretty happy about it myself.'

'I thought you'd never get there,' Fleur said. 'It's about time you got yourself a nice man.'

'Steady on… It's only a first date and there are no guarantees.'

'But I have a good feeling about this… From what you've told me, it sounds promising. You must think it does too – look at the start you've had. It's not like he's sidled up to you drunk in a bar and asked for your number…' Fleur grinned. 'The best romances always start like this.'

'Like what?'

'You know each other first. You already have a feeling about what sort of person he is and he has the same about you, so you have that head start when you set out on your date. All that awkwardness where you try to figure out whether he's a dickhead or not is already out of the way. You also know you like his sister, so he comes from a good family and that has to be a good sign, doesn't it?'

'But,' Cathy said, trying to throw some calm into the mix, 'he does also have a sister who sounds like a nightmare and a niece who is very hard to like. So what if he's like one of them?'

'You already know he's not like his niece because you liked him the first time you spoke to him. As for the other sister… I think you would have been able to tell by now too. You must have a good idea, otherwise you wouldn't have said yes to him, would you?'

Cathy allowed herself another soppy grin. 'I suppose not.'

'So,' Fleur asked, her gaze resting for a moment on someone who was inspecting the Christmas wreaths displayed at the front counter. Seeming to decide that they could look for a moment, she turned back to Cathy. 'Have you got something to wear?'

'I don't even know where we're going,' Cathy said, her grin fading now. 'Oh, heck, I don't know what kind of thing I need to wear! I don't know if it's going to be smart or casual… Fleur – what am I going to wear?'

'Maybe you could send him a text to ask where he's taking you? Or even suggest somewhere you want to go?'

'Yes, I should do that. Fleur, you're a genius!'

'I don't think so but thanks.' Her gaze went to the browser at the front of the stall again. This time, the old lady seemed to want their attention. 'You do that,' she added, 'I'll be back shortly to see what he says.'

'I'll make a start on the poinsettias too,' Cathy said.

'You're a love,' Fleur called back as she went to the customer. 'Whatever would I do without you?'

Chapter Twenty-Two

How do you feel about the theatre?

Cathy read the text again with a smile. She loved the idea of the theatre for a first date. She hadn't been to see a play for years and it seemed so much more romantic and different from going to the cinema or a pub, but it had given her a real quandary over what to wear. It was only a small local theatre, Matthias had explained in subsequent texts; he happened to know one of the supporting actors and they'd offered him tickets to the show any night he wanted. He thought maybe this was a pretty good night to take them.

Cathy had asked what was on, though she didn't really care as long as she was out with him, but when he'd said it was Twelfth Night she was even more excited. She'd never been to see Shakespeare performed live before – in fact, the one and only Shakespeare play she'd ever seen was a movie version that had Mel Gibson in it, and she'd been forced to admit that she hadn't really understood a lot of it. At least it sounded as if Matthias would know what was going on tonight, and if she got a bit lost he didn't seem the sort of man who would make her feel silly as he explained it to her.

But when she turned her mind to her choice of outfit, she realised that she just didn't have a clue. Did she go formal, or was it more casual than that? If it had been a pub she'd have had just the thing, and if it had been something posh she had an old dress she'd worn to a cousin's wedding a few years before – a little dated, but a fairly classic style that would work. But this was somewhere in between, she guessed. She didn't want to go for the dress because she didn't want to feel as if people were staring at her for overdoing it, but she didn't want to look scruffy and embarrass Matthias. She'd asked Fleur for advice, who'd told her that he wouldn't care what she had on. Then she'd phoned Erica, who'd said pretty much the same and then spent the remainder of the conversation telling Cathy how excited she was and how she could tell that her brother really liked her. All that was lovely to hear, of course, and filled Cathy with an even greater heightened anticipation, but it didn't help solve the outfit conundrum.

Currently laid out on her bed she had four choices: a pair of black wide-legged trousers and a silk shirt; a lace tea dress that was a bit pulled in places but always made her feel cute when she wore it (not that often these days); a pair of smart jeans and a chiffon top; and a maxi dress that was perhaps a bit summery for this time of year but maybe she could get away with it if they were going to be inside for the majority of the time. She wasn't really happy with any of them, but as she hadn't had time to find anything during her lunch break at work or go to the shops afterwards, something from this pile was going to have to do.

Out of desperation, she went to the wardrobe and got out the fancier dress she'd worn to her cousin's wedding. It was royal blue and had a calf-length chiffon skirt, the halter-neck top studded with embroidered, sequin-embellished flowers. Was it too fancy? Did it matter if anyone else thought she looked overdressed if she felt good in it? And, if she was very honest, she wanted to make the sort of impression on Matthias that would cause his jaw to drop – anything less than that would feel like a failure. She wanted him to be proud to walk into that theatre with her.

Making a snap decision, she shook off her bathrobe and pulled the dress over her head, going to the mirror as she squirmed around to reach the back zip. Last time she'd worn this dress her mum had been there to do it up for her, and this time she struggled. Eventually, she got it all the way up and took a long, critical look at herself. She'd put on a little weight since she'd last worn it and she'd probably have to breathe in all through the play, but it didn't look too bad. In fact, it looked good. And besides, it was going to be a nightmare to get off again with nobody to start the zip off so perhaps that was a problem she could spend time dealing with later rather than now, when time was a bit more precious, because she still had her hair to do and make-up to put on, and Matthias was due to pick her up in half an hour.

With a last look in the mirror and a nod of approval, she went to heat up her curling tongs.

The knock on the front door was bang on time. Cathy had been sitting on her sofa for the last ten minutes, completely ready and watching the clock. Was that a bit sad? Perhaps, but as there was no one around to witness it, what did it matter?

She leapt up from her seat now and rushed to the door to open it and find Matthias smiling on the doorstep. But then his easy smile disappeared and he stared at her.

'What?' Cathy looked down at herself, suddenly uneasy. 'What's wrong?'

'Wow,' he breathed.

'It's too much, isn't it?' she asked, gesturing her dress. 'I've overdone it, haven't I? I'll go and get changed... Have I got time?'

'Don't do that!' he said, his smile returning. 'I only meant: wow, you look incredible!'

Cathy relaxed. 'I do?'

'God yes! I mean… absolutely stunning!'

'Oh…' Cathy waved away the compliment, blushing violently. 'It's an old dress.'

'It's the person wearing it I'm bowled over by, not the dress.'

Cathy's blush became deeper still, and she was quite sure a passing troop of scouts would have been able to toast marshmallows on her face if they'd had a sudden hankering for them.

'My lady,' he added, offering his arm. 'Verily, we should make haste, lest we miss the start of the performance.'

Cathy giggled. 'Forsooth, my lord,' she replied. 'I would not… OK, you got me, that's about the only bit of old-fashioned talking I know.'

'That's about my limit too,' he said. 'I expect we'll be reciting sonnets when we come out.'

'I wouldn't bank on it,' Cathy said, taking the coat she'd made ready from the hook in the hallway.

'No,' he said with a wry smile, 'neither would I.'

Cathy had been past the theatre plenty of times over the years, but she had to admit to not taking all that much notice of it and she'd never been inside. The few shows she'd been to see – the obligatory Christmas panto, the odd musical or band tour – had always been at Linnetford's larger main theatre. The one that Matthias drove her to tonight was housed by a tiny rococo building that had once been a rather grand bank. When the bank had closed its doors for the final time, at some point during the seventies, the building had stood empty for another decade until some enterprising soul with more vision than Cathy ever could have had saw its potential and set about turning it into an alternative arts venue. The stone of the exterior had been sandblasted to its former dove grey, the roof, doors and windows had been replaced, and the derelict land that lay behind it had been paved to provide a small car parking space, enough for the five hundred or so patrons that the auditorium was able to hold. As they stepped inside, Cathy found herself in a sumptuous interior with painted frescoes on the ceiling depicting Greek and Roman myths, stone columns, stained-glass windows, plush red carpets, a heavy rosewood bar and brass fittings.

'It's gorgeous in here,' she exclaimed, gazing around. 'I can't believe I've been walking past it for all these years and never came in. If I'd known how lovely it was, I'd have done it years ago.' She looked at Matthias. 'Do you come here a lot?'

'I've been half a dozen times,' he said. 'Not as often as I'd like to.'

Cathy recalled briefly that Erica had said her brother was quite arty – was this the sort of thing she meant? If it was, Cathy hoped she wasn't about to show herself up because she'd hardly taken a lot of interest in stuff like this before and she felt she was mostly quite ignorant about it. She also thought, however – and she hoped she was right – that Matthias was far too kind to make her feel silly, even if she did say something that sounded silly and uneducated.

'I just hope you like it,' he said. 'I know Shakespeare isn't to everyone's taste, but I think we'll be alright with this – it's one of the lighter plays. I definitely wouldn't subject you to Richard III – it would put you off for life.'

Right now, Cathy wouldn't have cared if they were watching the cleaners sweep the aisles as long as she was here with him, but she wasn't about to say that.

'I'm looking forward to it,' she said. 'I'm interested to see what I've been missing.'

'I won't be offended if you don't like it,' he said. 'It's not to everyone's taste. And please, don't be afraid to say so at the interval – if you're really hating every minute then we'll leave and find something else to do. I won't mind at all and wouldn't like to think that you've suffered in silence.'

'I'm sure I will like it,' she said.

'But promise me you'll say so if you don't. I realise that I've sprung this on you without really asking.'

'But you did ask. You asked and I said I'd be up for it – remember? And I'm happy you've thought of something a bit different – left up to me we'd be drinking tea at Sainsbury's café.'

He burst out laughing. 'Much as I'd usually avoid that sort of thing, I think even that would be OK if I was with you.'

Cathy smiled up at him, caught almost instantly in those soft hazel eyes, the hustle and noise of the foyer melting away. She felt herself drawn in again, desperate to feel his lips on hers, but even now, at the back of her mind was a little voice that warned her she'd have to wait, no matter how much she wanted to. That was right and proper, wasn't it, even though she didn't feel much like being proper where Matthias was concerned. In fact, the more time she spent in his company, the more she felt like being very improper indeed…

'We've got time for a quick drink before we go and get our seats,' he said. 'Can I get you something from the bar?'

'Hmm, yes, that sounds lovely. I don't know what I want – how about you surprise me?'

'You still trust me to surprise you after I've brought you here?'

Cathy giggled. 'I like it here! So far at least. I absolutely trust you.'

'OK…' he said, looking doubtful. 'You like gin?'

'Who doesn't?'

'Right… something with gin coming up.'

Cathy still had the smile stapled to her face as she watched him walk to the bar. It didn't matter if she hated this play, if she hated the drink he brought back for her, because she was certain she was going to love this night, here with him. She was certain that she would have loved it wherever they'd gone.

She took a moment to glance around the room as he talked to the bartender. There were more young people than she'd imagined there would be: early twenty-somethings, teenagers, even parents with children that couldn't have been older than nine or ten. She'd expected it to be full of older couples, people who looked cultured and professional, who might have big-shot, well-paid jobs, but for the most part, everyone looked fairly ordinary, a lot more like her. At least she didn't feel out of place in her best dress, because there was a mix of outfits too, everything from smart casual characterised by blazers teamed with dark, sharp denim, to sequined metallic tops and frocks. It didn't seem to matter what anyone was wearing and nobody seemed to care that they'd all gone for a totally different level of formal.

After a few minutes, Cathy looked to see Matthias coming back to her with two glasses.

'I took some advice from the guy at the bar,' he said, handing her one of the glasses. 'So if you don't like it I'll go and shout at him for you.'

Cathy laughed as she took it. 'I'm sure it will be lovely. What's in it?'

'I'm not altogether sure. I know he mentioned lemon and mint… I think it's called a Southside or something.'

'It sounds nice – I love lemon and I love mint leaves, so…'

'When he said what was in it I thought most people probably like those things.'

'You've got the same?' Cathy asked, looking at his glass.

'I figured: what the hell? Why not give it a go? It looked good.'

Cathy took a sip and it was good. It was dry and bitter and sweet all at the same time, zingy from the lemon and fresh from the mint, though she couldn't figure out where the sweetness was coming from. It was a bit like trying to unravel the ingredients in a slice of cake when she tried something for the first time without knowing what was in it. If she could figure it out, maybe she'd try to make this for herself at home. She didn't usually bother drinking much in the house because it was just no fun alone, but maybe having this would bring back fond memories of tonight. And who knew, maybe in time, she wouldn't be drinking it alone…

'Ladies and gentlemen, the auditorium is now open if you'd like to take your seats. Tonight's performance of Twelfth Night will begin in ten minutes.'

'Wow, does that mean we'd better drink up quick?' Cathy asked as the public address announcement came to an end. 'I might be drunk if I knock this back all at once!'

'Don't worry,' he said, 'we've got ten minutes yet. And anyway, even if you do get drunk I'll look after you.'

'I might be a bit embarrassing, though.'

'You could never embarrass me.'

She smiled. 'We'll see if you're still saying that when I've asked for the hundredth time what's going on in the play.'

'Ah, but you're missing the point of Shakespeare.'

'What's that?'

'Nobody really understands what's going on – they're just here because they think it makes them look clever.'

Cathy giggled. 'Does that apply to you too?'

'Of course! How else was I going to impress you?' He took a sip of his drink and fixed her with a smouldering gaze that made her want to forgo the theatre and find somewhere private to spend the rest of the evening with him. 'So, tell me,' he continued, still gazing at her, 'how's that working out? Am I impressing you yet?'

'You were impressing me the moment you said hello by the canal,' she said, and then snorted with laughter. 'Oh, God, that sounds like a line from some cheesy romantic comedy, doesn't it?'

'You impressed me at hello?' he replied with a grin. 'A little bit but I'm more interested in the fact that my ploy is working.'

'It's a ploy? So you're not really this clever at all?'

'Nope.'

'I don't believe you. Erica says you're clever.'

'Erica thinks that chair is clever,' he said, nodding at a nearby barstool.

Cathy grinned. 'I won't tell her you said that.'

'You can tell her – she's heard it enough times from me so she wouldn't be surprised.'

'I think you're secretly clever too, but you're trying not to make a big deal of it,' Cathy said. 'I mean, I know that you have a very clever job.'

'Me?' he pointed to himself and grinned. 'It might sound clever but it really isn't.'

'I don't believe you. Erica says you save lives.'

'Well… I suppose I have been known to assist in the odd bit of lifesaving.'

'Like what?'

'If I started to tell you now we'd miss the start of the play. Do you think you can stand the suspense of waiting for a while to hear me flex about my own coolness?'

Cathy laughed. 'I can't wait!'

'Well, I'm glad to see I'm managing to impress you.'

'You are,' she said. 'And you're not even having to try…'

Chapter Twenty-Three

Cathy had been mesmerised from the moment the curtains opened. Her original doubts had proved valid because half the time she didn't have a clue what was going on, but that didn't seem to matter. She became swept up with the lavish staging, the sumptuous costumes, the massive performances, daft songs and rhymes, the poetry of the speeches, the enthusiasm of the audience and the general atmosphere. Every so often Matthias would whisper in her ear to ask if she was OK, or to clarify something he thought she might not have quite got – though this never made her feel stupid because he did it in such a subtle and respectful way that she couldn't possibly have felt insulted. Besides, whatever his reasons for leaning in close, his breath in her ear and his scent did things to her that made her forget the play more than once.

During the interval he got them more drinks and insisted on paying – even though Cathy had argued that it was the twenty-first century and there was no reason he ought to be footing the bill for the entire date. They chatted easily back in the foyer, mostly about how she'd found the play so far and about which part Matthias's friend was playing. (One of the ship's crew, as it happened. Cathy didn't like to say that, even though Matthias had told her, she'd probably struggle to tell who he was because there were quite a few of them and their costumes were very similar.)

Shortly after the beginning of the second half, Cathy felt a hand settle on hers with a gentle squeeze. It was the grown-up equivalent of the yawning-hand-around-the-back-of-the-seat at the cinema, but Cathy didn't care. A quiver of pleasure sent the hairs at the back of her neck on end, and she wanted to kiss him more than ever. It would have to wait, and although she was still enjoying the play, now she wanted it to finish quickly too because she was sure that the evening would end with that kiss and she couldn't wait. All she could offer him right now was a smile as he glanced across to check that his attention was being well received, and the one he sent in return almost set her on fire. She hadn't felt like this in so long, not since Jonas, and the anticipation was enough to make her feel drunk.

Before Cathy knew it, the play was over and they were filing out of the auditorium. Matthias reached for Cathy's hand again and she smiled, that delicious feeling of barely contained excitement creeping over her once more.

'What now?' he asked as they stepped out onto the street, the cold air like a slap after the warmth of the packed theatre. 'Would you like to go on somewhere for a while?'

'Would you?' Cathy asked, trying to sound cool even though inside she was shouting: YES!

'There's a nice bar not far from here. We could get a snack, maybe another drink… At least you could get another drink and the designated driver here could knock himself out with lemonade.'

'That sounds good,' Cathy said, nuzzling into him, the action so natural she hardly realised she was doing it. But then she shot up again as she heard her name being called.

'Cathy…?'

She turned around to see Jonas with a woman. His wife, she had to presume. His manner was open and friendly but he was still the last person she wanted to see right now.

'Cathy...' he said again, staring towards them. 'I thought it was you. You've been to see the play? I never had Shakespeare down as your sort of thing.'

'I didn't think it was yours either,' Cathy said. She glanced at his wife, and then Jonas did the same to Matthias.

'Oh,' Jonas said, 'you haven't met Eleanor, have you?'

Jonas's wife smiled. 'Hello.'

'No, hi, Eleanor. This is Matthias,' Cathy said.

The situation was getting more awkward by the second but Jonas just couldn't seem to grasp that. She wanted nothing more than to get away, but perhaps that would make it seem weirder to Matthias, and she didn't want to be raising those sorts of questions this early in their new relationship. She'd felt certain that tonight would be the first of many nights, but it might not be if Matthias was put off by the thought of complications.

Was Jonas a complication, though? She couldn't – at this precise moment – figure out how she felt about him, apart from the fact that she really wanted him and his wife to get lost.

Perhaps Jonas got the body language, because his next sentence was to that exact end.

'We really ought to get going,' he said. 'I just thought we'd say hello.'

'It was nice to see you,' Cathy replied. She glanced up at Matthias. He didn't seem to have noticed anything untoward in the exchange and for that, at least, she was very glad.

'You too,' Jonas said. 'Bye, Cathy... Matthias.'

Matthias gave an airy smile. He turned to Cathy as they walked away. 'A friend of yours?'

'An old friend,' Cathy said. 'Someone I knew years ago. I don't know about you,' she added, determined to get back to where they'd been just before they'd been interrupted by her past, 'but I'm ready for that drink.'

Eventually Cathy got her kiss, and it had been worth waiting for. Gentle yet intense, respectful and lustful all at the same time, she could barely recall the last time she'd been kissed, but she could never remember being kissed like that.

Matthias had been spot on again with the bar he'd chosen for their follow-up drink. It had been Spanish-themed, full of warm wood, bright tiles and soft lighting. They'd spent the last hour until the bar shut sitting close, nibbling on tapas that Cathy hadn't really cared about. Not that it wasn't very good, and ordinarily she would have been marvelling at the flavours, but tonight all she wanted to do was drink in everything Matthias did and said.

She'd had two more cocktails and so Cathy had added a vague tipsiness to the heady feeling of being with him. Still in that good phase when she was drunk enough to enjoy it, and not too far gone to wish she hadn't had the last one after all, it undid any remaining inhibitions she might have had, so that when he did kiss her, as they said goodbye on her doorstep, she didn't think about it. There was no uptight doubt, no concentrating on whether it was right, on what he thought about the way she did it; it was only easy and passionate.

On reflection today, as she opened her eyes and her mind immediately went back to it, she might have thought that it was the alcohol that had made it seem so good, but something told her that when they met up again (they'd arranged a second date for the weekend) it would be just as good, alcohol or no alcohol.

Still, she knew that Erica was bound to call her first thing wanting gossip. Cathy could hardly blame her for that, though she wasn't sure how much was appropriate to reveal or how much Matthias would be happy for her to give away.

As she got out of bed – more through habit than the fact she needed to, as it was her day off – she glanced at the clock and wondered how long Erica would leave it before she phoned. Perhaps it was more a case of how long she was able to leave it, because she'd seemed almost more excited about the date than Cathy or Matthias – and, for Cathy at least, that was very excited indeed.

To her credit, Erica managed to wait until just gone ten. Cathy was eating a slice of toast, still in her dressing gown at the table, when the phone rang next to her.

'Hi,' Cathy said, a grin spreading across her face, just knowing that what would issue from Erica next was a squeaky demand for information.

'So what happened?' Erica asked. 'How did it go? Do you like him? Matthias won't tell me anything!'

'He won't?' Cathy asked, her grin spreading. 'Then maybe I shouldn't either.'

'Don't you dare!' Erica cried. 'You don't get the same let-off as he does.'

'Why not?'

'Because he's my brother and you're my friend – it's different. Friends tell each other everything.'

'Everything?' Cathy raised an eyebrow that showed in the tone of her voice, even though Erica wouldn't see it.

'Well, not everything, of course… that would be weird.' She paused for a moment. 'Oh my God you didn't…?'

'NO!' Cathy said, snorting with laughter. 'I know I've been on my own a while but I'm not quite at that stage yet!'

She could hear Erica laughing too. 'But you like him?'

'Yes.'

'You're going to see him again at the weekend.'

'He told you that much then.'

'He really likes you,' Erica said.

'He told you that too?'

'He doesn't have to; I can tell. I've got such a good feeling about you two; and I never had a feeling like this about any of his other girlfriends.'

Cathy wondered if that good feeling was based more on the fact that she and Erica were already friends rather than any hard evidence, but she smiled and didn't say so.

'I have a good feeling about it too.'

'Didn't I tell you he'd be right for you? Didn't I say so?'

'Yes, I should have listened to you in the first place.'

'Although, I have to admit that your way of meeting was far more romantic than me sending you both on a blind date. Actually, that would never have worked because Matt would have flat out refused to go on a blind date. It didn't go so well when he did it before.'

Cathy's smile faded for a moment. 'You know when you said before that he'd had a lot of bad luck with women… how much, exactly? What kind of bad luck?'

She wasn't sure she wanted to know because she was half afraid knowing would provide things to put her off Matthias, but she was beginning to realise now that they were questions she needed to ask. Maybe they were questions that were easier to ask Erica right now than Matthias himself, and maybe she'd get more frank answers from her too.

'Oh, you know, the usual... selfish girlfriends, the odd cheating incident – her, not him – ones that just fizzled out, the ones that ended in friend-zoning...'

Cathy frowned at Erica's suddenly careful tone. Was there something else she wasn't saying? Something bigger than the things she'd mentioned? Perhaps she felt it wasn't her place to tell that story – if it even existed at all. Right now, maybe it was better that Cathy didn't push it. And she felt certain that if it had been something that could really threaten her and Matthias's fledgling relationship, something that could kill it dead if Cathy found out about it in the wrong way, Erica would have found a way to say it, if only to make sure it didn't jeopardise what she clearly hoped Cathy and Matthias might eventually have.

'None of them was the right woman, though,' Erica added, her tone upbeat again. 'You're different.'

'Hmm, let's not get ahead of ourselves,' Cathy said with a light laugh, though she loved the faith Erica was placing in her.

'So you're seeing him again at the weekend?' Erica continued. 'Where are you going this time?'

'I think we're going back to the bar we ended up at last night,' Cathy said. 'It was lovely but we didn't have a lot of time to try much of the food.'

'That's Aguilar's, isn't it? I love it in there.'

'I'd never been in before but it was nice. Never had tapas either before last night. So that's two firsts – Shakespeare and tapas...'

'It's three if you count Matthias.'

Cathy laughed. 'That's true.'

'I'm so happy it went well,' Erica said, and Cathy could hear the warm smile in her voice. 'I really felt it would, and I hoped so, but you can never tell if my stupid brother is going to manage to put his foot in it somehow and ruin what should have been as easy as falling off a log.'

'What's easy?'

'Getting along with you, silly! If he managed to cock that up I really was going to wash my hands of him.'

'Well you don't need to because we got on really well.'

'I really am glad. Listen, do you want to meet up today for coffee?'

'So you can grill me about the date properly?'

'Yes,' Erica said, laughing. 'But it would be lovely to see you too.'

Cathy smiled. 'There isn't that much more to tell that you don't already know, honestly. It was lovely, but it was a first date so it was all a bit polite. But if you really want to meet up then I'm free. I could show you the new recipes I've got for the book anyway.'

'Ingrid's at twelve then?'

'Sounds good to me!'

Chapter Twenty-Four

Cookery club had rolled round again, and while Cathy always loved having her new friends to what had begun to feel like her own kitchen to do her favourite activity, today she had even more to smile about. Even though they'd arranged their second date for the coming weekend, Matthias and Cathy had spoken on the phone every night since their date, sometimes for an hour or more. It was mostly small talk but it came easily and it was fun. A bit of how's your day been, a bit of flirting and a healthy dollop of cute and harmless innuendo had gone a long way to making those calls almost as enjoyable as seeing him in person.

This morning Erica came in beaming too. She winked at Cathy. 'Good morning!'

Cathy grinned. Tansy was with Erica again today.

'Good morning Tansy,' Cathy said. 'Good to see you again.'

Tansy gave the vaguest nod and headed straight to her usual spot at the worktop to start getting ready to bake. It was hardly friendly but it was definitely an acknowledgement. Cathy wondered whether anyone had told Tansy that she was dating Matthias yet. Was this a Tansy who knew, or would a Tansy who knew react with even more coldness than she had today? Or was this only marginally less frosty version of Tansy the one who knew and was making an effort to be nice to Cathy, or was it just Cathy's imagination that she was less cold than usual? If she didn't already know, she was bound to find out soon. How would that work out? Cathy wondered. Tansy was so closed and unreadable all the time that she couldn't even begin to guess.

'I spoke to Matt last night,' Erica said as Cathy bid her a more private good morning. 'I don't think I've ever heard him sound so happy.'

'Really?' Cathy replied airily. 'Why would that be?'

Erica grinned. 'I think you know exactly why that would be.'

'We've only spoken on the phone a few times.'

'Well, whatever it is you've been saying it's good...' She lowered her voice further still as she threw a glance at Tansy, who was unpacking ingredients from a bag. 'Please keep doing it – it's nice for me to have only one sibling to worry about for a change instead of two.'

Cathy could only assume she meant Tansy's mum, Michelle. Neither Erica nor Matthias had said a lot about Michelle but, knowing how close they were to each other, the fact that they hadn't spoke volumes about how difficult that relationship obviously was for both of them. Cathy had wanted to ask on more than one occasion, but she always got the impression that opening a discussion on that subject might be unwelcome.

Maybe later, when she knew them both better, she might learn more, and it might make her understand Tansy a little better too. She was just as much of an enigma in her own right, and though she seemed to hate everything and everyone, including the cookery club, she kept turning up. When she first arrived she always looked as if she couldn't have cared less about it, but once settled in, she suddenly began to take every task very seriously. It was such a strange juxtaposition, and Cathy wished she could work it out.

She was prevented from asking more by Beth and her sister, who came over to ask whether she'd baked the barmbrack they'd given her the recipe for and whether she'd liked it. Cathy didn't need much encouragement to wax lyrical about something she'd enjoyed making and eating, and it didn't take her long to get so involved in a conversation about it that she hardly noticed Erica wander off to get set up for today's bake. When she finally did, she realised that she'd been talking about barmbrack for so long that it was time to start the session. Anything else would have to wait for now.

They were making two cakes today: some were making Eve's pudding, and those who didn't like apple were doing pineapple upside-down cake. Everyone had been getting along well, as they always did, the room full of good-natured but fairly low-level chatter as Cathy busied herself talking people through problems, offering advice on how to do something more easily, or just congratulating them on a job well done. But that was shattered about an hour into the class with a shrill squeal. Cathy was with Colin trying to figure out why his cake batter was so runny, but she looked up sharply, along with everyone else, to see Iris standing in front of one of the ovens with a look of absolute horror on her face.

'Someone's taken my cake out!' she cried. 'It's nowhere near cooked! Look at it – it's a horrible mess!'

Cathy rushed over, as did Myrtle and Dora. Erica exchanged a look of confusion with Lindsey. Only Tansy didn't look up, calmly getting on with washing her mixing bowl as if nothing had happened.

'It was on that shelf,' Iris said, pointing to a spot where another cake now sat. 'Someone has taken it out to put theirs in.'

'Are you sure?' Cathy asked. 'You couldn't be mistaken at all? Maybe you thought you'd put it in and you hadn't?'

'Of course I'm sure!' Iris snapped. 'I know I put it in!'

Cathy looked through the glass door into the oven again. She wasn't happy about a situation that might have someone pointing a finger of blame at someone else here, and her question had been aimed at heading an awkward eventuality like that off; she hadn't meant to offend or insult Iris. But she really had been hoping that it was a mistake that Iris might suddenly recall making.

'That's a red tin,' Iris said. 'Who's using red?'

They'd bought colour-coded silicone baking tins so that people could recognise their own cakes and take the right one home. Some were white, some pink, some sage green, some powder blue and some red.

'Not me,' Beth said.

'Not me either.' Myrtle looked guilty, even though Cathy could see her cake still in front of her, waiting to go into the oven. It might have been funny if the situation wasn't so excruciating.

'I've used red,' Colin said. 'But my cake isn't in yet.'

'Yes, we're still working out your batter, aren't we?' Cathy reassured him. Who did that leave?

Everyone else called out what colour they'd used, and when they'd all but done, there was one person who hadn't contributed to the investigation at all.

'Tansy…' Cathy said gently.

Tansy looked up now, seemingly surprised to find everyone staring at her. 'What?' she said, her lips twisting into a challenging sneer. 'It wasn't me!' she growled.

Erica put a hand up to halt Cathy's next sentence. 'Tans… come take a walk with me, eh?'

She led her niece outside, and Cathy could only assume it meant the cake that was in Iris's spot was indeed Tansy's, but that Erica knew better than to have this conversation with her in a crowded room where everyone would be listening in. She obviously knew what Tansy's reaction might be, and that it was one best handled in private.

Cathy let out a sigh. She felt sorry for Erica, who seemed to be on edge whenever she had her young charge with her, and yet continued to make the effort. She thought about how hard that might be, what a burden it was for Erica, and saw that this was what love looked like. She must care deeply about her niece to keep persevering with her when she had no real duty to. What was the role of Tansy's mother in all this? Did she even have a role to play, or did she leave it all to other members of the family? From what Cathy had seen so far, it looked as if the latter was the case and Michelle didn't bother with her daughter at all.

She barely had time to process that thought – Tansy and Erica had only just closed the kitchen door when Iris launched into another verbal attack.

'She did that on purpose! She's had it in for me since she arrived!'

'I'm sure that's not the case,' Cathy said, trying to keep a calm tone even though she felt the class unravelling. All the friendship and camaraderie they'd built up over the last few weeks was in danger of evaporating with this one careless act. Because it was obvious to Cathy, whether Tansy had done it deliberately or not, that she had taken Iris's cake from the oven to put her own in, and to deny it when an apology might have defused the situation had only made things worse.

'It was probably a misunderstanding,' Colin agreed. 'I can't imagine anyone would have done that deliberately.'

'She would – little snake!' Dora chimed in. 'The way she looks at everyone... I don't know why she comes – she clearly hates us all.'

'Perhaps she only meant to make room and took yours out so she could jiggle things about?' Cathy suggested helplessly. 'She might just have got distracted and then forgotten to put it back in?'

'If there was no room on the shelf then she should have gone to one of the other ovens,' Iris snapped back. 'She had no right taking my cake out at all – it would have sunk and been ruined anyway, even if she had put it back in, and I would have thought that was my fault.'

Cathy couldn't argue with that logic, but still she had to try to keep the peace. 'She wouldn't have known your cake would sink – she's very new to baking.'

'She'd know,' Dora said.

The door opened and Erica came back in alone. She took Cathy to a quiet corner, away from the others, but everyone watched anyway. So Cathy turned her back to them and leaned in close to hide Erica from view.

'I'm going to take Tansy home,' Erica said quietly. 'She's a bit upset… I think it was a genuine mistake but… well, she's not very good at taking criticism and I can see it blowing up if we stay. Best if I remove the touchpaper from the firework stack… so to speak.'

'What about your cakes?' Cathy asked, her heart sinking. Of all the people she didn't want to have trouble with today, it was Matthias's sister and niece.

'I don't know. Maybe the church can have them for a coffee morning or something. Not that they'd be any good for that.'

'They were looking good to me,' Cathy said with a smile she hoped was encouraging and non-judgemental. 'How about I take them with me today and drop them off for you?'

'You could give them to Matt,' Erica said. 'You're seeing him tomorrow anyway so he could get them to us – save you a job.'

'I don't mind coming tonight with them,' Cathy said. 'It's only twenty minutes on the bus.'

Erica shook her head. 'Don't make a special bus journey on our account. Listen… I've got to go; I've left her in the car. I'll phone you later.'

Cathy nodded, and Erica went to hastily gather up her belongings. Cathy helped her, and while everyone else went back to their cakes, a defiant Iris opened up the oven, took Tansy's half-baked sponge out and put hers back in its place. As Erica hurried out, Cathy rushed over to try to save it. A cake was a cake, and it had looked like a good batter – to waste it would be a crime. She found a vacant spot in one of the other ovens and slammed it in, hoping it wouldn't suffer too much from the time cooling on the side. Then she let out a sigh. If this was how cookery club was going to be from now on, maybe she wasn't so keen on it after all.

The atmosphere was tetchy as Iris, Dora and Cathy cleared up at the end of the morning. Iris still hadn't forgiven Cathy for sticking up for Tansy (as she saw it), and Dora was firmly on Iris's side this time. Cathy hated confrontation in any form, so she'd really been caught between the devil and the deep blue sea. She hadn't wanted it with Tansy and Erica and she didn't want it now with Iris and Dora.

They'd worked in silence for ten minutes when Cathy took a breath and broke it. 'I think I might make next week the last cookery club.'

At this, Iris's head whipped up. 'What did you say?'

'It isn't fair to spring it on everyone over Facebook, so I'm going to announce it next week.'

'But you can't!' Dora squeaked. 'Everyone loves it!'

Cathy looked sadly at her. 'Do they? As far as I can tell they didn't love it today.'

'If you got rid of that girl we'd be just fine,' Iris said.

'But that's just it,' Cathy said. 'No exclusions. It's supposed to be inclusive and open to everyone – wasn't that our mantra when we first started it? To be there for people who were lonely or needed that bit of human connection to get through the week? To help people to help themselves, no matter who they were or what their situation? If we ask Tansy not to come back that goes against everything we set out to do.'

'But she's the cause of all the trouble,' Dora said.

'She might be, but she clearly wants to come because she keeps turning up. And when she gets down to it she's a good baker and she wants to learn. I can't ask her to leave. More to the point, I won't ask her to leave.'

'So you'd rather ask everyone to leave?' Iris said tartly.

'It's not asking everyone to leave – it's calling it a day. We can still keep in touch via the Facebook group and people can share their baking stories on there. You could even run one without me if you really wanted to – that way you can invite who you like to join. I'm not going to do that – if someone wants to come then they're welcome as far as I'm concerned. If you want me to continue then that's my deal.'

'She makes everyone uncomfortable,' Iris said. 'Nobody likes her.'

'I'm sure that's not true.'

Iris held her in a challenging gaze. 'Name one person who's said they do.'

'Erica,' Cathy said.

'Pah!' Dora chipped in. 'Of course she's going to say so. But I'm not sure even she likes her when it gets down to it. Blood is thicker than water, but it doesn't mean you have to like who you're related to.'

Cathy shook her head slowly, but she didn't reply. Instead, she went over to fetch the mop and bucket from the cupboard. She could hear Iris and Dora talking softly to each other as she went. She wasn't all that bothered about what they were saying – it wouldn't change how she felt about today. She'd agreed to this club on the terms she'd just laid out, and nobody was going to persuade her to continue it on any others. Much as she loved being here, she would disband it if she was forced to, even though she secretly hoped that Iris and Dora would back down and it wouldn't come to that.

By the time she'd filled the bucket with soapy water they'd stopped talking and were watching her expectantly.

'Perhaps what happened today was a genuine mistake,' Iris said. 'I'm willing to put it behind us if Tansy is.'

'That's good of you,' Cathy said. 'I'll let Erica know next time I speak to her.'

'So you'll carry on with the club?' Iris asked.

Cathy paused for a moment. 'Yes,' she said finally. 'I'll carry on.'

Dora and Iris both looked relieved.

'I wouldn't have wanted to be the one to tell Myrtle,' Dora said.

'Or Colin,' Iris added as she opened an oven door to wipe it down. 'He loves coming here on a Friday morning – highlight of his week now.'

Well, Cathy thought, *if that's the case, let's just hope everyone behaves from now on.*

Cathy phoned Erica as soon as she got home, but there was no reply. She sent her a quick text instead.

Please call me when you can, need to talk. I'm sorry about today x

Then she put the kettle on to boil and, while it bubbled away, took the cakes that Tansy and Erica had left behind out of her bag and put them into tubs to keep cool in the larder. If Erica would let her, she'd feel much happier about taking them over to her house than keeping them here, especially if she forgot to give them to Matthias when he came to pick her up tomorrow night. And it would give her an opportunity to iron things out with Erica. Not that she thought Erica was angry at her, but she still felt somehow responsible for what had happened. Regardless of the circumstances, it had all kicked off on her watch and if she'd been paying better attention she might have seen enough to stop it before it got as bad as it did.

And she'd meant what she'd said to Iris and Dora afterwards too. The last thing she wanted was to disband the cookery club, but if they started to exclude people when they took a dislike to them (even if that person had brought it on themselves to some extent) then Cathy didn't want to be a part of it anymore.

The kettle had just boiled when her phone pinged the arrival of a message. It wasn't Erica though; it was Matthias.

> *How's your day been so far? Work is hell today, clinic was overbooked and patients are spilling out of the door – might have to phone you much later tonight. That ok? X*

Cathy tapped out a reply to the affirmative. It wasn't like she had much else to do so it didn't really matter to her what time he called. If he wanted to call at three in the morning she'd wait up for it. Talking to him would have been one bright spot in an otherwise fraught and difficult day, if only it didn't make her think quite so much about how annoyed his sister might be with her. She just hoped she could get to iron things out with Erica before he phoned.

She didn't have to wait long. As soon as Cathy sat at the table with her mug of tea her phone rang and she saw Erica's name on the display.

'Erica... I'm so sorry about today,' she said.

'I was about to say the same to you,' Erica replied, and Cathy was glad to hear the warmth in her tone.

'I spoke to Iris afterwards and she's realised that it was a genuine mistake.'

'About that...' Erica paused, and her tone was more uncertain when she resumed. 'I'm not sure it was. Tansy can be... well, it can't have escaped your attention that she can be a bit difficult.'

'I suppose not,' Cathy admitted, realising that there was no point in doing otherwise. Erica had opened the discussion, indicating at last that the time for turning a blind eye or pretending nothing was wrong had passed.

'None of that is her fault,' Erica added. 'The things she does – she often does them deliberately but the fact that she does them... that's not her fault really.'

'You don't have to explain,' Cathy said. 'Whatever Tansy needs we can be there for her.'

'I'm not sure that's true of everyone.'

'Well... I'll admit that Iris and Dora have been a bit judgemental, but they said after you'd gone that they were willing to put today behind them.'

'The thing is, I know Tansy loves cooking with you – I can see it's doing her so much good. It's the first thing I've ever seen her concentrate so well on and the first thing I've ever seen her do that makes her forget for a while that she doesn't have to be angry at the world all the time. I'd hate to be the one to take that away from her, but I would have to if it was going to make it hard for you to run the club.'

'It won't,' Cathy said.

'But you'd tell me if she was causing so many problems that it was becoming a real issue for you? You've been so kind to her, I'd hate that. She doesn't see it yet, but one day I think she will. At least, I hope so.'

Cathy didn't think she'd been especially kind to Tansy – in fact, she'd mostly done her best to stay off the girl's radar. But she smiled and nodded.

'I'd tell you, but right now there's no problem as far as I'm concerned. And if she's getting as much out of it as you think, then I can only be happy to be a part of that.'

'Thank you.'

'While we're being so open…' Cathy began as another thought occurred to her, 'the missing blender… that wasn't you, was it? That was Tansy too, wasn't it?'

Erica gave a chuckle. 'Nothing gets past you, does it?'

'I thought it was strange at the time, that you'd managed to somehow drop it into your bag.'

'She only took it because she thought it would be funny that Iris would be looking for it – she didn't mean any real harm. I found it and confronted her, but it didn't seem worth bringing up at the time… I mean, all I've just said to you about her getting a lot from the club… I was worried you'd kick her out if you thought she was a thief.'

'So you took the blame? You are a good aunty.'

'I try,' Erica said, 'but never having had any kids of my own to practise on, I don't know that I'm very good at working out what your average teenager wants or needs. Not that I'm convinced Tansy is your average teenager.'

'I don't have any kids but I'm not convinced she is either,' Cathy said. 'And I don't mean that in a derogatory way…'

'Most would. It's nice of you to be diplomatic but I know what people tend to think of her and – if I'm totally honest – I know she doesn't do much to help herself there either. People think she's sulky and aggressive and it's a message she takes great pains to send out, but when you really know her…' Erica let out a sigh. 'It's hard to explain.'

'It's OK,' Cathy said. 'I understand, and you shouldn't have to explain it to anyone anyway, least of all me. Was she alright when you left? Iris didn't upset her too much? She wants to come back?'

'She said she didn't care what Iris thought and she would carry on doing exactly what she liked because she hadn't done anything wrong – which includes coming to the cookery club. I think she was lying about Iris, but the rest… I think she probably doesn't see that she did anything wrong.'

'But she did take the cake out of the oven deliberately?'

There was a pause, and Cathy seemed to sense a helpless shrug at the other end of the line. 'With Tansy, you never know what's going on in that head of hers.'

Chapter Twenty-Five

Cathy had been shopping, this time having had more warning about their next date, and she had on a new dress. It was a navy-blue floral with chiffon bell-sleeves, a flattering sweetheart neckline and a mid-length skirt. It showed her figure at its best, skimming over her belly and thighs, and, as she'd made a final check in the mirror, she'd felt sexy for the first time in a long time. Matthias's reaction had certainly done a lot to boost that too – as soon as she answered the front door he'd joked that she looked so incredible that they shouldn't bother going out to dinner but should stay in together instead, a flirty, cheeky look on his face.

But, just like a perfect gentleman, he'd escorted Cathy out anyway, back to the bar they'd tried briefly on their first date, only this time they could order a full meal and make the most of the warm, ambient atmosphere.

'I love it in here,' she said as they settled at their table. 'Do you come here a lot?'

'Not really – I've been to a couple of work socialising things here but that's about it.'

'Erica says you're a physiotherapist… Do you like your job? You were going to tell me about it at the theatre and…'

'I got distracted,' he said, smiling. 'Hardly surprising considering the company I had. I'd much rather hear about you than talk about my job.'

'But I'd like to know. It sounds interesting.'

He raised his eyebrows and grinned. 'You're sure about that?'

Cathy laughed. 'Yes!'

'Well, there are physiotherapists for more things than anyone realises. I specialise in rehabilitating people with heart conditions.'

'Erica said that. She's very proud of you.'

He looked vaguely surprised and Cathy laughed. 'She is!' Cathy said through her laughter. 'She said so!'

'She could try saying that to me once in a while.'

'She doesn't?'

'I think it's a sibling thing. You're not supposed to say things like that to your brother.'

'I wouldn't know – I'm an only child.'

'Do you wish you'd had brothers or sisters?'

'I always wished for a brother or sister but I never got one. But you seem close, closer than a lot of siblings I know of. I'm envious of that.'

'Your parents didn't want any more children after you?'

'It wasn't that simple.'

'Erica told me about your mum… I'm sorry. What about your dad? Is he…?'

'He died when I was five. I find it hard to remember him now. Mum got ill a few years later. It wasn't too difficult to manage at first, but then she got sicker and sicker… I had to start looking after her. I wouldn't have had it any other way, of course, but I don't mind admitting it was a lonely time of my life. My friends moved on, I lost boyfriend after boyfriend and then I decided it just wasn't worth bothering with any of it. It became too painful to see people move on and disappear from my life so I cut myself off to a point.' She shrugged. 'It was just easier to cope that way.'

'So it was just you and your mum?'

Cathy nodded.

'She must have been so grateful to have you.'

'I think she was and that made it a lot easier to bear, knowing I'd made her feel safe and cared for.'

'I know a lot of people who care for others in my line of work, and I know that it's never easy. I don't honestly know that I'd be able to do it; you must be one amazing person.'

She smiled up at him. She'd never seen herself that way, but to hear it from him now warmed her in a way she hadn't felt in a long time. It made her feel that maybe what she'd done for her mum had been worth something after all, that it was something to be proud of.

Her hands rested on the table in front of her, and she glanced down as she felt him cover them with his own before looking up to meet his gaze again. There was that now familiar thrill of excitement as she fell into those eyes and the world around her disappeared.

'I suppose we ought to have a look at this menu…' he said in a husky voice.

'I suppose we should,' Cathy replied, but she didn't move her gaze from his, utterly trapped, mesmerised… not that she would have wanted to be rescued.

He smiled. 'This is weird, isn't it?'

'Is it?'

'The way we met… how quickly I feel I know you… how quickly I feel as if we could be…'

He cleared his throat and reached for the menu with a sheepish grin. 'Ignore me – I'm talking rubbish as usual.'

'No – no, you're not,' Cathy said, reaching for his hand again. 'It's not just you. I feel as if I've known you for years not days. I mean, it's all new and that's wonderful, but at the same time, it's like you've always been there.' She blushed and reached for her own menu. 'If that's not what you'd been about to say then I sound pretty stupid right now.'

'It was,' he said. 'That's exactly what I was trying to say and you saying it has only proved I'm right.'

Suddenly aware they were no longer alone, Cathy looked up to see the waiter at their table.

'Had time to look over the menu, folks?' he asked brightly.

Cathy glanced at Matthias and they grinned at each other.

'Could you give us five more minutes?' Matthias asked. 'I promise we'll stop talking long enough to give you an order when you get back.'

The waiter nodded. 'Sure thing – no need to rush.'

He walked away, Cathy hardly noticing, her gaze trapped in Matthias's again.

'We're never going to get any food at this rate,' he said, laughing, though he made no move to do anything other than look into her eyes.

Eventually, she managed to tear herself away and blushed as she put her attention to the menu again. 'We should probably...'

'We should,' he said, but when she looked up he was still gazing at her.

'Menu!' she said and laughed, making him chuckle too.

'Right,' he said, finally making a move to read his. 'Let's see what there is.'

Matthias was a lot more knowledgeable about Spanish food than Cathy. She'd spent a lot of time over the years cooking as well as baking, but she tended to concentrate on the things her mum would like and usually ate the same. As Miriam got sicker their choices had become smaller because her appetite had waned and she'd found fewer and fewer foods tempting or palatable, and so, to some extent, Cathy's choices had shrunk too. It had just been easier to go with what her mum wanted rather than cooking separate meals, but it meant that she'd stopped experimenting with different cuisines and had baked a lot more of the sweet treats that her mum would always eat.

Cathy had been torn about what to order as she'd wanted to try so much, so in the end they'd gone for small tapas-style portions, as they had the first time they'd come here, but this time they chose more varieties including garlic shrimps, a meatball dish called *albondigas*, *patatas bravas*, chicken wings and even some octopus.

But despite enjoying what she'd tried, and even making a note to find recipes so she could replicate some of it at home, if anyone had asked her to describe what she'd eaten afterwards she'd have found it difficult, because all she could think about was the man sitting across from her. She hardly registered the tangy tomato sauce that came with the meatballs, or the sharp green olives with the shrimp, but she'd memorised every line on his face, the way his nose wrinkled when he laughed, the resonant timbre of his voice, the way one lock of hair in his swept-back fringe refused to sit with the rest, the feel of his hands whenever they'd crept to meet hers, the woody scent as he'd leaned close to share a joke or a stolen kiss.

As the evening drew to a close, they had another friendly disagreement over the bill and Matthias, again, insisted on paying, but only once Cathy had made him agree that next time they met he'd let her cook for him because she didn't want him to keep paying for her and he didn't want her to splash out on him. So he settled up and they stepped out onto damp pavements made glassy by a sharp frost, his arm around her shoulders to pull her close as she shivered at the sudden change of temperature.

'I don't suppose you want to go somewhere else?' he asked. 'I don't know about you, but I'm not ready for the night to end yet.'

'You're making a habit of that,' she said, laughing. 'I seem to recall you saying the same thing when we went to the theatre.'

'Yes, but that was early to be going home...' He looked at his watch. 'I suppose around now there won't be much open except for nightclubs.'

Cathy wrinkled her nose. 'If you're going to suggest a nightclub then I'm afraid, for the first time tonight, I'm going to have to disagree. I think my days of clubs are long gone.'

'Mine too,' he said. 'I was hoping that would be your answer. In which case... we could grab a coffee?'

'There won't be anywhere open for coffee.'

'My house is always open,' he said with a hopeful smile. 'I promise no funny business and I'll take you home as soon as you want to go.'

'We could go to mine for that matter,' Cathy said.

'We could,' he agreed, 'but... well, I need to take Guin out for a last pee before he settles for the night.'

Cathy laughed. 'Oh, I completely forgot about poor Guin! Of course, let's go back to yours; we might as well. I don't mind coming with you to walk him.'

'I'd like that,' he said. 'I think Guin would too.'

Half an hour later Matthias's car came to a halt outside a darkened house in a terraced street. Cathy knew the neighbourhood, characterised by eighteenth-century terraced houses, though she'd rarely visited anyone who lived there. Her cottage was almost at the opposite side of the town.

Unclipping his seatbelt, he smiled at her. 'Here we are,' he said. 'No palace, I'll admit, but at least I had the foresight to clean up earlier today.'

'I wouldn't have cared,' Cathy said.

'Oh, I think you would,' he said, laughing. 'I'm pretty sure you wouldn't have wanted to come back. Guin makes enough mess of his own with all that hair, let alone mine.'

'What, your hair? Do you lose it that quickly?'

He grinned. 'Cheeky. I could change my mind about this coffee, you know.'

'You could.'

'But I wouldn't.'

'I'm glad to hear it.'

With another grin he got out of the car and Cathy followed. But then he stopped dead on the pavement, staring at his front door. For a moment, Cathy couldn't understand what had halted his progress, until she made out a shadow and then someone who had been sitting on the step get up and walk towards them.

It was Tansy. Her face was in gloom, but there was just enough light from the nearby streetlamp for Cathy to recognise her. She looked from Matthias to Cathy and then back again.

'What's she doing here? Are you two…?'

'What are *you* doing here?' Matthias asked.

Tansy rammed her hands on her hips and stared at him. 'Are you *seeing* her?'

'Does it matter?'

'Yes, it matters! When did this happen? How long ago? Why didn't anyone tell me?'

'Because it's none of your business, Tans.' He frowned and positioned himself, ever so subtly, between her and Cathy. 'It's almost midnight. How did you get here?'

'Walked. It's not that far.'

'In the dark? Alone? Anything could have happened to you!'

'I couldn't stay at home, could I?'

'Why not? What's happened this time?'

'I'm not saying anything in front of her.'

'Whatever you've got to say, you can say it in front of Cathy.'

'She's not family.'

'Then don't say it. Go home and call me tomorrow.'

'What, so you can shag her?'

'Tansy!' Matthias snapped. 'If you're going to be like that I'll call a taxi for you right now!'

Tansy looked as if she might argue, but then clamped her mouth shut.

'Let's start again,' he said. 'Do you want to tell me what's happened or am I wasting my breath asking? If you've got nothing to say then there's no point in being here.'

'What do you think happened? Mum kicked me out.' Tansy glared at Cathy as she answered him.

Matthias sighed. 'Again?' he asked, his voice betraying that fact that this was a regular occurrence. Then he looked puzzled for a moment. 'Where's your stuff?'

'Didn't have time to pack it. Shane was gunning for me; he said he'd…' She glanced uneasily at Cathy as she continued, seeming to think better of uttering the rest. 'You know. What he normally says when he's in one of his moods… I didn't have time to pack anything, I just got out.'

'Ah.' One small word of understanding and Matthias's whole body appeared to stiffen; his tone hardened and his jaw clenched, animosity suddenly seeming to radiate off him in waves. Cathy had never seen a mood darken so violently in someone. Gone was the charming, relaxed man of only a few minutes ago to be replaced by a seething mass of anger and resentment. She would never have imagined that this side of him could exist if she hadn't seen it with her own eyes.

He turned to Cathy. 'I'm sorry… do you mind if I take you home after all?'

'Of course not. I mean, I could call a cab if you need to be here—'

'No, of course not; I'm not going to let you do that. It won't take long.' He unlocked the front door and nodded to Tansy. 'Wait inside; I'll be back as soon as I can.'

'I'll come with you.'

'No you won't.'

'Why not?'

'Because Guinness has been on his own all night and he'd appreciate a friendly face right now. If you really want to make yourself useful you can let him into the back garden for a quick pee, otherwise he'll be bursting.'

'Right,' Tansy said, and this seemed to smooth over any argument she might have been thinking up. 'Want me to change his food too?'

'Just his water – he's eaten today.'

Tansy went inside and, as the door closed, Matthias turned back to Cathy. 'I'm really sorry about this.'

'It doesn't matter.'

'No, it does. I'll make it up to you somehow – I promise.'

She followed as he began to walk back to his car. 'Really, it doesn't. Family has to come first; I understand that.'

The mood was flat as they made their way along darkened and quiet roads to Cathy's house. Questions tumbled over one another inside her head, though they all seemed too personal to ask, especially when very little was being volunteered. After ten silent minutes Matthias spoke.

'I bet you think this is really out of order.'

'Of course I don't. I wish I could help, but I realise it's something that's probably personal. Is it something to do with Tansy's mum?'

He looked sharply at her before turning his eyes back to the road.

'I only ask because Erica has mentioned a couple of times that Tansy and her mum don't get along all that well, and that you and Erica worry about both of them. You don't have to tell me anything, of course. You could just tell me to mind my own business.'

He shook his head. 'I'd never do that, but I feel as if this is too big and nasty to drag you into.'

'It wouldn't be dragging me in to just tell me about it. Not that you have to… only, if it helped to talk…'

'Let's just say Michelle has interesting taste in men, and they don't often take kindly to the fact that she has a daughter. The latest one is about the worst in a long line of assholes.'

'That's Shane… the man she mentioned just now? Does he hit them?'

As soon as she'd asked the question Cathy wished she could take it back. Matthias's expression darkened further, hands gripping the steering wheel so tight that Cathy saw them turn white as they passed under the streetlights.

'Sorry…' she said hastily. 'None of my business… Forget I asked.'

'It's alright.' He dragged in a long breath, trying to calm down. 'I don't know. I've asked and Michelle tells me to keep my nose out. There's only so much I can do there, but Tansy… I don't know what he's done to her or what he's threatened, but I think she's scared of him. She won't say either, though.'

'But she…? You haven't seen her injured, have you?'

'No,' he said. 'And I can't prove anything. All I know is the way Tansy looks when she mentions his name, and that every few weeks or so either Michelle throws her out or Tansy leaves of her own accord and turns up at my house or Erica's… Mine more, since Malcolm put his foot down about her moving in and out of there. He said they didn't know whether they were coming or going with her and I get that. She can be a handful and as a couple they have to think about each other too.'

'Doesn't Michelle worry for her if he's that bad? I'd be terrified if I thought someone was putting my daughter in danger and I'd be just as unhappy if I thought my boyfriend was making her so miserable she felt she had to keep running away from home.'

'But that's where you're very different from my sister. Michelle is only concerned with the new man in her life. Always has been, always will be. Tansy has pretty much brought herself up for the last ten years because her mother's always too busy doing something else to care.'

'Is that why you and Erica do so much for her?'

'I don't do nearly enough, but there's only so much you can do, which is as much as Tansy will let you. She's built a wall around herself. It's hard to get through, and even when she's crying out for help she won't let you in.'

'Sounds like she doesn't know how to,' Cathy said.

He turned to her again. 'I think you're right. Or she's so used to keeping her defences high she's forgotten how to let them down.'

'I wish I could help.'

'You are helping.'

Cathy looked to see his eyes still on the road, though his expression had softened a little and, despite the nature of their conversation, it warmed her to think that she might have done that. 'I don't know how,' she said doubtfully.

'Erica told me how you tried to stick up for her at your cookery class and how tolerant you've been. We're grateful for that – it's very easy to judge Tansy when you don't know her situation. Any support is appreciated.'

Cathy wondered if Erica had been too generous in her assessment of Cathy's part in the drama at cookery club or whether Matthias was being generous in his recollection of what Erica had told him. Either way, she didn't feel that she'd done all that much to defend Tansy, but in light of what he was telling her now, she resolved to do better in future. Although, it wasn't going to be easy because she clearly couldn't tell people what she knew about Tansy, and because they didn't have that information, they wouldn't see anything but a sulky and belligerent young girl with a chip on her shoulder and no respect for anyone or anything. Even knowing what she did now, and even seeing how it mattered to Matthias, it was still hard for Cathy to feel more kindly disposed to her.

She hadn't even realised they'd arrived at her house until he stopped the car and yanked on the handbrake.

'I'm really sorry about this,' he said.

'There's no need to be. Like I said, family has to come first.'

He gave her a bleak smile, and Cathy had to wonder – perhaps a little selfishly – whether family would always have to come first and how much of that she was willing to take before the situation became untenable. She liked him a lot, but was that enough? Did this have something to do with the fact that his previous relationships had never worked out? Maybe that hadn't been an issue before Tansy's troubles had become his, but perhaps his niece had got in the way since then.

'I'd better get back. Thanks for being so understanding.'

'You'll call me, won't you?'

'Of course I will…' He cupped a gentle hand behind her neck and guided her lips to his. Then he let her go, and she fought the urge to grab him again. 'I'll call you tomorrow.'

'Alright.' Unclipping her seatbelt, she pushed open the passenger door.

'Goodnight, Cathy,' he said.

She turned to him with a smile full of regret. 'Goodnight,' she replied, before getting out and shutting the door behind her. She watched for a moment as he restarted the engine and the car slowly left her street, and then, with a heavy sigh, she unlocked her front door and went to get ready for bed.

Chapter Twenty-Six

'Are you OK?' Erica asked.

Cathy swished the last drop of tea around in her cup, staring into the depths, phone to her ear. On the kitchen table in front of her, the cookery book was open. She was copying a recipe Dora had brought in – at least, she was trying to. Dora's handwriting was a bit difficult to decipher – she seemed to go off on tangents with irrelevant notes and her spelling was abysmal. It didn't help that Cathy was finding it hard to concentrate too, her mind full of what had happened the night before with Matthias and Tansy.

'Of course I am,' she lied. 'I ought to be asking you that. What did Matthias say when he called you this morning? I mean, if it's not too personal to ask.'

'Of course you can ask,' Erica said. 'I think if anyone's entitled to ask it's you. I expect Matt will phone you himself this morning, I just thought I'd call now while it was fresh in my mind.'

Cathy reached for a biscuit from an open pack. It was her third or fourth of the morning and, despite the fact she'd promised herself she was going to cut back, she was in the mood to eat many more. She nibbled on it as Erica continued.

'I'm not sure what happened between her and Michelle, but from what Tansy has told Matthias she's completely blameless.' Erica's voice contained more than a note of scepticism at this; at least she wasn't utterly blind when it came to Tansy's faults. 'It seems that whatever was done or said, Shane took offence and came wading in. It ended up with either Michelle throwing Tansy out or Tansy walking out or maybe even Shane having a hand in it. Tansy says it's the first option but you can never be sure she's remembering it exactly how it happened.'

'Have you spoken to your sister yet?'

'There's no point. She'll only stick up for Shane, no matter what happened.'

'So Tansy couldn't go back to her and work it out? She won't move back in?'

'Oh, I expect so – this isn't the first time she's left home and she usually ends up back there. Mostly because Matt and I try to impose rules to straighten her out and she doesn't know how to deal with that, so she goes home where there are no rules, where she knows how her world operates. She doesn't realise that, far from being as good as it seems, that lack of rules is damaging for her.'

'When you say lack of rules…?'

Erica sighed. 'It's just Michelle finds it hard to give her attention when there's a man on the scene. I don't know what comes over her, but she sort of seems to forget she has a daughter.'

Cathy recalled Matthias saying something similar. She couldn't imagine ever doing that if she had a child of her own, but she didn't have a child and so, perhaps, she'd never really know how she'd act. And it sounded as if Tansy wasn't entirely blameless and that she wasn't always telling things exactly how they'd happened.

'Apart from that,' Erica continued, 'I was calling to find out how your date went… Obviously you can spare me the details, but it was good?'

Cathy smiled. 'I would hardly be telling you if it wasn't good, would I?'

'Yes, but—'

'It was lovely. He's great.'

'You're going to see him again?'

'If he wants to.'

'Oh, he definitely wants to.'

Cathy wondered what he'd said about it, but it didn't look as if Erica was going to volunteer the information because she took the conversation back to Tansy.

'I'm sorry, I don't think Tansy is coming back to cookery club.'

Cathy couldn't say she was entirely sorry about that, but she understood that it meant a lot to Erica. 'That's a shame,' she said. 'Is this about what happened last week?'

'I think it's about a lot of things. She needs time to sort her head out and I think it's probably best for now that she stays away from volatile situations while she does that.'

'Of course. But you'll still come?'

'If I can, yes.'

There was a caveat – what was that? Erica was usually a lot more enthusiastic about cookery club. Was this to do with what had happened last week? Had it offended Erica more than it had Tansy? Was she annoyed that people had ganged up on her niece?

'I hope you can,' Cathy said. 'I'd miss you if you weren't there – I think the others would too. You're like a part of the original squad; it's just not the same without you.'

Erica laughed. 'I've never been part of any squad before.'

Cathy smiled. 'Neither have I. But I feel like I am now.'

'I'm glad,' Erica said. 'If anyone ought to feel they belong somewhere, it's you. Listen, I'll get off the line; I expect Matt will want to phone you to tell you about last night himself.'

'OK. Thanks for ringing.'

'I just wanted to make sure that brother of mine hadn't already cocked up the best thing that's happened to him in ages.'

Cathy's smile grew. Did Erica really think that? Was that how Matthias felt? Had he said so to his sister? Cathy certainly felt that way about him and loved the idea that she could be secure in the knowledge it wasn't one-sided.

'Thanks, Erica,' she said. 'I'll text you later.'

Matthias did call around ten minutes later, and although Cathy was happy to hear from him, the news that he was going with Tansy to pick up some belongings from her home so she could move in with him for a while was less welcome. It meant obstacles in the way of their blossoming relationship, and although she felt selfish to think that way, she couldn't help it. But she put a brave face on the situation, told him she was glad he was doing that if it felt like the right thing, reassured him that the way the previous evening had ended hadn't put her off and they arranged to go out again the following night. At least that was something to look forward to, as long as Tansy didn't manage to throw another spanner in the works. She was getting very good at that lately.

'So…' Fleur handed Cathy her usual early mug of tea. It looked as if she'd been there for hours already because the stall was almost set up, the displays bursting with seasonal arrangements of holly, ivy and mistletoe, some with scarlet roses and berries or pine cones sprayed silver and gold. There were also early daffodils, snow-white lilies and more delicate narcissi along with the usual fare of more traditional, year-round bouquets that included carnations and orchids. 'Firstly, where's my cake?'

Cathy laughed and gave Fleur the Tupperware tub she'd filled with rocky road.

'Oh, you're a good girl!' Fleur grinned as she took a square. 'And second, how did the big date go?'

'Interesting,' Cathy said, taking a sip of her tea.

'Now that's not an adjective I've come to expect when hearing how a date went. Interesting how?'

'Oh, it was lovely until the end.'

Fleur wrinkled her nose. 'Oh God, he didn't try to push things too far, did he?'

'Oh, no! He was a perfect gentleman. But when we got back to his place for a coffee his niece was on the doorstep.'

'Trouble?'

'That's her. And she had more trouble. She'd left home and wanted his help. So, of course, that was the end of the evening.'

'Well' – Fleur bit into her chocolatey square – 'at least the rest of it went well. Are you going to see him again?'

'Tomorrow,' Cathy said. 'As long as nothing happens to get in the way, I suppose.'

'You think it will?'

'Well, she's moving in with him for a bit as far as I know.'

'So? Surely his niece isn't that needy? She's older, isn't she? Old enough to look after herself for a few hours if he goes out?'

'She's seventeen so yes, but I think he worries about her. I think Erica does too but she can't do as much because her husband isn't very keen.'

'He might worry about her but surely that won't affect him seeing you?'

Cathy put her lips to her mug again. Fleur's appraisal of the situation was as practical as she was, and it was bang on the mark. Tansy staying with Matthias shouldn't affect his time with Cathy, but somehow she felt it wasn't going to be that simple. She'd seen already how easily Tansy seemed to wrap her uncle around her little finger and she wondered how far she'd go to make certain she was always his top priority. She craved affection and attention; that much was clear from what she did and what Cathy now knew about her, and to a certain extent Cathy sympathised – the poor girl probably deserved a bit of TLC. But she felt Tansy didn't always go the right way about getting it, and how far she'd push to get what she wanted was anyone's guess.

'I don't suppose it ought to,' she said finally. 'I'm probably worrying over nothing. It's just… I really like him, Fleur. I suppose I'm scared something will come and ruin it for me.'

'It sounds as if he likes you too, so maybe you ought to try to relax and let things happen. You know, I always think that if something is meant to be then it's meant to be, and nothing in the universe will stop it. And if it's not meant to be, then the universe will see that it stops, no matter what anyone else does.'

'Hmm,' Cathy said, smiling now. 'Sounds a bit fatalistic.'

'But it takes the stress out of things,' Fleur said, reaching into the tub for more cake. 'There's no point in worrying about things that will take their own course whether you worry or not.'

'I don't like the thought that the universe doesn't want me to find a good man like Matthias,' Cathy said.

'Oh, I think it does. That's why you're never here right now when your ex comes for his flowers.'

Cathy looked sharply up from her mug. 'What?'

Fleur shrugged. 'He came in again as I was packing up last Friday. Did I not mention it?'

'No.'

'Oh, I must have forgotten. Jade served him this time – she's doing extra hours to save for Christmas,' Fleur added in answer to Cathy's slight frown, guessing that she was wondering what their Saturday girl was doing in a day early, 'but I could tell he was looking for you.'

Cathy searched her memory. This must have been after he'd seen her out at the theatre with Matthias. There had been nothing strange in his demeanour that she could recall, though. He'd been cheery, friendly, as interested as an old acquaintance would be, even if Cathy had found it excruciatingly awkward. Cathy also had to question whether he really had been looking for her or whether Fleur was just choosing to see it that way because she was rather enjoying the drama.

'He probably just thought he'd say hello if I was here,' Cathy said. 'I saw him out at the theatre with his wife after the play had ended,' she added. 'And he came over to introduce her, so he probably just thought we're sort of friends now and he ought to be polite.'

'Yes,' Fleur said, 'I'm sure that's it.' But her expression told Cathy that she didn't believe that for a minute.

Cathy looked up to see someone at the counter holding a wreath they'd picked up from the display.

'How much is this one?' the woman asked.

Cathy, glad of the distraction, put down her tea and went over to help. With a bit of luck they'd start getting busy around now and Fleur would forget all about the fact that Jonas had been to the stall again.

*

Matthias and Cathy had agreed on somewhere more low-key for their next date and gone to a cosy local pub. He had seemed distracted at times, but she'd tried to dismiss it, realising that he had a lot to think about right now and she hoped that it was nothing to do with her. He seemed to rally, however, when Cathy took over the conversation to talk about the progress of her recipe collection and the book she was writing to safeguard it. She'd wondered if it was a subject that would bore him, but he'd seemed genuinely interested when he'd asked, telling her what he knew from Erica, and listening intently as she explained her thoughts on how it was a way of maintaining connections with the past and with family members no longer with them.

'So what will you do with it when it's finished?' he asked.

'I don't know. Lots of people have said they would like photocopies so I suppose I'll make some to give out.'

'Seems a bit of an anti-climax for something you've put so much work into.'

'Not really; it's more of a labour of love than anything else. Maybe I'll ask for donations or something to give to the cancer charity, but it's really not worth that much to anyone but me.'

'I think you underestimate its worth.'

Cathy shrugged and reached for the white wine spritzer he'd just brought back to their table. The pub was quiet, only two other tables occupied, but then, it was a weeknight. Besides, she liked it this way – it meant they could talk properly without having to shout over the noise of a jukebox or quiz machines or rowdy drinkers, and it meant they could each listen properly too.

'Fleur said that— My boss at the flower stall,' she clarified at the look of vague confusion on Matthias's face. 'She says I ought to get one set properly by a printer – glossy pages and photos and all that.

She offered to sell them on the stall in the run-up to Christmas if I got copies.' Cathy sipped her wine. 'It's probably a bit late for that now though, Christmas is only a couple of weeks away and I'd never get them printed on time.'

'I think she was right – it's a shame you never got it done before now. The shops are full of recipe books right now.'

'Yes,' Cathy said with a light laugh. 'From celebrity chefs people actually care about. I don't think I fall into that category.'

'People care about you,' he said.

Cathy raised her eyebrows. 'I'm hardly a celebrity.' And then she smiled. 'People care about me, do they?'

'Yes,' he said.

'Who?'

'Erica… your boss… *me*.'

He reached for her hand, lifting it to his mouth to kiss her fingers, the tiny action sending shockwaves through her.

'I think I could get to like that,' she replied. 'The caring bit, I mean, although the kissing's not too bad…'

He leaned in further, this time to kiss her on the lips. Cathy had always been slightly embarrassed to kiss in public, but Matthias did something to her that made her stop caring what anyone else thought.

But when he pulled away, he looked somehow grave.

'Cathy… I feel as if we're getting so close so fast…'

She frowned. 'Is that a bad thing?'

'No, of course not. It's just that… if we're going there, I should probably tell you some things about my past that you don't yet know.'

Her insides suddenly turned cold. Why so serious? What could he possibly say that might affect where their relationship was going? And if it was that heavy, capable of damaging what they had, did she really want to know? Maybe, sometimes, ignorance was bliss, because if it was anything that would jeopardise what they'd got going here she'd choose ignorance every time. But she also realised that whatever it was troubled him and he wanted to come clean. This was Matthias – it couldn't be that bad, could it?

'OK,' she said. 'I'm ready.'

He paused. 'I've—'

His phone began to ring. He waited for it to stop and after a minute or so it did. Then he opened his mouth to begin again, only for the phone to start ringing once more.

'Sorry… I'm going to have to get this,' he said, groaning as he looked at the display. Cathy could see Tansy's name flash up. Talk about bad timing. Or perhaps it was good timing – at least, as far as Tansy was concerned. She'd take great delight in interrupting their date; Cathy was under no illusions about that. Tansy had made her displeasure about the fact that Cathy and Matthias were dating known, mostly stemming from the fact, Cathy suspected, that nobody had told her straight away, a fact that would have been perfectly reasonable to anyone else. At first there had really been nothing to tell and might not have been for some weeks, so why would they go to her and explain anything?

'Is everything alright?' Matthias asked as he took the call.

His expression darkened as he listened. Cathy couldn't tell what Tansy was saying but judging by how long it was taking it wasn't straightforward.

'OK,' he said finally. 'I'll be there as soon as I can. Don't touch anything until I get back.'

He looked up at Cathy as he locked his phone and put it back in his pocket. 'Something's happened. I can't tell what but Tansy says there was a tiny explosion and all the power's gone off in the house. She sounds terrified to be honest. I'm going to have to sort it out.'

Cathy nodded. What else could she do?

'Sorry,' he added. 'It feels like every time we're out at the moment the universe seems to have other plans for us.'

'It does, doesn't it?' Cathy replied, thinking about what Fleur had said and wondering what this meant for her and Matthias. Did this mean they shouldn't be together?

They arrived at Matthias's place twenty minutes later. The house was in darkness, Tansy waiting at the open front door wrapped in a huge woollen jumper. Guin was at her side like a sentry, stock-still, eyes trained on the street. But at the sight of Matthias, he leapt up, his tail whirring like a windmill.

'Alright, Guin,' Matthias said, ruffling the dog's fur. He looked up at Tansy. 'Are you OK?'

'I was just scared,' she said. 'I thought the house was going to blow up or something.'

'I doubt it,' he said, following her into the darkened building. The gloom was pierced by a beam of white light from his phone torch. 'What on earth did you do?'

'Oh, I knew it would be *my* fault,' Tansy said, and Cathy could just make out the teenager glaring back at her as she followed them in, gingerly putting one foot in front of the other in the blackness, Guin's cold nose nuzzling her hand for a fuss.

'I'll be going home as soon as your uncle has sorted the electricity for you,' Cathy said, feeling the need for an explanation even though she owed none. 'We just thought it was better to come straight here first.'

'Nobody is saying it's your fault, Tans,' Matthias said patiently. 'I was just asking what had caused it. What were you doing when it went off?'

'Putting the oven on,' Tansy said sulkily. 'I was going to make a cake for you.'

'Oh, what were you going to make?' Cathy asked, seeing the chink of light from some common ground. 'Something we've done at cookery club?'

'No,' Tansy sneered. 'I got the recipe out of a *proper* book.'

It stung, even though Cathy knew she'd walked right into a trap that Tansy had meant to spring and even if she knew better than to take any notice. Without another word she searched the gloom of the hallway to see the shadow of a door open. It looked as if it housed some kind of understairs cupboard.

'The trip switch is in here if it happens again, Tans,' he said. 'Just in case I'm not here.' He shone a torch up to a box on the wall. 'See…? All you've got to do is pull this…'

Suddenly the hallway was flooded with light. Cathy stepped back towards the front door, suddenly feeling desperately unwelcome as Tansy's gaze was turned to her properly now and she looked her up and down with some distaste. 'So you're going to take her home now?' she said to Matthias.

'I'd better go and check the kitchen first,' he said, striding down the hallway. 'If something has burned out in the oven's circuits we ought to make it safe before I go anywhere else.'

Tansy followed him, but Cathy stayed by the front door, absently running a hand down Guin's back. A moment later Matthias's face appeared at the door again. 'You can come in, you know,' he said with a smile.

'But I thought…' she began.

'If you like, as we had our night cut short, I could make you some supper and then take you home.'

'But the oven…?'

'I don't know what happened but it seems alright now. I just turned it on and it's working.'

Cathy could take a wild guess at what had happened, but it was a theory she could never air – at least, not here and now.

'I don't think…'

Tansy's head appeared now too, and her face wore the strangest expression. She was *smiling*.

'Yes, stay,' she said.

Cathy stared at her. Was she hallucinating? What had been in that spritzer at the pub? She'd never seen Tansy smile in all the weeks she'd known her, and certainly had never been able to envisage a day when she might actually be invited to spend time with her. There had to be more to this than how it looked. Cathy hated to be suspicious but she couldn't help but feel Tansy was up to something. If she was, what on earth could it be? But she could hardly refuse the offer now because of how it would look to Matthias, and if Tansy really was suddenly in the mood to hold out an olive branch then Cathy wouldn't want to jeopardise that either.

'I suppose I could stay for a short while,' she said, feeling a bit dazed. 'I wouldn't want to keep anyone up late, though.'

'I'll put the kettle on,' Tansy said. 'You do want tea, don't you? You always drink tea at cookery club.'

Without waiting for Cathy to reply, Tansy went back into the kitchen again.

'What happened?' Cathy asked Matthias.

'I have no idea. Something must have shorted, overloaded the circuit somehow, but I can't see what it was. I'll have to get an electrician to have a look at it, just to be certain it isn't a dangerous loose connection or something.'

Cathy nodded, although she hadn't actually been asking about the power cut, more about his niece's strange transformation into someone who actually might like her.

'I could have perhaps talked Tansy through flicking the trip switch back on over the phone but I wanted to make sure it wasn't something more serious… I'm really sorry we had to come back so early.'

'Of course,' Cathy said. 'If it was my house I'd want to check too – you can't be too careful, especially with Tansy and Guin in here.'

'I knew you'd understand,' he said.

Cathy wished she could say she did, but right now she didn't understand any of it. One thing was fairly obvious to her – Tansy had tripped the electric deliberately. Cathy didn't know how but she was sure of it. Why was a different matter, and why she was suddenly being pleasant to Cathy was even more of a puzzle.

'Come on through,' he said. 'What do you want to drink? I've got gin and brandy in.'

'I don't mind,' Cathy said, following him into the kitchen. 'Surprise me.'

'One day you're going to regret telling me to surprise you,' he said with a chuckle.

Matthias's kitchen was small but cosy, an old wooden table taking up most of it, with heavy oak units and Spanish wall tiles. It was a bit dated, and suggested to Cathy that he'd either lived here alone for a long time, or moved in and not cared too much about how long it had been since it was last decorated. But it was clean and neat and he obviously took pride in keeping it that way. Tansy was back at the table, staring into a laptop, but she looked up as Cathy took a seat.

'Where did you go?' she asked.

'Oh, nowhere special,' Matthias said.

'But where?' Tansy closed the lid of her laptop and looked at Cathy now.

Matthias put a glass of amber liquid in front of Cathy and she detected the smell of brandy and perhaps lemonade in there.

'What was that pub called?' Cathy asked.

'Oh, it was just the Keys,' Matthias said.

'The Cross Keys?' Tansy asked carelessly. 'Oh, there... Isn't that where you used to take Aunty Sidonie?'

'No,' Matthias said firmly.

Cathy stared at him, realisation hitting her like a brick. Who was Sidonie? He'd never mentioned any sister other than Erica and Michelle and neither had Erica. In fact, Erica had very definitely stated that there were only three of them.

He looked suddenly uncomfortable.

'Oh,' Tansy said. 'I thought it was.'

'No, it wasn't. Tans...' he added, 'do us a favour and take Guin outside; I think he wants to go to the toilet.'

'No he doesn't,' she said. 'I took him just before you got back. So, where was the pub where you used to take Sidonie? She used to love it, didn't she?'

'Tansy, not now...' he growled, throwing her a warning look.

'What do you mean?' Tansy replied, a look of pure innocence on her face. 'You don't usually tell me I can't talk about Sidonie and Beau. We talk about them all the time usually... Oh! Is it because Cathy is here?'

Cathy looked from one to the other, the cogs in her brain whirring at speed. Matthias looked as if he wanted to kill Tansy, but she simply gave a serene smile. Tansy was clearly up to something, but what?

'Sidonie used to cook amazing dishes, didn't she?' Tansy said. 'You used to say it was the best food you'd ever had.'

'Tansy…' he warned, but she ignored it.

'I suppose it's because she's French and they make the best food, don't they? And she never got fat no matter how much she ate, did she? She's still thin now. She was thin after she had Beau too, wasn't she? I don't think anything would make her not thin and not pretty. So pretty. And she had a lovely French accent too. We all loved her, didn't we? Erica misses her too – she said so. Said she was the best—'

'Tansy!' he roared. 'I know what you're trying to do and you'd better stop right now!'

'I'm not trying to do anything.'

'Go to your room please.'

'I don't have a room.'

'To the spare room then! The one you're using right now!'

'But I'm talking to Cathy.'

'It's alright,' Cathy began, but Matthias cut across her.

'No, it's not. These things are for me to tell you and I was going to. I was trying to tell you tonight.'

'I thought you would have done already,' Tansy said, and the look he gave her now was enough, even for her. 'I've just got to go and…'

She scurried off, but not before Cathy had caught a fleeting look of satisfaction on her face. Whatever stunt she'd been trying to pull – and Cathy was beginning to think she'd worked out what it was – she'd obviously thought it a success.

'I'm sorry,' he said. 'You must think this is the most dysfunctional family you've ever come across and I wouldn't blame you if you ran now and didn't look back.'

Cathy tried to give him an encouraging smile, even though the ground felt very unstable beneath her right now. 'Why would I do that? Show me a family that isn't dysfunctional in some way and I'll show you a lie.'

'Yes, but some are definitely worse than others.'

'It's alright. I think I know who Sidonie is and I don't care.'

'Please, I need to explain—'

'You don't. I trust you.'

'I know. But let me explain it to you anyway. I wanted to tell you earlier, before Tansy rang. Cathy, I feel that we're getting somewhere and I hope you feel the same way.'

'You know I do.'

'And what I didn't think you needed to know before I feel that you do now. I'll be honest, I've had so many pointless dates that never went anywhere that I got sick of telling the story, so I stopped. But with you... well, I feel as if I need to tell it maybe only once more. At least, I hope so.'

'OK,' Cathy said, her emotions torn between warmth for his words, for his faith in what future they might have together, and trepidation about what he was about to tell her. She'd guessed at it, but what if it was a lot more than what she'd guessed? What if it was something that she wouldn't be able to deal with?

'Sidonie is my ex-wife. She's French, and she moved back to France when we split up. It was a long and messy divorce and it took me a good few years to get over it. Tansy was very fond of her and they still keep in touch.'

'And Beau?'

'Sidonie's son.'

Cathy frowned. 'But not your son?'

'He was two when we got together. I suppose, for all intents and purposes, I became his father because he didn't see his own back in France. I was fond of him and eventually we decided I should adopt him so that we were an official family.'

'Do you still see them?'

'Not as often as I should,' he said, the regret and guilt obvious in his expression. 'It's difficult. Sidonie and me... it was complicated and hard to be in the same room, which wasn't Beau's fault, of course, but it means that it's also difficult to see him too.'

'She doesn't like you seeing him?'

'I don't know. I don't think she'd be that obtuse but it's not that simple really.'

'I suppose not,' Cathy said.

He studied her for a moment. 'So,' he said finally, 'where does that leave us?'

'Exactly where we were,' she said. 'It doesn't matter to me. Everyone has a past and if you tell me that's where Sidonie is, then I believe you.'

'I'm sorry you had to hear it from Tansy...'

'It's alright.' Cathy wanted to say that she thought Tansy had rather enjoyed the way it had all unfolded and she suspected he thought the same, but that would give Tansy even more of a victory than if she pretended she didn't care and it hadn't been a big revelation at all.

But the fact was, part of her didn't believe that. Not about Tansy's enjoyment of her little game, but about not being bothered. Cathy shouldn't have been bothered – Sidonie was in his past and there was no doubt he liked Cathy a lot – but why had everyone been so reluctant to tell her about Matthias's ex? Did she buy Matthias's reasons? And even if she did, why had Erica felt the need to hide it from her? Her friend had mentioned that women had let her brother down, but never that he'd been married or that he'd actually adopted his wife's child, which, in itself, said a lot about how he'd felt about her. Was he still in love with Sidonie? And if he was, where did that leave Cathy? A consolation prize when he couldn't have the woman he really wanted? Her rational thoughts told her no, and everything he said and did with her told her no too, but there was a part of her, that insecure, paranoid part, that kept asking the question.

'While we're on the subject of pasts, I should tell you something too…'

'OK,' he replied carefully.

'Nothing terrible,' Cathy said with a nervous laugh. 'At least I hope not. It's just… Jonas… the man we met at the theatre with his wife… well, Jonas is more than an old friend. In fact, we were engaged once. About five years ago, but still… does it bother you? I'm sorry I didn't say something at the time—'

'Of course it doesn't bother me. I understand why you didn't – for the same reasons I didn't mention Sidonie straight away. We've all got a past and I wouldn't have expected anything else. What matters is that we're willing to move forward.'

'I think so too,' Cathy said, relaxing into a more natural smile now, glad she'd finally said something. It felt like the last secret and now that everything was wide open and honest they could really build something worth having here. Or so she hoped.

'So we're still good?' Matthias asked, though he looked as uncertain of that right now as Cathy was.

'Yes,' she said. 'Of course we are.'

Chapter Twenty-Seven

'Cathy… I'm so sorry.'

Erica had called earlier that day to say that Matthias had told her about how Tansy had tried to stir up trouble by mentioning Sidonie. She had said, more than once, how sorry she was that she hadn't told Cathy herself, how she'd felt it was for Matthias to tell her but now realised that she'd made the wrong call about it and hoped it wouldn't affect their friendship or the way things were going with Matthias. She had also said that they'd both be having a stern word with Tansy (Matthias already had) and that Cathy really didn't have anything to worry about. Then she'd asked if Cathy wanted to meet her at Ingrid's to talk it over. Cathy had agreed, though she really didn't think there was anything to talk over, only for them to sit down with their coffees and for Erica to say more or less the same things all over again.

'Honestly,' Cathy said. 'It's alright. Matthias was going to tell me himself before Tansy phoned to get him home. She didn't do anything wrong.'

Cathy had been very careful not to draw attention to the fact that she thought Tansy had done it all on purpose because she didn't want to offend Erica. It was hard to know why they persevered with a girl who was clearly so ungrateful and so resistant to their efforts. But Cathy understood that they must love Tansy very much and that it pained them to see what she had to put up with at home, always coming second to whichever man her mum had around at the time. The one way Cathy could make sense of their dedication to Tansy was comparing it to the way she felt about caring for her mum. It had been hard, often thankless as her mum never got any better no matter what Cathy did, and in the end, she'd done it because that was what families did. Both Matthias and Erica appeared to go out of their way to help Tansy and she did nothing to thank them – she only got more demanding and didn't seem to recognise their kindness at all. Perhaps she was different when they were away from outsiders to the family, but Cathy couldn't imagine it.

There was only one thing for it. The prospect was hardly appealing, but Cathy was going to have to spend a lot more time with Tansy. If she could get to know her, gain her trust, even perhaps get her to like her a bit more, then it would make life with Matthias a lot easier. The last thing she needed was Tansy constantly trying to drive a wedge between them, because, much as Cathy didn't want to think so, one day she might just succeed, and Cathy was beginning to feel that what she might have with Matthias was worth too much to abandon when they'd only just begun.

'If it makes any difference, he hasn't been to see Beau in about a year now,' Erica said, breaking into Cathy's thoughts.

Cathy gave a small smile as she reached for her coffee and blew to cool it down. There was one burning question in all this that she hadn't asked. She was afraid to ask it but she wanted to, and she wasn't sure she'd get a completely honest reply from Matthias himself. Not because he would want to deceive her, but because he might be afraid to hurt her. Cathy wasn't sure she'd get much more honesty from Erica either – for pretty much the same reasons – but maybe there was a greater likelihood of getting to something like the truth. She braced herself and decided to go for it.

'Did Matthias leave Sidonie or was it her who ended the marriage?'

Erica shook her head sadly. 'That was one thing I didn't keep from you – all the women in his life have let him down in one way or another.'

'And that includes Sidonie?'

'Yes. He was a mess when he moved back to England.'

'So he lived in France with her?'

'They'd started out living here when they were first married, but she got restless and wanted to go home. Matthias would have done anything for her so he agreed and they spent the last couple of years in the village where she was born. I think he hated it, but he wanted to make her happy. Turns out, nothing he did made her happy.'

'Did you like her?'

'I tolerated her. She was alright, but sometimes I found her demands frustrating and I wanted to tell Matthias what a pain I thought she was but it was none of my business. Sometimes I wish I'd made it my business – I might have spared him a lot of heartache if I could have made him see what she was really like. Not that he would have listened, I expect; he was besotted.'

'Does he…?' Cathy hesitated. No, she decided, it didn't matter and it wasn't a question she was going to ask. She wasn't going to put Erica on the spot like that. Whether he still had any feelings for his ex or not, it did look to Cathy as if she was firmly out of the picture.

'So,' Cathy said instead. 'It doesn't look as if Tansy is going back home any time soon?'

'Is that wishful thinking?' Erica asked, the hint of a wry smile on her lips now.

'It might be,' Cathy admitted, smiling herself now. 'Does that make me a bad person?'

'No, I wouldn't blame you. She's a handful for us; I can't imagine how she'd be for you, especially when she…' Erica shook her head. 'I don't know. I've spoken to Michelle and she says Tansy overreacted. She says she can go home any time she likes but she's not going to beg her and she's not going to apologise because she says she's got nothing to apologise for.'

'Do you think that?'

'I don't know what went on so I'm not going to make a judgement. I know what my sister's like when she gets in with a new man, but I think Tansy often makes herself quite unpopular too. I wouldn't like to comment on what happened between her and Shane.'

'Matthias seems to think Tansy was scared of him.'

'I think sometimes Matthias misses having Beau to care for. Obviously, Beau wasn't his own son but he raised him as if he was and I think Tansy is an outlet for those paternal instincts. If he feels she's in trouble, he's there, and she takes advantage of that too. I think she plays up to him a lot more than she does me.'

'How old is Beau?'

'He'd be about twelve now, I'd say.'

'And how long is it since Matthias and Sidonie split up?'

'About two years now. He was going over to visit at first, but then Sidonie started to see another man and she asked him not to go because she said it was confusing Beau. I don't personally agree and I think she was using Beau as an excuse because she didn't want to keep having to deal with Matt's visits. I think he knows that too, deep down. But he always did do everything she asked and this was no different.'

'Do you think he feels guilty about not seeing Beau?'

'Oh God, yes. I think he'll feel guilty for as long as he lives.'

Cathy was thoughtful for a moment. 'You know you said you didn't think Tansy wanted to come back to cookery club? Do you think you could persuade her to change her mind?'

'I'm not sure,' Erica said with a vague frown. 'You'd really want her back there after everything that's happened?'

'I just feel like it's a good place for us to bond. It would be a bit obvious if I started going over and asking her to spend time with me, but I do think that we need to do that. Maybe if we knew each other better she wouldn't be against me seeing Matthias. Being at cookery club is a way to do that without her realising I'm trying to do that. Do you think it could work?'

'I'll mention it to her but I can't promise anything. What about Iris and Dora? I'm sure they won't be thrilled to see her back.'

'They'll be alright,' Cathy said, as certain as she could be that her previous threat to pull the plug on the cookery club would still be enough to keep the opinions of Iris and Dora on the matter private, if not completely in check. 'I'll have a quiet word with them.'

Erica reached for her coffee. 'Well, if you're sure…'

'No, I'm not sure at all,' Cathy said with a small smile. 'But I've got nothing else up my sleeve right now so it has to be worth a try.'

Chapter Twenty-Eight

By some miracle, Erica did persuade Tansy to come back to cookery club, and they arrived together the following Friday. Cathy beamed as she went over to greet them and Erica was her usual bright self, whereas Tansy – though not quite as closed as usual – was more cautiously reserved.

'Hello!' Cathy said. 'Got everything you need?'

'We have!' Erica held up a bulging carrier bag. 'Raring to go, aren't we, Tans?'

'I don't like carrot cake,' Tansy said.

'Yes, but Matthias loves it,' Erica replied cheerily. 'It'll be a nice surprise for him when he gets home from work, won't it?'

Erica glanced beyond her and gave a little wave to Iris, who was watching them closely as she unpacked her ingredients. Cathy had briefed Erica on a need-to-know basis about what Iris had said the last time Tansy had been there and sabotaged her bake (inadvertently or not). She wasn't planning to tell her but, considering they couldn't discount the possibility of more trouble with Tansy's return, she'd decided that she probably had to give Erica a bit of warning. Erica had nodded gravely and seemed to understand that she had to let it slide for now. She was no fool when it came to her niece.

'I'm really glad to see you here,' Cathy said, smiling warmly at Tansy, who seemed confused by the sight, which gave Cathy a private moment of amusement. If Tansy thought Cathy was going to fight fire with fire, she was in for a shock. Cathy had decided on the complete opposite tactic – the more difficult Tansy was, the nicer Cathy was going to be to her. She was going to get through to this girl if it killed her.

Almost everyone's carrot cake had turned out well. Cathy had definitely seen an improvement in the quality of the bakes at the club over the weeks, and a massive surge in confidence too. People had started to believe that they were bakers and, rather than getting fazed or upset when they found something tricky, were far more inclined to roll up their sleeves and give it a go anyway – whether it turned out to be successful or not. As a consequence, they usually did a pretty good job. Only Colin's looked a little worse for wear today but, Cathy had reassured him, that was only because he'd put his cream cheese frosting on before the cake had cooled and it had melted. She was sure it would taste just fine, even if it did look like a lump of goo.

As she started her usual tidy and clean, Erica and Tansy came to bid her goodbye.

'How did you find today?' Cathy asked. 'There was a bit more to think about with today's bake but everyone seemed to get on well.'

'Good,' Erica said. She looked at Tansy. 'Don't you think it was good today?'

'Yes,' Tansy said – it was about as close to praise as Cathy was ever going to get so she'd take it.

'In fact,' Erica said, 'Tansy wants to do some baking at Matt's house over the weekend. You get a bit bored, don't you? It's a bit too far to see your friends—'

'They're all bitches anyway,' Tansy cut in.

Cathy's smile held, despite the acid in Tansy's tone.

'I could help,' Cathy said. 'If you wanted some help, of course, I mean, if you wanted to get on with it then of course that's fine. But if you like, I could show you some new things to make. You've got natural talent – I think you'd be able to handle far more complex bakes than we do here.'

'I think that might be good,' Erica said, looking at Tansy for agreement. 'Sounds like fun. I think you're good too – better than I am.'

Tansy nodded. 'Alright,' she said. 'You could. I suppose you'd be coming to see Matt anyway.'

Cathy had been planning to see Matthias and, in fact, he'd booked a day off work to do just that, but it certainly hadn't involved spending time with Tansy. But this seemed like a good opportunity to make those inroads she'd vowed she was going to make, and she didn't think he'd mind. She hoped he'd see it as a good thing. She half wondered if it would have been this hard trying to get on with an actual daughter rather than just his moody niece. Anyone who had to go to such lengths to ingratiate themselves with the son or daughter of a new partner had her deepest sympathy.

'Great!' Cathy said. 'I'll talk to your uncle and we'll fix something up!'

Before her day with Matthias, Cathy had a day at work. Ordinarily she'd look forward to spending time with Fleur, but today she was filled with a vague impatience as she stood at the stall, hands in the front pocket of her green tabard, eyes fixed on the doorway to the market hall. They'd finished their usual morning cup of tea and cake and there had been a flurry of customers which had tailed off about half an hour ago. It was almost midday. Cathy had told Fleur to go and have her lunch first and she'd follow. Fleur often argued that she didn't need lunch and it would have been no surprise if she'd done so today. However, surprisingly, she seemed to jump at the chance.

'I'll go in ten minutes or so,' Fleur said. 'Just let it get to a respectable time – can't have my lunch when it's not even afternoon.'

'Nobody will care if you're hungry,' Cathy said absently, eyes still on the doorway.

Fleur clicked her fingers in front of Cathy's face. 'Earth to Cathy!'

Cathy turned with a grin, shaken out of her daydream. 'Sorry.'

'No prizes for guessing what you're thinking about.'

'Actually I was thinking about what I was going to bake with Tansy tomorrow,' she said.

Fleur raised her eyebrows.

'OK,' Cathy said, laughing, 'I was thinking about Matthias a little bit too. But I promise there was some baking in there.'

'Are you taking your little recipe book?'

'I suppose I'll have to; otherwise, most of it's in my head and I think Tansy will find the idea of me dictating quite random measurements and staring at the bowl for ages until I decide if it looks right quite frustrating.'

'She certainly wouldn't be doing much of it herself. Why don't you go and buy her a proper recipe book? She might like that.'

'She might,' Cathy agreed. 'I think that's a brilliant idea, actually. A token of friendship and all that. I might take mine anyway in case there are recipes she wants out of there, but I think I'll get her something that's her own for when I'm not there.'

'Is your book finished yet?' Fleur asked.

'More or less. People are still coming to me with recipes, but I suppose I'll have to have some kind of cut-off point or we'll be going at it forever.'

'You still don't fancy getting a few printed for sale on the stall?'

'I think it's too close to Christmas now.'

'We have two weeks.'

'What if they don't sell and we've got a load left?' Cathy shook her head. 'It's a lovely idea but I think I'd rather just give copies to people.'

'Like whatshername…?'

Cathy frowned.

'Oh, you know, that woman who's in charge at the church hall.'

'Iris?' Cathy smiled. 'She thinks she's in charge… actually, come to think of it, she's probably the closest thing to a manager they've got. Whatever they pay her – and I'm not sure they do pay her – it's not enough. She's always there no matter what day it is and I'm pretty sure she doesn't need to be.'

'That's dedication,' Fleur said.

'It is.'

'So she's already got a copy of your book?'

Cathy resisted the urge to frown. 'Yes… a rough one. Why do you ask?'

'Oh, no reason,' Fleur said airily. 'Do you know what…? I might have my lunch now after all. If I'm late back hang on for me – might have to run an errand or two.'

'Oh, right…' Cathy began, but she wasn't even sure that Fleur heard that much because without another word she grabbed her coat and dashed off.

Cathy arrived at Matthias's house the following day with everything she thought they might need and he wouldn't have for an afternoon of baking. He'd seemed a touch sceptical on the phone when Cathy had explained their plans and what she'd hoped it would achieve, but he was happy that she was making an effort. He was even happier that Tansy seemed to be making an effort too.

Matthias greeted Cathy at the door with a tender kiss. They both understood that it would probably be the only one of the afternoon, unless Tansy decided to make herself scarce, though Cathy thought that was very unlikely. Even if she'd wanted to go out, she wouldn't have wanted to make life easy for anyone, least of all Cathy.

'Hello,' Cathy said, breathless as he pulled away.

'Hello,' Matthias replied with a warm smile. 'Well, this is new, isn't it?'

'What?'

'I sort of feel as if you're on a date with both me and Tansy.'

'So do I,' she said with a laugh. 'Like I'm on approval and if she doesn't like me she can send me back.'

'Not on my watch she can't,' he said. 'This is as much about her making an effort as you – don't think otherwise.'

Cathy didn't believe that for a moment; Tansy – as far as Cathy could tell – had never heard of the word compromise. You either played her way or you didn't play. It was a cycle that needed to be broken and there was no way the stick method was going to work so it would have to be the carrot. That was what today was about – carrots and lots of them. Or one big one, if you really wanted to stretch the analogy.

Matthias took a bag from her and winced. 'What the hell is in here? It weighs a ton!'

She laughed. 'It's not that heavy.'

'I wouldn't have fancied carrying it on the bus. If you'd told me you were dragging so much over here I'd have insisted on picking you up.'

'I didn't know I was bringing this much; I got a bit carried away. I looked in the cupboards and it just felt as if I needed everything.'

'Well, I hope she appreciates the effort,' he said, and Cathy didn't have to ask who he meant.

'I got her this too…' Cathy opened one of her bags and showed him a glossy hardback book.

He offered a silent question.

'A present,' she said. 'A recipe book of her own. I thought she might prefer something put together by a real cook so she could bake when she feels like, here. When I'm not here, I mean.'

'You *are* a real cook!' he said with a chuckle.

'Oh, you know what I mean.'

'So that's not yours then?'

'God no!' she said, laughing. 'Mine looks nothing like this!'

He kissed her lightly. 'That's such a kind thing to do; I'll bet it cost a fortune. It's just the sort of thing I'm learning to expect from you – I think she'll love it.'

'I hope so,' Cathy said.

'Come on through,' he said, pots clanking in the bag he was carrying as he continued down the hallway. 'She's upstairs; I'll call her down.'

As Cathy unpacked her bags Tansy came in. She was wearing leggings and a slouchy sweatshirt, and her usual harsh make-up and tight ponytail were missing. With her hair tied in a loose plait over one shoulder and her face bare she looked a lot younger. Pretty, actually, Cathy thought; if she'd only drop the permanent look of confrontation she'd be prettier still.

'Hi,' Cathy said.

'Hi.' Tansy took a seat at the table and watched for a moment as Cathy got things out of her bags. 'What's all that?' she asked finally.

'Stuff I thought we might need. There are a few things I have twice at home and don't need. You could keep them here... In case you decide to do a lot more baking. I don't think your uncle has much of this.'

'I have none of it,' Matthias said, turning round from where he was filling the kettle. 'You're lucky to find a spoon and bowl for your breakfast around here.'

'Oh,' Tansy said, and although she didn't offer any thanks, Cathy thought she detected just the tiniest softening of her expression.

'I got you this, too,' Cathy continued, pulling the professional cookery book from her bag now. She pushed it across the table to Tansy, catching a smile from Matthias as she glanced up.

'What is it?' Tansy asked, making no move to pick it up.

'What does it look like?' Matthias said.

He leaned back against the worktop and folded his arms, regarding them both with a pleased look. Cathy wondered if he thought this was progress. He'd know better than her, of course, but if this was progress, it was going to be slow and painful because Tansy hardly looked thrilled with her gift.

'Thanks,' she said in a toneless voice. She twisted round to look at Matthias and caught a slip in his smile, and, perhaps for him more than anyone else, she eventually took up the book and thumbed through its pages.

'Do you like it?' Matthias asked.

'Yeah.' Tansy put the book down again. 'It's good.'

'I brought mine with me too,' Cathy said. 'It's obviously rubbish compared to that but we can look through it if you decide you'd rather do something you've tried at cookery club before. Or we can go through the new one and have a go at something in there.'

'I don't mind,' Tansy said. 'Whatever.'

'Right…' Cathy threw an uncertain look at Matthias as he stood behind Tansy. He shrugged. 'Maybe you want to look through the new one for a bit? There's no rush to start anything. I could chat to your uncle for a while.'

'What do you think we should make, Matt?' Tansy said, twisting to look at him again. 'You choose and you can eat it.'

'All of it?' he asked with a grin. 'How greedy do you think I am?'

'Well,' she said, the ghost of a genuine smile now, 'you ate all that carrot cake.'

'I did not!' he said, laughing.

'Almost all of it,' Tansy said.

'Did you like it?' Cathy asked.

'It was amazing,' he said warmly. 'Best carrot cake I've ever had.'

'Shall we make that again then?' Tansy asked with the vaguest hint of enthusiasm – nothing crazy but certainly more than Cathy had ever witnessed.

'That sounds good to me,' Cathy said.

'Shall we use your recipe?' Tansy asked.

Cathy got her own exercise book out and looked for the page. 'Will you have all these ingredients in?'

'I might have some left over from when I brought the stuff to cookery club,' Tansy said, getting up to look in the cupboards. One by one she brought the ingredients to the table as Cathy read them out.

'Maybe there's not quite enough brown sugar there,' Cathy said, looking them over when they'd finished. 'We might want a bit more dried fruit too.'

'I could go foraging,' Matthias said. 'Make a list for me – make it *very* clear because I don't know the first thing about cake ingredients and anything could come back with me. You two can make a start while I'm gone.'

The prospect of time alone with Tansy hardly filled Cathy with glee, but she realised that this was probably the best solution. Matthias had his car and he could be at the shops and back far quicker than she could walk it. Besides, the point of this visit (apart from the fact that any excuse to see Matthias was one she'd grab willingly) was for Cathy to get to know Tansy better and to get her to open up a bit. Being left alone with her could go one of two ways, but she hoped that if she handled it right, it would go the good way and not the bad.

'Tansy… would you like to check the recipe and write down what your uncle needs to get? I think your handwriting might be a lot better than mine.'

'Here… you'll need a writing pad,' Matthias put in, pulling one from the drawer and dropping it onto the table with a pen.

Cathy handed her recipe book over and Tansy began to check what they had, making notes of where there wasn't enough. Cathy smiled up at Matthias and he smiled back. The fact that Tansy hadn't complained or pulled a face was good, surely? That was progress?

When she'd finished she tore off the page and gave it to Matthias.

Cathy followed him out to the hallway and stood at the front door as he got his coat on.

'Just as if you live here,' he said, smiling down at her as she saw him out.

'Not quite,' she said, but she liked the image anyway.

He leaned down to kiss her lightly. 'I won't be long. Try not to get into a punch-up while I'm gone.'

'I've never been in a punch-up in my life and I'm not about to start now.'

'Glad to hear it – see you shortly.'

He closed the door behind him, throwing the hallway into gloom again. Cathy made her way back to the kitchen to find Tansy already weighing out the things they did have. She glanced up as Cathy came in but said nothing, turning her attention back to her task.

'So...' Cathy began, scrabbling for a conversation opener, 'how's it going staying with your uncle?'

'Alright,' Tansy said.

Cathy reached for the tea Matthias had just made for her and waited, but there was nothing more.

'Do you think you'll stay long term?'

'Don't you want me here?'

'It's none of my business,' Cathy said. 'I can't tell Matthias who to have here.'

'No, you can't. He's always got my back and I've got his.'

'I'll bet you have,' Cathy said. 'It's lucky you're so close and you have good family around you.'

Tansy glanced up with the sneer that Cathy was far more used to seeing.

'But they are,' Cathy insisted. 'I've got nobody.'

'You've got a house – Matthias told me.'

'Yes, but there's just me living in it.'

'At least that's somewhere to live. If I didn't have Matt I'd be living on the street.'

'I'm sure your mum would never allow that to happen... she's your mum, after all.'

'Have you met my mum?'

'No, but—'

'Then you don't know what she'd allow.'

Cathy was silent for a moment. She sipped at her tea while Tansy poured the flour she'd just weighed out into a bowl.

'Have you spoken to her since you left?' she asked finally. She suspected her question would be met with the usual sullen rebuff but she asked it anyway. She had to make some kind of conversation and she didn't know anything about Tansy except that she quite liked to bake and that she had just left home and moved in with Matthias. They'd pretty much covered the baking topic – at least they would throughout the afternoon. The second one seemed like a conversation more worth having.

'No,' Tansy said. 'I'm not going to either. If she can't be bothered to phone me then I'm not going to bother phoning her.'

'She hasn't even phoned you? But you've been gone for days!'

Tansy straightened up and regarded Cathy coldly. 'Look, you don't have to pretend you care. I'm not going to get in the way of you seeing my uncle so you don't have to be my friend. I don't need to get in the way…' she added, putting her head down to the recipe book again. 'It never works out.'

'One day it will,' Cathy said firmly.

'Yeah, you keep thinking that,' Tansy said. 'You'll see.'

Cathy put down her mug and folded her arms. If they were going down this road then *come on*, she thought, *bring it on. Let me know what's in store*. 'OK. Why don't they work out?'

'Well,' she said, in a tone that implied Cathy must be a bit slow if she needed Tansy to enlighten her, 'he loves Sidonie, doesn't he?'

'They're divorced.'

'So?'

'He can't go back to her.'

'Doesn't mean he doesn't want to.'

'He seems happy enough now.'

'Yeah, well, he's not going to cry to you about it, is he?'

'I can tell.'

'How?'

'I just can.'

'Whatever…'

Cathy picked up her cup again. For all her bravado, she couldn't deny that the thought of Matthias still being in love with Sidonie had rattled her. It didn't matter that it had come from Tansy and that it might well be a lie to stir up trouble – Tansy's favourite pastime, apparently – the prospect of any nugget of truth in it was unnerving. What if he did still love his ex? It would explain why none of his relationships since then had worked out.

No! Cathy gave herself a mental shake. That wasn't it at all. A man who looked at Cathy the way he looked at her couldn't still be pining after someone else. If his relationships thus far since Sidonie hadn't worked out, it was because they hadn't been the right relationships for him.

She looked down at her mug to see it was almost empty. As it so often did, the act of clutching a warm cup seemed to soothe her in times of crisis or uncertainty, and she decided quickly to make another one.

'Do you drink tea?' she asked Tansy.

'Yeah.'

'I'm going to make another one – do you want one too?'

'If you want.'

'Do you take sugar?'

'Two.'

Cathy set about making drinks, the kitchen now silent once more. She'd seen which cupboards Matthias had gone to for the cups and teabags so it wasn't too difficult to locate them again. When she was done she put Tansy's on the table next to her and sat down with her own.

'Did you do any cooking before you came to the club with Erica?' she asked.

'I cooked my tea at home most nights.'

'But not cakes?'

'Mum doesn't buy in food like that. She mostly gets frozen and stuff in tins.'

'You know, if you're resourceful you can make good cakes with things out of tins.'

'Maybe I'm not resourceful then.'

'What I mean is I could show you.'

'I'm never going home again so it doesn't matter now.'

'You're going to live here permanently?'

Tansy looked up. 'Why not?'

'Won't your mum miss you?'

'She won't care.'

'I think she might.'

'You don't know her!' Tansy snapped. 'Stop thinking you know what's going on here because you don't!'

'I want to help, that's all. If I knew more about it maybe I could.'

'So you can get me out of the way and have Matt all to yourself? You're just like her!'

'Like your mum?'

'She got what she wanted – I'm out of the way and now she has the house for just her and Shane.'

'I'm sorry,' Cathy said. 'But that's not what I want. I think your uncle would choose you over me every time.'

'He wouldn't.'

'He's doing all this for you – what does that tell you?'

Tansy pressed a peeled carrot to the grater and started to scrub viciously. Cathy watched her. Everything about her was spiky and full of resentment, and, right now, she just didn't see any chink in that armour. And even if Cathy could breach it, how on earth would she press home that advantage when she was so hopelessly out of her depth?

She was beginning to realise that this whole mission was foolish. She'd wanted a breakthrough with Tansy, a way to make her understand that not everyone was out to get her, that they could be friends, but she didn't have kids and she hadn't been a teenager herself for a very long time. She doubted she'd been your average teenager, even then. She had no clue how a girl of Tansy's age thought or felt, even the ones with stable home lives and sunny dispositions. Perhaps the best course of action here was to sit and wait for Matthias to come back and resume his role as go-between. Maybe the best outcome Cathy could hope for was a cold tolerance from the girl who looked set to be around for the foreseeable future.

Tansy reached for another carrot and, as she did, her arm caught the mug sitting next to her. The contents flew out, soaking everything. It dripped from the edges onto the floor, it soaked into Tansy's leggings, it speckled the bowl of flour and spread a steaming puddle across the wood of the table.

Cathy leapt up to find a cloth, but when she came back to start mopping, she saw that most of it had tipped over her handwritten recipe book, the very same book she'd spent hours working on – the one that had all those precious connections in its pages.

'Oh!' she cried, desperately trying to mop the worst from it, although the pages were already mushy and some of the writing fading. She glanced up at Tansy, tears pricking her eyes. 'Why don't you watch what you're doing?'

'It's just a book,' Tansy snapped.

'It's not just a book!' Cathy snapped back. 'You know how hard I've worked on this!'

'You can make another one…'

'I could make another one but it wouldn't be this one!' Cathy cried. 'That's not the point! I could make another one but that's not the point… Why don't you get it?'

'I just don't see what the big deal is.'

'No,' Cathy growled, turning back to her mopping, 'you wouldn't. You don't get the point of anything unless it's about you.'

'What?'

'You're not the only person who can be hurt, you know. You're not the only person who's had a hard life. You think you've got problems with your mum – try giving up everything to look after a mum who only goes and dies on you anyway! Try being left alone by your mum and not even being able to phone her to ask if you can come home! Try having nobody to run to!'

Tansy's face contorted into a grimace, and for one moment Cathy thought she was going to launch a counter-attack. But she just ran from the room, and a second later Cathy heard the front door slam shut.

As she began to cry she felt warm breath on her hand and looked to see Guin next to her. She'd almost forgotten he was there, he'd been so quiet in his basket. Perhaps even he'd had more sense than her – enough to know when he ought to keep his head down and stay out of the way.

Giving his head a quick fuss, she sniffed hard and turned back to her cleaning. The book was beyond salvaging now and there was no point in wasting any more time on it. Perhaps, if she dried it out, it might look better later, so she took it to a radiator and perched it on top. Then she went to the sink to look for a damp cloth and some detergent.

As she was searching she heard the front door slam again, but this time it was Matthias coming in. He appeared at the doorway of the kitchen and the smile on his face faded instantly as he saw the mess.

'What happened?' he asked, though still with humour. It wasn't until he really looked at Cathy's face that he realised something more than just a clumsy spillage had happened. 'What's happened, Cathy? Where's Tansy? Did she do this? Has she upset you?'

'It was an accident.'

'Then why are you crying? Why isn't she helping to clean up?'

'I… I lost my temper. It was silly… the tea… it went all over my recipe book and I was so annoyed, I couldn't help it.'

'So rather than take it on the chin she ran out? That's about right.'

'It's not her fault; if anything it's mine.'

'No, it's not yours. Did she even try to apologise?'

'I didn't really give her the chance.'

Matthias strode across the room to take Cathy in his arms. 'She might be my niece and I might be very fond of her, but even I know she can be a complete pain in the backside. When she comes back I'll have a word.'

Cathy pushed away from him and rubbed her eyes. 'No, I'll talk to her. I made her feel as if her situation wasn't worth anything and that isn't right. I made out like she had no right to feel sorry for herself and that wasn't right either. Her feelings are as valid as anyone else's and if they hurt then that's valid too, no matter whether you think her situation is worse or better than anyone else's.'

'She has to be told or she'll never change. Just look at your book. She knew how much that book meant to you.'

She shook her head. 'It's just a silly book. I can write it again.'

'That's not the point.'

'It's exactly the point. Eventually we all have to move beyond our past; we can't let it define us. Maybe that's what the book was for me, and maybe if I don't have it I can't keep clinging to that past.'

'It's not a bad thing to keep some connections though. Remembering and honouring the past doesn't have to mean you're trapped there.'

Cathy looked up and she felt that maybe Matthias wasn't talking about her book now. Was he talking about his connection to Sidonie and Beau?

'I feel terrible about shouting at her,' Cathy said.

'I'll go and find her – I think I might know where she's gone. There's a brownfield site up at the back of the old factory and she goes to see some horses that run loose on there. I reckon that's where she'll be now. It's only a couple of minutes away on foot, and even if she's not there I don't think she would have got much further than that anyway.'

'Horses?' Cathy blinked. 'Whose horses?'

'No idea. They just run about on there. There's a fence so they can't get out but nobody seems to know who owns them. I think maybe that's why she likes them so much – I think secretly she feels they're a bit like her.'

'If anyone should go to her, it should be me.'

'I'll bring her back and you can talk.'

'What if she says she doesn't want to come back and talk to me?' Cathy shook her head. 'If I go then she's got no choice but to talk to me.'

'She can run off again.'

'She can – that's true, but I can at least try. Let me do that at least. I'll clean up the rest of this when I get back.'

'Tansy can clean the rest of this,' he said firmly.

'So this field,' Cathy said, 'how do I find it?'

Chapter Twenty-Nine

It took only a matter of minutes to get there. Cathy's mind raced as she walked, wondering if she would find Tansy there, wondering how she'd open this conversation, whether she could say the right thing. Part of her wondered why she was bothering at all. Tansy clearly didn't want to engage, and it almost felt like the harder anyone pushed to help her, the harder she pushed back against it. Perhaps she was beyond anyone's help now. More importantly, perhaps she'd pushed it so far almost nobody wanted to help now. Cathy only knew that she wanted to try for Matthias's sake, if not for Tansy herself. It was clear that he cared for her – as Erica did – and that to be a part of his life meant Cathy would have to be a part of Tansy's in some capacity too, and it was better that they understood each other than constantly being at war.

The path that ran along the back of the old factory was overgrown but still just about visible. It had once been a railway line that had taken goods in and out of the factory compound, but the cuts of the sixties had closed it and seen the sleepers and tracks stripped away so that now only the ghost of the route remained. Most of the trees and shrubs that shrouded it from view were bare and dripping from a melted frost, but some were evergreens, leathery leaves still hanging from sturdy branches. Cathy was forced to move them out of her way every few yards, one occasionally catching at her foot where she hadn't noticed it snaking over the path. She'd seen a couple of joggers, but apart from that it was deserted. Matthias had wanted to come with her but she'd asked him to give her at least ten minutes alone with Tansy, and then he could come to find them. She had the ringer volume on her phone whacked up high so she could hear it if he needed to call her and had assured him that if she was safe anywhere in Linnetford, it was probably going to be there.

The path gave way to a clearing and almost immediately Cathy saw the field. The horses were shaggy-haired and hardy-looking, with stocky legs and broad shoulders. Some were piebald with striking black and white markings, some with the same in brown, some almost entirely black or dark bay with the odd strip of white. There were perhaps a dozen of them wandering amongst the coarse grass of the site. Cathy wondered why someone would leave them to live here – it was hardly lush or sheltered – but someone had.

A second later, Cathy made out Tansy, standing at the chain-link fence and looking in. She had her back to the path and Cathy walked as quickly and as quietly as she could. If Tansy saw her coming she might not wait around to find out what she had to say.

But as she drew closer she could see that there was a horse at the fence and Tansy had her head close to it, staring intently at something. It looked as if her hands were working at something too, though Cathy couldn't make out what. She looked to be concentrating so hard that Cathy wondered if she would have heard her coming no matter how much noise she'd made. In fact, she jumped as Cathy spoke.

'Tansy…'

Tansy spun around to face her. 'What are you doing here?'

'I came to talk to you.'

'I don't have time for that.'

Cathy frowned as Tansy turned her back and started to fiddle at the fence again. Then Cathy realised that she wasn't fiddling at the fence but at the horse's mane. Somehow, it had got caught up and it looked as if Tansy was trying to free it.

'Stupid…' she mumbled.

Cathy could see that the horse was getting restless, starting to pull away, as impatient as Tansy was.

'Need some help?' Cathy asked.

'No. I've got it. You'll scare him.'

'He's scaring me,' Cathy said. 'I'm terrified of horses. I mean, I like them but they make me nervous.'

'That's stupid.'

'It's because they're so big.'

'These aren't even big – they're like ponies. They're just doing their thing on here, not bothering anyone.'

'What's happened there?' Cathy asked, nodding at the horse, though Tansy was still concentrating on her task.

'It's stuck on the fence.'

'I can see that but how?'

'I don't know – it was like that when I got here.'

The horse blew out impatiently and stamped a hoof on the ground.

'It's getting pissed off,' she said. 'Going to pull a load of hair out.'

'I think that's the only way he'll get free,' Cathy said.

Tansy turned to her with a scowl. 'That would hurt! Would you like it if I pulled a load of your hair out?'

'No, sorry. I only meant I don't know how you're going to get it free – looks really stuck to me.'

'Must have got it caught and then made it worse wriggling about or something. I don't know how.'

There was a sharp whinny and Cathy could see that the horse was definitely getting more distressed. It was trying to pull away from the fence more violently now.

'Shhh,' Tansy whispered, a hand to the tip of its nose to calm it. 'We'll have you out in a minute.'

'Keep him still,' Cathy said, moving closer and rooting in her handbag as she did. She produced a manicure kit and took out the scissors.

'What are you doing?' Tansy asked, glancing down at them and then at Cathy.

'I'm going to cut him free.'

'I thought you were scared of them.'

'I am. Just hold him still and I'll take as little hair off as I can. If we can get the main knot then the rest might just come away.'

Tansy didn't argue; she just moved closer to shield Cathy's approach, whispering soothing words to the horse as she did.

Cathy's heart was beating wildly, her legs suddenly weak. When she'd told Tansy that she was terrified of horses she hadn't been lying. They'd always scared her – their size and their power – no matter how many times people had told her they were mostly gentle animals. And she could see why others loved them because she could appreciate they were beautiful… just as long as she was looking from a distance. It went against her every instinct to reach out now and grab the tangled mane. She worked as quickly as her trembling hands would allow, all the time the sound of the horse's heavy breaths and the smell of its hair filling her head. She could hear Tansy talking to it, gently and calmly, and a little of that calm seemed to rub off on her too because, ordinarily, she'd have run a mile from this situation but today she carried on cutting.

'There!' she gasped finally as the final strand came free. She backed away from the fence and watched as Tansy gave the horse's nose a final rub and stepped away too. The horse paused for a moment and, whether it realised it was free or not, started to walk away too as if nothing had happened.

'There's gratitude for you,' Cathy said, brushing her hair away from her face as her breathing slowed again.

To her complete and utter shock, Tansy smiled. Not the usual mocking smile, but a warm and genuine one.

'You're pathetic,' she said.

Cathy gave her a quick grin. 'Don't you think I know that? I hate that I'm so scared of something so daft.'

Tansy shrugged. 'You're scared of what you're scared of.'

'What are you scared of?'

'Lots of things.'

'Listen…' Cathy said, serious now. 'I'm sorry about before. I shouldn't have shouted at you.'

'I ruined your book.'

'It's just a book – not even a good one. I can write it again; it doesn't matter.'

'It won't all be ruined, will it?'

Cathy shook her head. 'I'm sure it won't be.'

'So you might only have to write a bit.'

'Yes.'

'I'll bet Iris will let you have her photocopy.'

'Not every recipe is in there but I think I could get most of them again.'

Tansy was silent for a moment, her gaze on the horse now further up the field. 'Has Matt seen it?'

Cathy nodded. 'Yes.'

'Was he mad?'

'I don't think so.'

'You have to be kind to him, you know.'

'I hope I am being.'

'Sidonie wasn't.'

'I heard that.'

'She didn't even care after the overdose.'

Cathy looked sharply at her now. 'Overdose?' she repeated, suddenly feeling dazed.

Tansy turned to her. 'You didn't know about that then.'

'Your uncle?'

Tansy nodded. 'We found him; me and Erica. She says it was just a cry for help, but I don't know. I think he wanted to die.'

'What happened?'

'He went to hospital and then we had to look after him. I mean, we had to make sure he didn't get lonely.'

'When was this?'

'When he first came back to England after Sidonie dumped him.'

Cathy quickly ran through what she knew. So that would have been about two years ago?

'When you say "we"… was that your mum too?'

'At first. But then she got with Shane. She said he was alright anyway and he probably wouldn't do it again. That's when he started going on dates with people, but we all knew none of them were right for him.'

'Tansy…' Cathy began slowly. 'I can't tell you if I'm right for him or not, but I can tell you that I really like him and I would never willingly hurt him. As for being lonely, I know exactly how that feels so I understand how to help him with that. I don't want to come and mess up your family; I just want to be a friend to you all.'

'All of us?' Tansy said, a note of scepticism creeping into her voice, the shadow of that old challenging expression again.

'All of you,' Cathy said. 'If you'll let me.'

Tansy nodded. She glanced up the path. 'We should go back.'

'Your uncle's probably on his way down here,' Cathy said. 'He told me he'd give me ten minutes and then follow.'

'Is he bringing Guin?'

'I don't know. I expect he will.'

'I love Guin.'

'You love all animals, don't you?'

'Yeah. Makes me angry when people are mean to them. They can't help being what they are.'

True, Cathy thought. *You could probably apply that to a lot of people too*. She felt that she might just be looking at one of them right now.

Matthias did have Guin with him and seemed pleased but very surprised to find Cathy and Tansy having a calm and civil conversation as they walked the path. He smiled warmly at them both but, as Cathy smiled back, it was tinged with sadness too. He'd hidden so much pain from her and it made her sad that he'd felt he'd had to. She could understand to some extent why he hadn't told her what the split from Sidonie had done to him but she wished he'd been able to. What did that say about their relationship? Did it mean he didn't feel as close to her as she did to him? That he didn't trust her as she did him? It was early days, of course, and it might have been no more than that, and she hoped so. Perhaps it was just too painful to talk about and Cathy understood that too, but she wanted to be there for him and she wanted him to know that. She glanced at Tansy, walking at her side. They'd finally made their breakthrough, but if she repeated what she felt Tansy had told her in confidence she might undo all that hard work.

So what did she do? Did she tell Matthias that she knew or not? Or did she wait and hope that he'd feel able to open up to her?

Chapter Thirty

Cathy and Tansy had managed to make their carrot cake. Cathy had put out the ingredients from memory and Tansy had followed her verbal instructions to combine them. Eventually the book had dried out enough to look through and, though they'd lost a few pages to the tea deluge, some of the pages were still intact and legible. While Cathy was fast learning that Tansy was never going to be the life and soul of any party, they at least had got along for the remainder of the day, and Cathy felt they'd finally reached a new understanding. Matthias had been pleased to see it and never once betrayed that he'd ever been anything but perfectly content with his life.

This morning, Cathy was back at work. For the first time she'd really noticed how bright and festive the town was as she'd walked through to the market. Every shop front was adorned with fairy lights or tinsel or fake snow or some other Christmassy motif, strings of lightbulbs stretched across every road, and Linnetford Rotary Club had their Santa out, collecting donations for various charities and entertaining the children. At the entrance to the market building a choir of local schoolchildren were gathered and singing uptempo Christmas songs in that adorably tuneless way that only school choirs did, bundled in scarves and hats and coats that still had growing room, breath rising as tiny clouds on the frosty air.

Linnetford was a small town by most comparisons, and even though they usually only managed a handful of visiting Christmas stalls, today the smallness of their number was more than made up for in the power of the aromas issuing from them. It was early, but already Cathy could smell roasting nuts and sugary pastries and the smoky scent of the charcoal as it fired up to cook bratwurst and burgers. And the town was buzzing with shoppers, the early birds eager to finish their gift lists and the more chilled finally prompted by the imminent arrival of the big day to get started on theirs.

Cathy and Fleur had a busy morning dealing with all these extra people, meaning Cathy barely had time to share recent events with Fleur. But when lunchtime came Cathy grabbed a sandwich and found a quiet spot on the stall to eat rather than go out, making the most of the odd lull to catch up with her boss.

'So where's this girl's friends?' Fleur said, leaning against the counter as she watched Cathy pull apart her sandwich to inspect the filling. 'Doesn't she have any of her own age?'

'I don't think she has many,' Cathy said. 'I don't know why.'

'Even they can see she's a miserable pain,' Fleur said.

'But at least I can see why a bit more now,' Cathy said. 'She is difficult to get along with but she's been through a lot.'

Fleur nodded. 'You don't think her being a bit nicer to you is another plot to try to split you and Matthias up?'

Cathy shrugged. 'I really couldn't say but I want to trust her this time. Besides, what she told me about him… makes me think she's only trying to protect him. They have a weird relationship when you think about it. She needs his help, and at the same time she needs him to protect her, but she feels like she ought to be protecting him too and keeping him safe. No wonder she's messed-up; there's a lot going on there.'

'And her mum sounds about as useful as a chocolate fireguard,' Fleur agreed.

'I don't know about that, but I'm convinced Tansy's not going home any time soon.'

'Which means you've got to put up with her.'

Cathy took a bite of her sandwich. 'If I want to be with him, yes.'

'Is he worth it?'

Cathy smiled.

'I'll take that soppy look as a yes,' Fleur said, laughing. 'Well, I'm glad to see you with someone who makes you look like that but I don't envy you the rest of it.'

'I'm sure it will work out eventually.'

'What are you going to do about your fella?'

'What do you mean?'

'Are you going to tell him what his niece said about him? She could be making it up – after all, this is the first anyone has said about it. Even his sister hasn't told you and she's a good friend of yours.'

'Maybe none of them liked to. It's not the sort of thing you break the ice with, is it? How do you do? And by the way, I tried to kill myself once...'

'I suppose not,' Fleur said. 'I still think it's something you should have been told once you were getting closer to him. You're sure this isn't one of Tansy's tricks?'

'If you'd seen her face, you'd have believed her. And I think she loves him too much to make something like that up. I believe it – even though Erica didn't tell me about that, she did tell me that he'd been pretty cut up after his split from his wife and that not seeing Beau hit him hard.'

'I just hope for your sake he's past all that now.'

'Me too,' Cathy admitted. 'I really like him, Fleur. I don't want to get this one wrong.'

'If it does go wrong I'm sure it wouldn't be your fault. As far as I can see you've been patient, the one to go the extra mile.'

'Hmm. It wouldn't be the first time I've done all that and still managed to cock it up,' Cathy said.

'Matthias seems like a very different proposition to your ex. Not that I know either of them well – it's just my impression.'

Cathy swallowed a chunk of chicken she'd fished out of her sandwich. 'Has Jonas…?'

'Been to the stall?' Fleur asked. 'Not since the last time. Maybe he's finally got the hint that you don't want to speak to him.'

'I haven't seen him the last few times so I don't think that's it. I wonder if he was just coming by to see me for old times' sake. You know, a trip down memory lane.'

'He ought to be keeping his eyes on the lane he's in now,' Fleur said. 'Stick to trips down today's lane.'

Cathy couldn't help but laugh lightly at the awkward analogy. 'Well,' she said, 'whatever was going on, it looks as if he's forgotten about me again.'

'Don't tell me you're upset about that? You sound almost disappointed.'

'Not at all!' Cathy said. 'Saves me a lot of stress.'

Fleur nodded. 'Only, when he first came in I thought…'

'I had feelings for him still? I suppose I might have done. It was the shock of seeing him more than anything, and I was feeling a bit low and vulnerable. I'll admit for a while I thought about what it might be like if we got back together.'

'I'm glad you weren't daft enough to do anything about it then,' Fleur said.

'It wasn't whether I was daft enough, but whether I was brave enough,' Cathy said. 'Turns out not being very brave might be a good thing after all – if I'd been a braver woman I might have.'

Fleur raised her eyebrows. 'I'd stick to the not being stupid line if I were you.'

Cathy laughed again. 'Maybe I will. Thanks for listening.'

'I haven't been listening for your benefit – there's been nothing good on telly over the last few weeks. Got to be entertained somehow.'

'Well then I'm glad to have been of service.'

Cathy popped the last of her sandwich into her mouth and screwed up the packaging.

'So your little book is ruined then?'

'Not quite but it's not looking too clever. It's funny; I was so upset at the time but it doesn't feel important now. I feel a bit silly for making such a fuss; it's only a book, after all. And not even a good one at that. Just a cheap exercise book filled with doodles.'

'It meant a lot to you so it doesn't matter that it's a cheap exercise book.'

'I'll get round to writing all those recipes down again at some point, I suppose. As long as they're in my head I can still cook those things.'

Fleur went off to the far side of the stall and reached into the space beneath the counter where they kept their belongings when they were working. A moment later she pulled out a flat package wrapped in thick paper. She brought it over and handed it to Cathy.

'So you won't be needing this, then?'

Cathy reached into the bag and pulled out a book. She stared up at Fleur. 'What's this?'

'What does it say on the cover, Dumbo?'

The outside of the book was thick glossy paper. There was a photo of a cake and it read 'Cathy's Special Recipes'. Cathy didn't know where the photo was from but it did look very much like a chocolate gateau she'd made and brought in to work a few weeks back, and the background appeared to corroborate that, as it was filled with flowers.

She opened it up and there were more photos, all of the same sort of phone quality, alongside recipes that she recognised as ones she'd written into her exercise book. Some of the photos had been taken in the same location as the one on the front; sometimes they were only slices of a cake but there was always a floral background. Cathy began to recognise each one as things she'd brought in for Fleur to try, though she had no idea when Fleur had taken the photos because Cathy hadn't seen it happen. Not all of the pictures were from the stall though, but Cathy quickly began to recognise bits of background that placed them at cookery club, and some had backgrounds that she didn't recognise at all.

Cathy flicked through, her mouth open and tears filling her eyes. 'I can't believe you got this done? How…?'

'I went to see your friend at the church. She was only too glad to get me some photos and lend me her photocopied recipes. I'm sorry not all of the ones you lost are in there but I got as many as I could – at least, all that Iris had.'

Cathy got to the last page, and on it there was a photo of her, head bent over a mixing bowl.

'Where did you get this?' she cried, laughing and crying all at the same time.

'Iris got someone to take it when you weren't looking. Do you like it?'

'Oh, Fleur, I love it! I don't know how you managed to sneak around to get all this but I absolutely love it!'

Fleur shrugged. 'I guess you must not be very observant,' she said with a light laugh.

'Obviously not,' Cathy said, laughing too through her tears.

'Happy Christmas,' Fleur said. 'Early Christmas anyway. I was going to save it until we closed up on Christmas Eve but seeing as your other one got ruined, I thought you might as well have it now.'

'How on earth can I find something as good as this for you?' Cathy said. 'It makes the perfume I was going to get look absolutely rubbish!'

'Cathy, you work for me… you're the best assistant I've ever had. I couldn't ask for a better gift than that! Besides, it's a bit amateur really. If I'd had more time and better resources we could have got some really good pictures to go inside.'

'It's lovely,' Cathy said. 'Perfect the way it is. I like that all the photos are stolen and sneaked from everywhere. Every time I look at it I'll think about how much thought and effort went into making it and I'll probably have a little cry.'

'Don't look at it too often if it's going to make you cry.'

'In the very happiest way,' Cathy said, running her hand across the glossy cover with a broad smile. 'It'll remind me of what amazing friends I have.'

Matthias's hand was wrapped around Cathy's as they walked. He'd driven her up to the forest where her mum's ashes were scattered. He'd wanted to see the place for himself as soon as Cathy had told him how beautiful and peaceful it was. Today it was more beautiful than ever, the mighty evergreens dressed in a glittering frost and the sun sending darts of light to the forest floor through gaps in the trees. The trade-off for all that fairy-tale beauty was a bitter temperature – the kind of cold that froze your lungs as you breathed it in – and the tip of Cathy's nose was numb and her cheeks were ruddy. But she was happy to endure it because Matthias was with her.

They easily found the tree where Cathy had left Fleur's holly wreath for her mum.

'It's lovely,' Matthias said.

'Fleur's so good to me; I don't deserve her.'

'Of course you do. You think she's good to you for no reason? She's good to you precisely because you deserve it.'

'I don't know about that. I know I'm lucky to work for such a great boss.'

'That's probably true,' he said. 'And worth a lot.'

Cathy fell silent for a moment as she looked at the wreath. Matthias gave her hand a quick squeeze but he didn't speak again until she did.

'How's Tansy?' she asked.

'She's good. A lot better these days… happier. I think some of that's down to you.'

'It's down to her. She just needed to settle.'

'She needed someone to understand her. She's complicated – I'll admit that. You took the time where nobody else would.'

'I wish I could say that but I don't think I did nearly enough.'

'She told me…' he hesitated. 'She told me…' he began again '… that you had a very frank discussion down by the horses.'

'Did she?'

'Yes.'

'What did she tell you?'

'I don't want you to worry about what happened when I came back from France,' he said slowly.

She looked up to see his expression was uncertain and she gave him an encouraging smile.

'I wasn't myself back then but I'm alright now; I'm happy. I'm more than happy.'

'So it's true? What she told me?'

'I don't think I really meant to do it.' He sighed. 'I don't know what I meant to do; I only know that I was glad afterwards that I hadn't managed it.'

'I'm glad too.'

'I just… I'd lost everything I knew and my life had changed so completely. It felt so empty. Erica and Malcolm were doing their best, and even Michelle came over once in a while with Tansy. Then she moved Shane in and Tansy started to come over with Erica…'

The uncertainty in his expression was now replaced with a look of pain and regret. 'I can't tell you how I wish it hadn't been those two who found me. When I think about it, I think that must have gone a long way to screw Tansy up. To see that at fifteen years old…'

He shuddered and Cathy nuzzled into him. 'It's not your fault,' she said.

'Then whose fault was it?'

'You were struggling; you needed help. I know you would never have done it to hurt anyone.'

'Except it did. It hurt everyone I cared about.'

'Maybe it's time you started to forgive yourself, just like everyone else has forgiven you. What's past is past.'

'I wish I'd been that philosophical back then,' he said with a wry smile.

'You really loved her…'

'Sidonie? Yes, I did. Beau too. I still miss him.'

'But you don't miss her?'

He bent to kiss her. 'Not anymore.'

Cathy smiled. She hoped that might have something to do with her.

Chapter Thirty-One

Cathy couldn't recall the last time her house had looked so bright and cheerful and been so full of noise. Erica had found a station on the radio playing exclusively Christmas songs during the run-up to the big day and she'd insisted they blast them out now as they worked together to decorate Cathy's living room. It was Cathy's day off and she'd been planning to do some much-needed organising of her kitchen cupboards – necessary, if a little dull even by her standards. She'd been thinking about asking Matthias over for Christmas dinner, though she hadn't yet. She'd been trying to gauge whether he'd appreciate the offer or not, or whether he'd really rather spend it with his family, which might make it awkward for him to say no even if he wanted to. She didn't want to put him in that position, but she'd decided that she'd give the place a good spring clean, just in case.

But then, just as she'd got started, Erica and Tansy had arrived to surprise her with a box of decorations Erica had picked up cheap from a shop that was closing down. A thank-you gift, Erica had said, although Cathy wasn't sure what she was being thanked for. It was a lovely thought, nonetheless, and Cathy was only too happy to let them come in and take over.

She found that they'd picked out some beautiful pieces for her too. Nothing was tacky and nothing screamed Christmas for the sake of it.

They'd chosen some baubles shaped like bright red apples and strings of gold beads and stars. There were wall decorations like woodblock carvings depicting snowy mountain scenes and a wreath of silver-sprayed holly for the door. Erica and Cathy hadn't known each other long – and Tansy and Cathy even less so – but she was touched that they'd clearly given such care and consideration to their purchases to try to make them the sorts of things they felt she might like. Cathy's taste in most things was modest and they must have completely understood this because she loved everything they'd bought for her. But then, perhaps she would have loved them anyway just because of the sentiment that had brought them into her home.

They'd just stopped to take a break and have a slice of the Christmas cake Cathy had made a few weeks before with tea made in a pot that had last been used so long ago she could barely remember where she stored it. Getting it out again and knowing that there were enough people in her house to warrant its use had been a nice feeling.

Tansy wasn't too keen on the cake, but she'd brought along a Madeira cake that she'd made using the new recipe book Cathy had bought for her, so they had a slice of that too, and Cathy said that Tansy was perhaps on her way to becoming a far better baker than she herself was. Tansy didn't smile and she didn't make a fuss over the statement, because – as Cathy was fast learning – that just wasn't Tansy's way. Even when she was happy she looked serious, but that was OK, because Cathy could tell she was flattered by the fact she immediately offered the plate around again with a cautious sort of pride on her face.

'I love those tiles,' Erica said as she looked around the kitchen. 'Bread-basket pattern… seems to be quite appropriate for someone who spends so much time baking. They're so cute and retro.'

'Retro would be the right word if I'd intended it as a style choice,' Cathy said with a smile. 'In fact, they're just plain old. They've been up since… well, I can never remember anything else being up in this kitchen. I think it's about time I changed them, though, and I was actually thinking I might redecorate after Christmas.' She swept a hand around the room. 'The blinds, the tiles, this flooring… this has all been up since my mum was here. Way before she was ill, in fact. It was just too hard to get anything much done once she got poorly.'

'Well, I like it,' Erica replied. 'But if you want any help just say so; I'll bring Malc around.'

'Will he be happy about being volunteered?' Cathy asked.

'Probably not,' Erica said.

Cathy laughed.

'I'll help,' Tansy said.

'Thanks,' Cathy replied. 'I'm sure I'll need all the help I can get. Decorating is not my strong suit.'

'It can't be that hard,' Tansy said. 'It's just painting and sticking things to walls.'

Erica and Cathy exchanged a quick grin.

'We'll let you do it all then, Tans,' Erica said.

Tansy wrinkled her nose and Erica started to laugh. 'Thought so.'

'I haven't showed you the book Fleur had made for me, did I?' Cathy said, jumping up from her seat. 'Let me go and get it!'

But as she made her way to the bookcase where she now kept Fleur's precious gift, there was a knock at the door. Another surprise? They just kept coming today. She wondered if it might be Matthias and was suddenly very aware of the dowdy sweatshirt and old jeans she was wearing. Having no time to do anything about it, she smoothed her hair down as best she could and raced to get the door.

But as she opened up she stopped and stared, the blood rushing from her face.

'I don't suppose you were expecting me,' Jonas said with a faint smile. 'I ought to be grateful you still live in the same house, or it could have been a very awkward moment just there.'

'But...'

'Could I come in?'

'Jonas...' Cathy began, gathering her senses again. 'What are you doing here?'

'I don't know,' he said. 'I just needed to see a friendly face. Can I? It's not a bad time, is it?'

And you had no other friendly faces? None of those people you've met since you were with me would do? What about your wife for a start?

'To be honest,' she said, her heart thumping as she recalled who was in her kitchen, 'it is.'

'Oh.'

'I'm not sure you ought to be here at all... What if your wife found out?'

'I won't keep you long.'

'You really can't come in,' Cathy said.

Despite meaning what she said, her heart went out to him. He looked deeply troubled and she still had enough feelings for him to want to help. In reality, no matter what past they'd had and how they'd split, she probably would always have helped.

'Oh... I'm sorry, I thought...'

'Hang on. I'll get my coat; we can walk and talk, but I can't be out long.'

He nodded. Cathy ran to the kitchen.

'I'm sorry...' she said, aware that she was about to arouse unwanted suspicion and not really sure how she was going to explain it all when she got back, 'I've got to go out for a few minutes.'

'Is everything alright?' Erica asked.

'Yes, yes… I just need to help someone out.'

'Is it something we can help with too?'

'No…' Cathy looked from one to the other and could see already Tansy narrowing her eyes. It probably did sound dodgy and she had half a mind to go back and send Jonas away. But whatever had brought him here had to be serious and she didn't think he'd give up so easily. Not only that, but in the back of her mind she still recalled how Matthias had needed help when he'd been at his lowest, and if help hadn't been there for him what terrible consequences could have arisen from that. Even though she didn't know what was wrong with Jonas, she couldn't bear to think that he might be at that place now and that a few minutes of her time might have saved him. 'I'm sorry… I'll explain it when I get back. Just… help yourself to anything you want for now.'

Without waiting to hear anyone's response she ran to the hall to grab her heaviest coat from the peg and hauled it around her shoulders. When she got back to the doorstep, Jonas was already on the pavement, pacing in little circles as he waited for her. He was about as agitated as she'd ever seen him, and that included the night they'd split up.

'I didn't know where else to go,' he said as they began to walk. The morning was frosty and their breath rose in plumes in the air.

'What's happened?'

'I've…' He turned to her and took a breath. 'I've left Eleanor.'

Cathy's mouth fell open. 'What?' she squeaked once she'd collected herself enough to reply. 'Why? And why come here to tell me?'

'I don't even know,' he said. 'It just stopped feeling right. And I'm here to tell you because…' He paused. 'Because I felt you were the only person who'd understand.'

Cathy narrowed her eyes. She didn't buy it for a minute. Maybe the reasons why he'd left Eleanor were sincere, but the rest of it… Would it sound arrogant to assume that it had anything to do with her? Did it just sound arrogant – was it actually arrogant and perhaps very misguided?

'But I thought you were happy. All those flowers you were buying, the time I saw you at the theatre…'

'We looked OK, didn't we? That's what everyone will say when they find out. But we haven't been OK. We've been arguing non-stop since we came back from Scotland…'

'Ah. And this is what all the flowers were about? Trying to make up for every argument? Was Eleanor trying as hard as you to make up?'

'She had nothing to make up…' He sighed. 'It was… I don't even know who is to blame anymore.'

'So what started all this?'

'She didn't want to leave Scotland and I kept pushing. In the end she came back to please me, but she hasn't been happy since we got here. I feel like that's where all the arguments started.'

'Then why not go back to Scotland? Wouldn't that solve everything?'

'I don't want to.'

Cathy stared at him. 'Not even if it would save your marriage?'

He shook his head. 'It sounds simple enough, doesn't it? But I'm not sure I even want to save it anymore – that's the problem.'

Cathy nodded and fell to silent thought. Jonas had never fought to save his relationship with her either and she had to have some sympathy for Eleanor, who was now set to go through the same thing. It appeared to be a pattern with him. If he was going to do this to every good relationship he had then she had to feel sorry for him too because he would end up a very lonely man.

After a few seconds he broke into her thoughts. 'I'm a bad person, aren't I? That's what you think? I'm not a nice guy…'

'I didn't say that.'

'You didn't need to.'

Cathy shook her head, trying to shake a little impatience with him. 'I don't see why you should worry about what I think. Surely the person you should be worrying about is Eleanor. When did all this happen? When did you tell her you wanted to leave her?'

'This morning. We woke up, got breakfast, got ready for work and suddenly, I don't know, I just felt as if I had to say something.'

'Where is she now?'

'At home.'

'Jonas, what's brought this on? You don't just decide something like this one morning when you're getting ready for work.'

'I know, but like I said, it hasn't felt right for a while now.'

'You talked it through with Eleanor at some point before you dropped this on her? I mean, you'd both be very aware of the increased arguments but have you actually said to her that you felt as if you wanted to leave?'

He fell silent.

'Oh God, Jonas,' she said. 'Why would you do this? She must be devastated right now. You should be with her sorting it out, not here with me.'

'I know. But I don't know how to sort it out and I felt like you were the one person who'd understand. Everyone else is too close to me or to Eleanor.'

'What made you think I'd understand you?'

'Because you always did. You always knew how to read me and you always knew what to say.'

Cathy frowned. That wasn't necessarily true. If it had been as simple as he made it sound then he might have been married to her now, not poor Eleanor. Although, today, for the first time, she was beginning to see that might not have been a good thing for her. Who was to say this wasn't how it would have ended between them if they'd been married – that one day he wouldn't have woken up just like he had today and decided it was over?

'Is this why you came home from Scotland? Did you know this was likely to happen?'

'I don't know.'

'Seems to me there's a lot you don't know,' Cathy said. 'Maybe you ought to work some of it out before you let this situation get any further. Could you go and talk to Eleanor now? I think it would help.'

'I'm not sure it would.'

'There you go again,' Cathy said with a tight smile. 'Another thing you don't know. Is there anything you do know?'

'I know that since I first saw you on the flower stall I haven't stopped thinking about you.'

Cathy froze. 'Is that why you kept coming in?'

'Didn't you realise?'

'Of course I didn't! Why would I think that? You're married!'

'You didn't suspect at all?'

'No!' Cathy cried. 'Even if I'd still had feelings for you I'd never have hoped for something like that because I have too much respect for the fact that you're married to someone else.'

'So you don't have feelings for me now?'

'Jonas… I'm seeing someone. You met him at the theatre!'

'You met Eleanor at the theatre; that doesn't mean anything.'

'It might not mean anything to you but it does to me!'

'Right… I'm sorry. I can see now I shouldn't have come. I'd thought… I guess I read the signs wrong…'

'No, you shouldn't have come if your plan was to get me back. I don't know what kind of signs I gave you but they were definitely accidental. And if I did, I'm sorry for them, Jonas.'

'This wasn't the plan – you have to believe me on that much at least. I didn't mean for any of this to happen.'

'But you did – you said you'd been thinking about ending your marriage for a while so you did.'

'I didn't mean to drag you into it.'

Cathy sighed. 'You can consider me well and truly dragged in now. You have to understand that there's no future for you and me, but I do care. What are you going to do?'

'What can I do? I suppose I'll find somewhere to live and get used to life as a single man again.'

'Don't say it in that tone…'

'What tone?'

'You know the one – the one that makes me feel guilty and sorry for you and like it's somehow my fault you're going to be living alone. We both know it used to work on me before, but it won't now.'

'I'm sorry – I didn't mean to.'

'*And* you're still doing it…'

'Sorry,' he said again.

There was a beat of silence. Cathy began to walk and he fell into step beside her.

'Tell me honestly,' he said after a moment. 'Did you feel anything when we bumped into each other again after all those years?'

'Of course I did – I'm not a robot.'

'But that feeling… it couldn't be more? You couldn't see us together again?'

Cathy paused. Perhaps at first she could have. When she'd been lonely and her life had seemed empty. But that was before Matthias, and despite the problems they currently faced, she understood now that the way she felt about him was different from anything she felt for Jonas, from anything she'd *ever* felt for Jonas. She'd loved Jonas once – she'd loved him deeply – but it had been a different kind of love. It had never really felt solid and the way it had ended had proved that to her; she saw it now more clearly than ever. It was too early to say for certain with Matthias where their future lay, but she could say already that she saw one and that it looked like something she might be able to depend on. When she thought about him, she didn't care that there were obstacles; she was willing to tackle them. If it had been Matthias instead of Jonas in her life while her mum was still alive and taking so much of Cathy's time, Cathy felt that maybe their love would have survived where her relationship with Jonas hadn't, and that was the difference.

'No,' she said. 'I'm sorry but I couldn't. Don't you remember how we broke up? Don't you feel any responsibility for any of it? Because if you do, how can you possibly come to me now with that knowledge and expect us to just pick up from where we left off like nothing happened?'

'I wouldn't expect that but… we had something good, didn't we?'

Cathy paused. Something that sounded sharper than she perhaps felt he deserved was going to come out of her mouth, but she couldn't stop it. And maybe it wasn't a bad thing that she said it. 'It was good for you as long as nobody got in the way.'

'What does that mean?'

'If you don't know then I'm not going to explain it. Jonas, you're a lovely guy but sometimes I think you find it hard to understand the world from anyone else's perspective. The world is good for everyone when it's good for you, and there are only problems for anyone if they're your problems. I'm sorry, but someone has to tell you this and you have to understand it, because if you don't you'll never make any relationship work.'

He stared at her. 'Wow… I had no idea you felt like this. You felt like this when we were together?'

'If I'd said it to you then would it have made a difference? Mum was always the problem for you when we were together – as far as you were concerned it was the only problem.'

'You're saying I was the problem?'

'You were more a part of it than either of us realised at the time.'

'And you were blameless?'

'Of course not; that's not what I'm saying. We both have to take some responsibility, but for a long time you made me believe that I was the only one who could have saved what we had and that I chose my mum over you. I didn't. I never chose her over you – you only let yourself believe that so you wouldn't have to face up to the reality that sometimes life is about more than what you want.'

'That's really how you feel?'

Cathy nodded.

'I can't believe you're telling me this now! I come to you because I need help and you give me this!'

'I don't know what you expected me to give you! Did you really think I'd instantly fall in love with you again and we'd run off into the sunset? You have a wife!'

'Then I'm sorry I came. I came because I thought you could help, not so you could list all the things that are wrong with me.'

'That's not what I've done at all. Jonas... there are many things that are wonderful about you too and many things I'll remember fondly. I just don't want you to view what we had through rose-tinted glasses because, for all the good things that happened, there was a reason we broke up. You might think that reason has gone with the death of my mum, but it hasn't, because she never was the reason. The reason we broke up was us, and no matter how we might want to, we can't blame anyone else. I'm trying to make you understand this because I care about you, not to hurt you and not because I want to punish you for our past.'

'Right... If that's the way you feel I'll leave.'

Cathy didn't argue because what was the point in giving him anything to latch on to? Any kind of hope would be a false one – better to let him see the grim reality rather than a rosy, misleading lie. She'd finally found the courage to say the things she felt he needed to hear, things that she ultimately thought would help him, and it was better for him to take those away with him and try to fix his marriage. She hoped he could because, despite all their past problems, she still cared for his welfare.

'Will you be alright?' she asked.

'I don't know...' he began, then he paused. 'I'm doing it again, aren't I?'

'A bit. You want to know what I think?'

'I suppose you're going to tell me anyway.'

Cathy gave a small smile. 'I think you need to go and talk to Eleanor before you do anything else. Accept that she deserves a little effort, because I feel as if that's one thing she hasn't had from you. Forgive me for saying this, but I feel like maybe you were having problems and you saw me as a handy escape route? Somewhere to run to? I think you made more of the feelings you had seeing me again than was really true.'

'I could never do that. I never stopped caring for you, and seeing you again after all these years reminded me of all the things I loved about you. But I shouldn't have assumed you'd feel the same, and I'm sorry for that.'

Cathy shook her head. She suspected he was wrong and confused about his current feelings for her and in time she thought he'd see that. She wasn't what he needed right now at all.

'I know I should,' he added, 'but I can't go home now.'

'Why not?'

'My head's a mess and I'd say the wrong thing.'

'You don't know until you try. And why do you assume you get to do all the talking? Isn't it worth going just to hear Eleanor out? You might not want to go home, but you owe it to her to give her a say too. Think about her for a minute; she might really need you to be there right now. You've left her this morning with barely a chance to understand what's gone wrong. Imagine how she's feeling right now after your bombshell. Go home, Jonas – go and talk to her. If you can't work it out, at least help her understand.'

'I don't know how to do that. With you, it might have been simpler, but Eleanor doesn't understand me like you used to.'

'Stop it, Jonas. Stop romanticising our past. It wasn't the way you remember it.'

'Isn't that the way you remember it?'

'No. I remember it being messy and confusing. Sometimes it was good and sometimes it was horrible. If anything tells you the truth about what it was, it has to be the way it ended. Neither of us even tried to save it. That's the truth about our past – it wasn't worth saving. You say it was wonderful, but you moved on without a single look back. If it was so great, why marry someone else and disappear from my life for five years?'

'I thought you didn't want me.'

'You didn't even take the time to check.'

'You were busy with your mum—'

'Don't drag my mum into this again.' Cathy sighed. 'I can't believe we keep having this conversation. It was five years ago and it should be ancient history. Why are you really here?'

'I've told you.'

'That's not it. You need to figure out what's really going on and you need to talk to Eleanor. Promise me you'll do that.'

'I can't.'

'Then I'm sorry, Jonas, but that's all I have. Please don't come here again. I've moved on and I have a life that I love – even if you can't fix your own please don't ruin that for me.'

He stared mournfully at her. But then he nodded. 'If that's what you want.'

'In time you'll come to realise it's best for both of us.'

When Jonas left her he'd agreed to go back and see Eleanor. Cathy felt drained somehow as she made her way back to her house. It wasn't as easy as she'd made out to turn him away like that and she'd no doubt fret and worry about him for weeks to come. She didn't know where he lived and she didn't still have a phone number for him, so unless he sought her out as he had done today, she might not get to hear for a long time how he was getting on or if he'd fixed the problems in his marriage. But she felt certain that fixing his marriage was what he needed to do. If she'd been the cause of its undoing in any way then she was truly sorry for that, but she couldn't take the blame and, for once, she wasn't going to allow herself to.

As she let herself back in she could hear Erica and Tansy chatting in the kitchen. It reminded her forcefully of all the reasons she'd sent Jonas home and instantly her mood lightened.

'All sorted?' Erica asked cheerily.

'Yes,' Cathy said. 'I hope so.'

Tansy was less easily put off. 'Who was it?'

'Just an old friend.' Cathy sat at the table and put a hand to the teapot to check if it was still warm.

'What kind of old friend?' Tansy asked, ignoring Erica's warning look.

'Just someone I used to know. He was having a bit of trouble… wanted some advice.'

'Did he used to be your boyfriend?'

Cathy looked up. She'd felt the need to hide this but perhaps being totally straight was the best way forward. What they'd make of it and what they might tell Matthias was another matter, but she'd done nothing wrong here. She was tired of feeling guilty for everything, especially things that were out of her control.

'Yes,' she said. 'But it's years since we were together.'

Erica's mouth dropped open as she slotted the pieces together.

'Don't worry,' Cathy said, 'he won't be back.'

'What did he want?' Erica asked.

'I don't think even he knew the answer to that,' Cathy replied.

But *she* knew what *she* wanted, and Cathy wasn't about to jeopardise that for anything.

Chapter Thirty-Two

It was the last cookery club before Christmas. Cathy was pleased to see a full turnout and a lot of excitement. Iris and Dora were sporting reindeer ears; Beth, Alicia and Lindsey had on matching jumpers that were covered in little flashing fairy lights; Colin had donned a Santa hat; Myrtle was wearing a halo; and Tansy and Erica had new Christmas aprons (though Tansy looked far from happy wearing hers). Cathy was wearing a jumper that Matthias had bought for her, half in jest, but that she loved. It had a Christmas tree covered in real baubles on it so that she clanked and jangled every time she moved.

'OK, folks,' she announced to the room, 'we probably ought to get started, otherwise we're going to run out of time.'

A cacophony followed as everyone got out spoons and bowls and measuring scales. Cathy was baking herself today and she did the same. She'd set a fairly simple challenge of Christmas-themed gingerbread and she was damned if she was going to miss out on her own batch of that. She hummed along to the radio that Erica had insisted on bringing in, still tuned to the station that played constant Christmas songs as she spooned syrup into a pan. She was going to miss her little gang of chefs over Christmas, but for the first time in a long time she was looking forward to the day anyway. Matthias hadn't waited for her to ask about Christmas lunch; he'd invited her to join him and Tansy. He wasn't much of a cook, he'd said, but he'd give it a bash. Cathy was only too happy to help (or take over) and she was sure that Tansy wouldn't want to be left out. It promised to be a pleasant day and, who knew, maybe she and Matthias would even manage to snatch a few minutes alone if Tansy could take a subtle hint or two.

She licked a blob of syrup from her finger and glanced up to see Erica smile across the room at her. Cathy smiled back. Erica, of course, was going to be spending Christmas Day with Malcolm at his parents' house. They were taking Erica's mum along too, so it meant that she wouldn't get to see Matthias, Cathy or Tansy that day, but they had arranged to meet up on Boxing Day instead.

Not long after they'd made a very rowdy start the vicar came in wearing his Christmas jumper and Iris very nearly passed out with excitement.

'Oh, that's lovely!' she squeaked, racing over to him. 'It's the nativity scene! Wherever did you get it?'

He grinned. 'Lovely Gladys Palmer knitted it – isn't she clever?'

Iris suddenly didn't seem quite so enthusiastic. Perhaps Gladys Palmer was a rival, or perhaps Iris was jealous that he was so pleased with something somebody other than her had done for him.

'Oh,' she said, visibly deflating. 'Yes, it's very good.'

'Oh, Gladys is good!' Dora called over with a wicked grin, never one to pass up on an opportunity to wind Iris up. 'What she can't do with a set of knitting needles isn't worth a postage stamp.'

'I wouldn't know,' Iris said. 'She doesn't come to church all that often.'

'She comes when she can,' the vicar said cheerily. 'I can't ask for more than that.'

'I come every week,' Iris said, puffing up, 'rain or shine!'

'And I'm grateful for it,' the vicar said, restoring some of Iris's spring as her look of annoyance transformed back into a smile. 'I'd think the world had come to an end if you weren't there on a Sunday.'

He had a young woman with him who hadn't spoken yet and Cathy wondered if he was going to introduce her because nobody else seemed to know who she was either, though there had been plenty of curious appraisals. Cathy didn't recognise her and supposed she must be someone who worked for the church.

'So have you finally come to join us?' Cathy asked brightly. 'We're making gingerbread today if you're interested.'

'I wish I could but it's a flying visit,' he said. 'I do actually need to have a quick word with you, though.'

He gestured to a quieter corner away from the rest of the group. Curious eyes followed as Cathy joined him.

'Oh...' Cathy wiped her hands on her apron. 'What can I do for you?'

He gestured to the young woman who'd come in with him. 'I'd like you to meet Lydia.'

Lydia stepped forward and extended her hand for Cathy to shake. 'It's lovely to meet you; Simon has told me so much about you.'

'Hello,' Cathy said, feeling slightly bemused, not least because she'd got so used to calling the vicar *the vicar* that the notion of him having an actual real name was somewhat of a surprise.

'I hope you don't mind,' the vicar said, 'but I thought I'd bring Lydia along to meet you because she's interested in your recipe book.'

'You'd like a copy?' Cathy began. 'I don't have the full one – that's at home – but I can do some photocopies of the ones you want to try...'

'I actually work for a publisher called Modern Traditions. We specialise in homey guides – things like sewing and crafts and cookery. How to paint or make pots or stencil... that sort of thing.'

'We worked together once before on an origami book that raised money for charity,' the vicar said. 'She also happens to be my cousin…'

Cathy smiled but still didn't really understand how any of this concerned her.

'Lydia had mentioned to me a few months ago she was looking for something a bit newer and fresher, something around cooking. She's visiting for Christmas and I thought, why not bring her along to meet you?'

'Me?' Cathy blinked, more confused than ever.

'I think your recipe collection might be just what I'm looking for,' Lydia said. 'Right now a book of wholesome, family-friendly and accessible cooking is what everyone is after – the right one is harder to find than you might imagine. Simon said he thought you might be the perfect face to front it too, and, having met you, I'm already fairly confident he's right.'

Cathy looked from one to the other, speechless. Was she hearing all this right or had someone laced her tea with a good glug of cooking sherry?

'I don't understand…'

'I'd like to take a look at your book, if I may, with a view to perhaps publishing it. I'd have to discuss it with colleagues at our next editorial meeting and that would be after Christmas now so there are no guarantees, of course.'

'I wouldn't expect any,' Cathy said, still not quite sure if she was dreaming or not. Things like this didn't happen to people like her. They didn't happen like this to anyone, surely? Publishers didn't just pitch up and say, hey, we like the sound of your book, can we publish it?

'I don't know anything about your company, I'm afraid,' she added, wondering if that sounded rude. She didn't mean it to be, but that old habit of talking rubbish on first meetings was one that would always be hard to shake.

'Here's my card,' Lydia said. 'The web address is there if you want to take a look at what we do. My email is on there too. When you're ready, feel free to send your book across.'

'I only have a printed copy,' Cathy said.

'How about you scan the pages and send them?' the vicar cut in. He looked at Lydia. 'Would that work for you?'

'I'd prefer a Word copy, but I suppose as an initial submission I could work with it. If we think it has potential I'd need to get something in a more appropriate format.'

'I could do that!' Cathy blurted out. She had no idea if she could or not but was fired by a sudden rush of excitement. Even if she couldn't, she was sure she'd find a way to get Lydia what she needed.

'Great,' Lydia said. 'It was lovely meeting you, Cathy. We'll let you get back to your class.'

'Thank you,' Cathy said.

The vicar gave her a good-natured wink before he turned to follow Lydia out. 'Thank you!' she mouthed to him. But then she called out: 'Merry Christmas!'

Lydia turned with a smile. 'Merry Christmas, Cathy. I very much hope to be working with you in the new year.'

'I still can't believe you don't like turkey!'

Cathy giggled as Matthias made an apologetic face. They were all wearing the obligatory rubbish paper crowns they'd pulled out of crackers and their best clothes. In front of Matthias was a plate piled with the usual crisp roast potatoes, honey-roasted carrots and parsnips, stuffing, pigs in blankets and Brussels sprouts. But instead of turkey he had two fat sausages.

'I'm afraid I might have to reconsider this relationship,' she added. 'I don't know if I can be with a man who doesn't like turkey – it's a bit suspect.'

'I happen to like sausages. What's wrong with sausages?'

Cathy grinned. 'Nothing on any other day. But sausages for Christmas dinner… that's just plain weird.' She turned to Tansy. 'You've done an amazing job on this turkey, by the way.'

She took a mouthful of wine. Her cheeks were rosy and her mouthfuls of wine were getting larger and less dainty the tipsier she got. Right now, she was at peak tipsy and heading towards full-blown sloshed. She hadn't been this drunk in a long time but she was rather enjoying it. She hadn't felt this relaxed in a long time either. She'd arrived early to share gifts and help prepare lunch and it had been reserved at first – happy and pleasant but a little awkward from newness – but it hadn't taken long to settle. They were soon getting on so well that Cathy felt as if she completely belonged.

Even the ever-dour Tansy managed to crack the odd smile, though, as was her way, she was never less than quite serious. The night before she'd pored over an online recipe instructing how to cook the perfect turkey and had made it clear that day it was going to be her job. Cathy would ordinarily have been longing to do it, but she realised that she was going to have to give Tansy this. Every little action, every little show of trust and respect brought Tansy out of her armoured shell that little bit further and it was wonderful to see. She'd spoken to her mother that morning on the phone, and Cathy had been afraid that it would set her back to the rude and insulting Tansy she'd first known, but thankfully her fears had quickly been dispelled.

'Sausages and pigs in blankets... Sausages and sausages,' Tansy agreed. 'Poor pigs.'

'At least I didn't make you cook some different meat,' Matthias said.

'What do you think sausage is?' Tansy's eyebrows drew together as she reached for her own wine.

'Well, at least I didn't make you cook something that would take a long time.'

'And who said you could make us cook anything?' Cathy grinned at Tansy. 'We're women so we do the cooking?'

'No, you do the cooking because my food wouldn't be edible,' Matthias said.

'We'll have to teach you, won't we, Tansy?'

Tansy nodded.

'I'm afraid you might find I'm unteachable.'

'Nobody is unteachable,' Cathy told him again. 'Everyone can cook if they put their mind to it – there's no great mystery to it.'

'I'll hold you to that.'

'Some people can cook better than others,' Tansy said. 'Iris is rubbish.'

Cathy laughed. 'Please don't ever let Iris hear you say that.'

'She thinks she's brilliant at everything but she's not.'

'She means well,' Cathy said. 'And she has been very kind to me so I'm not going to comment on that at all. She lives on her own, don't forget, and she's an old lady now. I think if it stops her from getting lonely and gets her out of the house, then let her get involved in everything St Cuthbert's has to offer. Believe me, I know what it's like to be lonely and feel as if there's no place for you in the world; I wouldn't wish that on anyone.'

'I hate to think of you feeling like that,' Matthias said.

Cathy turned to him, a smile full of affection and gratitude. 'But I don't anymore.'

Tansy rolled her eyes. 'If you're going to do that, I'll go and eat my lunch in another room, shall I?'

'Sorry…' Cathy said, blushing.

'One day this will happen to you and then you'll understand,' Matthias said, chuckling.

'What? One day I'll turn into an idiot?' Tansy fired back.

'No, you've already done that,' he returned.

Tansy pulled a face and he roared with laughter. 'Round one to me!'

'Believe what you like, loser,' Tansy replied, but she was stifling a grin just the same.

Cathy chewed on a mouthful of turkey. 'Tansy, this might be about the best turkey I've ever had.'

'Really?' Tansy looked doubtful.

'Really. You should have more confidence in your abilities – you're a natural cook.'

'I thought you said anyone could cook,' Matthias said.

'Yes, anyone can cook, but it's like art or music. Anyone can learn it, but some people have a gift that lifts them above everyone else.'

'You think I have a gift?' Tansy asked.

Cathy smiled. 'I do… Tansy… you know how you told me you hate your college course…?'

'I don't see the point in it. What am I going to do with A levels when I don't want to go to university?'

'I don't know about that, but what if you did something you enjoy? Would they let you swap onto a different course?'

'Like what?'

'Like catering. You like cooking and it might lead to a job you like. At least it might feel like less of a waste of time.'

'That's a brilliant idea!' Matthias said, beaming at them both. 'What do you reckon, Tans?'

Tansy was thoughtful for a minute. 'I always thought the thickos did catering.'

'I think perhaps that's a bit unkind,' Cathy said gently. 'Look at it objectively and forget your preconceptions for a moment. What job could you see yourself enjoying? What would you be happy to go in and do, day after day?'

'I don't know,' Tansy said, and Cathy sensed a little impatience in her tone now. Perhaps this was the wrong day to talk about this and perhaps Cathy was the wrong person after all. She and Tansy were getting along better but she couldn't expect miracles and she couldn't expect a transformation of their relationship overnight.

'You should give it some thought,' Matthias said. 'I think it might suit you a lot better than what you're doing now. You said yourself that you don't see the point in your A levels. If you don't know what you're going to do with them, is it worth doing them at all?'

'It's always worth doing these things,' Cathy said. 'If they make you happy and get you to where you want to be. That's the real question you've got to ask yourself... Anyway...' She picked up her wine again. 'That's probably a conversation for another day. One when we've had less wine.'

'I'll think about it,' Tansy said, looking from one to the other. 'I'd have to talk to Mum too.'

Cathy was surprised to hear that Tansy would want to discuss anything with her mum after all she'd said about her, but maybe it was a good thing. Maybe she was getting to a place with Michelle where they could get along, even if they weren't living together. She half wondered if Tansy might go back to her mum's house in the new year, though Matthias had made it clear that Tansy was going to be with him until she finished college at least. This hadn't been as much of a problem as Cathy might have thought, considering they could at least get moments of privacy at her house if they couldn't at his, and so she hadn't made much of a comment on this. Matthias still wasn't completely convinced that it was good for Tansy to be in the same house as Michelle's boyfriend, Shane. Tansy had come clean and admitted that she'd been as much to blame for the animosity as him and that he'd never threatened her with violence of any kind, but their relationship was still far from healthy and Matthias was of the opinion that there was no need to subject her to that at close quarters when there was a perfectly good alternative available.

'I wonder where we'll all be if we're sitting around this table again this time next year,' Cathy said.

'I should hope we will be,' Matthias said. 'Got plans elsewhere, have you?'

'I'll be here if you are,' Cathy said.

'Ugh!' Tansy cut in. 'Seriously, if you two are going to do this all day…'

'I'm afraid you might have to get used to it,' Matthias said. 'We've had a lot to drink.'

'True,' Cathy said.

'God, then I'll have to go to Erica's.'

'You can't,' Matthias said. 'I've had too much wine to drive you over there.'

'I'll walk.'

'Good luck with that.'

Cathy giggled. Tansy looked like she wanted to bang their heads together as if they were a couple of naughty kids.

'You're right,' Cathy said as she managed to stop laughing. 'We're being very silly.'

Tansy looked sceptical for a moment. But when Matthias offered no comeback, she seemed satisfied and cut into a roast potato. Cathy sent a steamy glance Matthias's way. They did need to behave today but, the way she felt about him right now, that was going to be very hard.

Epilogue

A year to the day had passed since that first Christmas lunch at Matthias's house. Cathy had remarked more than once on how quickly it had flown by and how she couldn't believe they were all sitting around the same table once again. But in that fleeting year, so much had changed in her life that she barely recognised herself as the same person who had laughed at Matthias's lowly Christmas sausages. They'd all changed: Matthias, Tansy, the folks at the cookery club. For a start, the members of the cookery club were all minor celebrities. At least, most of them felt like it, and it had done wonders for their confidence.

On the shelf in Matthias's living room, Cathy's cookbook took pride of place. Not the old exercise book, still tea-stained and largely illegible, nor the copy Fleur had given to Cathy last year, filled with amateur photos of cakes taken on phones and Comic Sans typeface – they were two of Cathy's most treasured possessions and were tucked away in a chest at her house. No, the cookbook on the shelf at Matthias's house was one of his most treasured possessions, because he loved completely the woman who'd written it.

Inside, the typeface was crisp and classy. Cathy had no idea what this one was called but it looked good. The pages were adorned with high-resolution photos of her creations (she suspected they'd been tampered with by the photographer to make them look better after she'd presented them but had let it slide) and photos of members of the cookery club hard at work in the kitchens of St Cuthbert's. They all looked as if they were having the time of their lives – the images of them frowning at their mixing bowl or each other, or looking less than delighted with their lives had been quickly deleted from the camera roll of the professional photographer who had come to capture the essence of what they and the cookery book were about. It was about community and friendship, about people coming together to make their lives better, to enrich their own and by doing so enrich each other's. And on the final page was a huge photo of them all together as a group, Cathy at the front with her hands tucked into the pocket of her apron and a beaming, welcoming smile on her face. It said, come on in everyone; you can all cook with us.

'How much money do you think the book has raised for the vicar's charities so far?' Matthias asked as he poured wine into Cathy's glass.

'I haven't had the exact figures yet,' Cathy said. 'They're done quarterly and the book only came out in October. I hope it's going to be a decent amount.'

'I think any amount is amazing. Most people would have taken the royalties for themselves.'

'Yes, but it was the vicar who made it all happen really. It was the least I could do, and I'm glad to be able to help some good causes. Besides, if the YouTube channel keeps on gaining subscribers at the rate it's doing right now I'll be able to live off the revenue coming from that quite comfortably. Not that I'd ever leave Fleur, of course. I still can't believe people want to watch me cook.'

'Neither can I,' Tansy said.

Cathy smiled at her. 'I can always rely on you to keep my feet on the ground.'

'Someone's got to do it,' she said. 'Don't want you getting all famous and big-headed.'

'I doubt a few YouTube followers will make me famous,' Cathy said.

'It makes some people famous,' Tansy replied.

'Youngsters maybe. I haven't been one of those for a long time.'

'Loads of people on my catering course have watched you.'

Cathy looked up from her drink. 'They have?'

'Yeah. They know I know you, see?'

'I bet they're having a right laugh too,' Cathy said with a wry smile.

'No, they like you.'

'They're going to say that to you, aren't they?'

'Some of them have the recipe book too. I hate that photo of me, though; I wish you hadn't said they could use it.'

'It's a great photo of you,' Matthias said.

'It's alright for you,' Tansy replied, 'you don't have to be in a book for the whole world to see.'

'I would have if someone had asked me.'

'You'd have been labelled as the only man in the world who's completely unteachable when it comes to baking,' Cathy said. 'You'd have come with a health warning.'

He grinned. 'I did try to tell you.'

'I'm going to phone Mum before lunch,' Tansy said.

'Tell her we said hello,' Matthias called after her as she left the room. They could hear her footsteps as she went upstairs and then the sound of her bedroom door shutting.

He turned to Cathy. 'She won't. And even if she did, Michelle wouldn't care.'

'Do you think they'll ever be able to get along properly again?'

'I don't know. I think Tansy's changed too much.'

'Yes,' Cathy agreed. 'I suppose she's a woman now with her own opinions and ideas and they don't seem to be very much aligned with any of her mum's. At least they're talking a lot more now.'

'It might be the most they ever do.'

Cathy paused, caught by that now familiar feeling as she fell into his eyes. They'd been together for a year but that feeling had never been less than all-consuming. She loved it and she craved it, but at times it had made her very afraid that she might not have it forever.

'So…' he said. 'We're alone…'

'Yes, we are…'

He leaned in to kiss her. 'Do you want your Christmas gift now?'

Cathy giggled. 'Depends what it is. Don't you think Tansy might have something to say about it?'

'Oh, your mind is filthy!' he said, chuckling before kissing her again.

'I thought we'd already done presents this morning anyway,' Cathy said.

'We did, but I was saving one for later.'

'Then give it to me later.'

'I can't wait… I want to give it to you now.'

'There you go again with those double entendres…'

He leapt up from the table and went to the hallway. A moment later he was back with a small gift-wrapped box in his hand. He placed it in front of her with a broad smile.

'That's cheating,' Cathy said. 'I feel bad now that I don't have anything else for you.'

'I don't care about that. Everything we opened this morning was supposed to be my lot too, but I saw this last-minute and I knew I just had to get it. I only wrapped it first thing if I'm honest.'

Cathy laughed. 'Did Tansy wrap the others by any chance?'

'It's that obvious?'

'They're a lot neater. For someone who appears to be this clumsy, I don't know how you rehabilitate people for a living.'

'That's funny, that's what people say at the hospital too!'

Cathy laughed, but then she turned back to the box, her heart beating just a little faster. She tore off the paper, and then her face lit into a huge, beaming smile as she opened the box.

'Oh, it's beautiful!' she cried. 'It's just perfect!'

'As soon as I saw it, I just knew I had to get it for you,' he said.

Cathy reached into the box and took out the bracelet. It was a charm bracelet, the chain sparkling silver, and every little charm that hung from it was a baking utensil. There was a tiny spatula, a mixing bowl, a whisk, a recipe book, a chef's hat, measuring spoons and even a food processor.

She looked up at Matthias. 'Oh, I love it so much!'

He reached for it, and Cathy held out her arm as he unfastened it and then did it up around her wrist. Then his hand slid to cup her face.

'I'm glad,' he said in a low voice as he moved closer. 'I'm glad you love it, because I love you.'

'I love you too,' she said. 'More than anything. I love you so much my chest hurts just to think about it.'

'Hmm,' he said, 'I think I know a physiotherapist who can help with that.'

'There's no cure for what I've got,' Cathy said. 'And I hope I never find one.'

'In that case,' he said, 'we'll just have to live with it.'

'Fine by me,' she said, melting into his embrace, breathing him in and knowing that if she could survive right here in his arms for the rest of her life, never moving, never sleeping or eating or doing anything else, she would.

A Letter from Tilly

I want to say a huge thank you for choosing to read *Cathy's Christmas Kitchen*. If you did enjoy it, and want to keep up to date with all my latest releases, just sign up at the following link. Your email address will never be shared and you can unsubscribe at any time.

www.bookouture.com/tilly-tennant

I'm so excited to share *Cathy's Christmas Kitchen* with you. This book was written during the Covid-19 lockdown and was a real test of my resolve, but, ultimately, I'm proud of my heroine Cathy and I think her caring nature reflects so much of the kindness I saw in the world during this difficult time. I'm so happy to share this book with my lovely readers who were an endless source of support and encouragement while I was writing it.

I hope you loved *Cathy's Christmas Kitchen* and if you did I would be very grateful if you could write a review. I'd love to hear what you think, and it makes such a difference helping new readers to discover one of my books for the first time.

I love hearing from my readers – you can get in touch on my Facebook page, through Twitter, Goodreads or my website.

Thanks,
Tilly

tillytennant

@TillyTenWriter

www.tillytennant.com

Acknowledgements

I say this every time I come to write an author acknowledgement for a new book, but it's true: the list of people who have offered help and encouragement on my writing journey so far really is endless and it would take a novel in itself to mention them all. I'd try to list everyone here, regardless, but I know that I'd fail miserably and miss out someone who is really very important. I just want to say that my heartfelt gratitude goes out to each and every one of you, whose involvement, whether small or large, has been invaluable and appreciated more than I can express.

It goes without saying that my family bear the brunt of my authorly mood swings, but when the dust has settled I'll always appreciate their love, patience and support. Unless you've spent the last twelve months under a rock, you'll be aware that 2020 has been a strange and difficult year for pretty much everyone on the planet and I, like so many other people, have spent much of it struggling to keep working while in a small house surrounded twenty-four/seven by my family who all had their own things to do too. They've been truly amazing, however, as supportive and patient as ever, willing to give me space and time to do what I needed to, even when it meant they had to sacrifice space and time of their own, and it's testament to them that *Cathy's Christmas Kitchen* ever got finished at all. My heroine, Cathy, is a carer by nature, a nurturer who gives the very best of herself at all times. She was inspired by so many of the people I've seen making the most incredible sacrifices this year to keep us all safe and well.

I also want to mention the many good friends I have made and since kept at Staffordshire University. It's been ten years since I graduated with a degree in English and creative writing but hardly a day goes by when I don't think fondly of my time there. I'd also like to shout out to Storm Constantine of Immanion Press, who gave me the opportunity to see my very first book in print. Nowadays, I have to thank the remarkable team at Bookouture for their continued support, patience, and amazing publishing flair, particularly Lydia Vassar-Smith – my incredible and long-suffering editor – Kim Nash, Noelle Holten, Peta Nightingale, Leodora Darlington, Alexandra Holmes and Jessie Botterill. I know I'll have forgotten someone else at Bookouture who I ought to be thanking, but I hope they'll forgive me. I'll be giving them all a big hug at the next summer bash whether they want it or not! Their belief, able assistance and encouragement mean the world to me. I truly believe I have the best team an author could ask for.

My friend, Kath Hickton, always gets an honourable mention for putting up with me since primary school and Louise Coquio deserves a medal for getting me through university and suffering me ever since; likewise her lovely family. I also have to thank Mel Sherratt, who is as generous with her time and advice as she is talented, someone who is always there to cheer on her fellow authors. She did so much to help me in the early days of my career that I don't think I'll ever be able to thank her as much as she deserves.

I'd also like to shout out to Holly Martin, Tracy Bloom, Emma Davies, Jack Croxall, Carol Wyer, Clare Davidson, Angie Marsons, Sue Watson and Jaimie Admans: not only brilliant authors in their own right but hugely supportive of others. My Bookouture colleagues are all incredible, of course, unfailing and generous in their support of fellow authors – life would be a lot duller without the gang! I have to thank all the brilliant and dedicated book bloggers (there are so many of you, but you know who you are!) and readers, and anyone else who has championed my work, reviewed it, shared it, or simply told me that they liked it. Every one of those actions is priceless and you are all very special people. Some of you I am even proud to call friends now – and I'm looking at you in particular, Kerry Ann Parsons and Steph Lawrence!

Last but not least, I'd like to give a special mention to my lovely agent, Madeleine Milburn, and the team at the Madeleine Milburn Literary, TV & Film Agency, who always have my back.

Printed in Great Britain
by Amazon